I0770951

ALSO BY Z.S. DIAMANTI

STONE & SKY
STONE & TIDE
STONE & RUIN
STONE & SKY PRELUDES COLLECTION

FABLES OF FINLESTIA

GUARD IN THE GARDEN
WAGONS & WYVERNS
ASSASSIN IN THE ALEHOUSE
(COMING SOON)

CHECK OUT ALL OF
Z.S. DIAMANTI'S
BOOKS AT:
HTTPS://ZSDIAMANTI.COM

FREE PRELUDES

AT

FreeFantasyFiction.com

WAGONS & WYVERNS

FABLES OF FINLESTIA

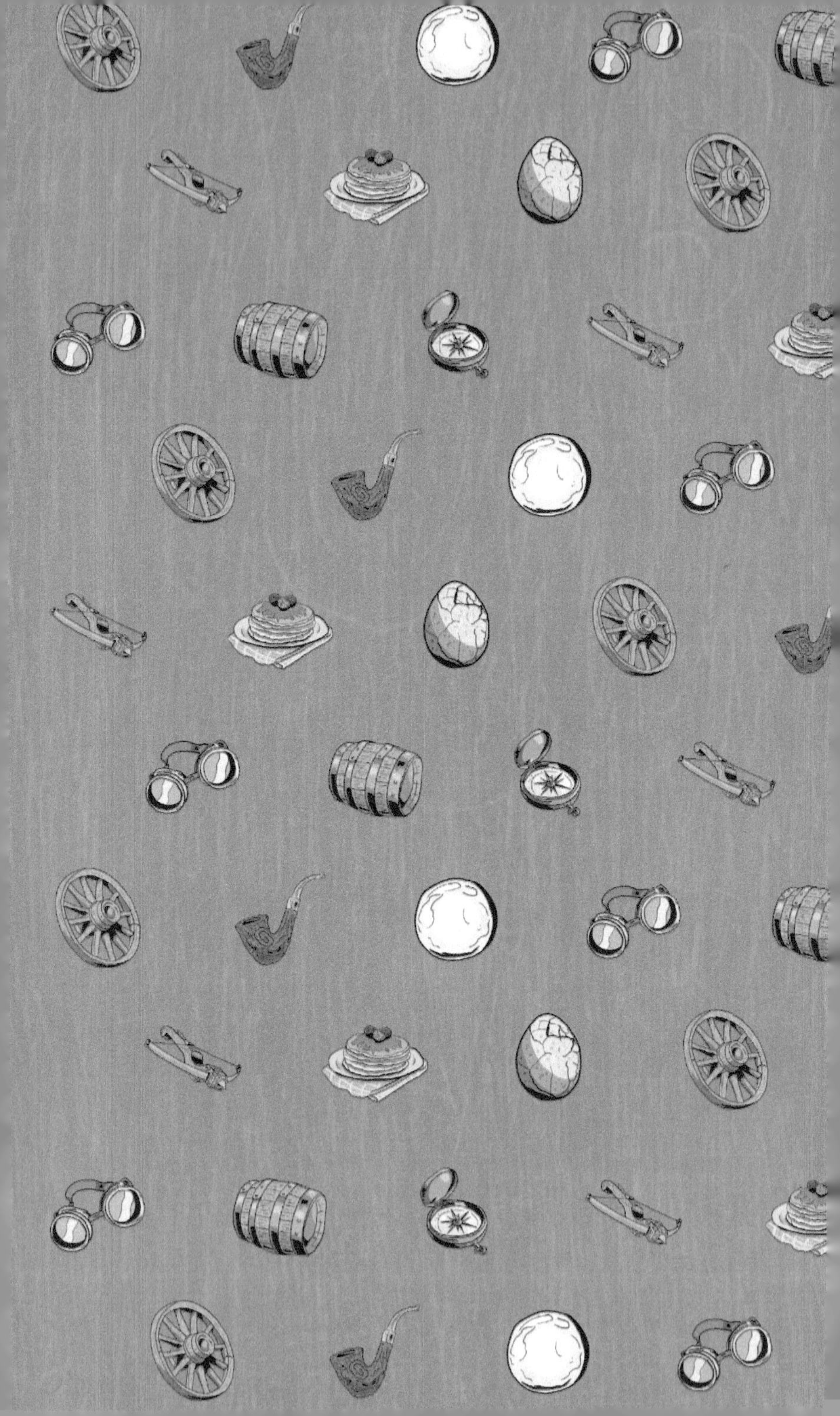

FABLES OF FINLESTIA

WAGONS & WYVERNS

Z.S. DIAMANTI

GOLDEN GRIFFIN

For Josh,
For the things I see in you
that you do not yet see in yourself

FINLESTIA
LAND OF TARRINE
TANDAL SEA
SEA
CHARTOK TUNDRA
DRELEK
ICE LAKE
BOROK
DAK-TAHN
RENJAK
RUK
EANT SEA
CROSSDIN
PORAK
LAKJO
IRK RIVER
CALROK
EALIUM
GHIN-RA
KANE HARBOR
EANT SEA NARROWS
LORALITH
HILL STOP
WHITESTONE
ELDERWOOD FOREST
WHITESTONE FOREST
PALORI RUINS
DAHRENPORT
EANT
TELRO
STRANDED COAST
RIVER
TAMARIA
SEA
ROLLIN
MARON
BLACKMAR FOREST
RIVER
LAKERUN
PEARL LAKE
VANDOR
PALORI
STALFORD
WILDLANDS
LASTTOWN
LAST LAKE
KALIMANDIR
MOON BAY
SEA
NARI DESERT
LIAMPORT
ELENPORT
SORELLO
VERFIN
TARN
PAW ISLES
ARELON
DENRIS
LETTO
DIRK
N

LAND OF KELVUR
SEA
CRAE WASTES
CRAES
FELL KEEP
EASTERN KNOLLS
VENTOLI
DUSKWOOD
LAKE KNOLL
DORANTOWN
ZORS
THE PALISADE
AIDEN'S DELL
ZOR LEDI
THE SHOALS
ANTALON
FOREST OF WIRRA
ZOR TOREIS
ZOR VELNIS
SEA
ELAIN'S SHOULDER
TALVIN
LAKE TORI
LANT
LOD MORAZ
SOLREH
ZOR PLEDIR
LAKE NEL
LOD ZIM
LORNASH POINT
ZOR LANTI
FAR
LOD KELPIO
FAR COVE
LOD POINT
LOD LAKE
LOD METO
LERIAN SEA

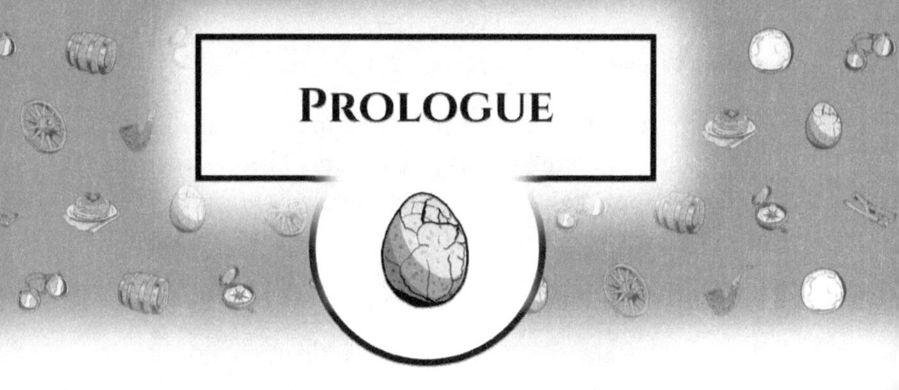

PROLOGUE

The mountain of Ruk shivered, absorbing the impact of great stones crashing into tunnel entrances and collapsing escape routes for the city's wyvern defenders. Zarnikorek squeaked before the large backhand of the orc King Sahr swung round and collided with his face. The small goblin sprawled across the throne room's stone floor, unable to keep his feet. His wiry goblin frame pressed against the cool stone as he worked to regain his footing.

Boom!

The mountain shook again as more tunnel entrances collapsed.

Zarnikorek shuddered.

King Sahr growled, but the noise soon turned into a wretched cough as he hollered. "The rebels have come!"

Rebels! Zarnikorek thought with horror. A million things ran through his mind as the orc king began to cackle.

King Sahr's quickly shifting moods had grown worse and worse as he'd continued his descent into madness. The condition had accelerated with the appearance of the wicked sorcerer that came from across the sea and bent the king's ear. Since, he'd led the orc nation of Drelek on a new crusade to destroy the other peoples of Tarrine. A rebellion had arisen, and now Ruk, the capital city of Drelek, was under attack.

Though growing terror welled within him, Zarnikorek couldn't deny the king deserved this fate. The destruction descending upon him now was not merely the result of the mad king leading the people of Drelek at the behest of a foreign orc sorcerer. Beside the resulting civil war, King Sahr had not been a good ruler for years. Perhaps ever.

A massive stalactite crashed to the throne room floor nearby, nearly squashing the king's little assistant, sending shards of stone skittering in all directions.

Zarnikorek yelped and jumped to his feet. His legs felt like lead as he forced them to move. He ran to a side table along the wall.

"What are you doing?" King Sahr hollered after him. The fat orc king pushed himself up from the floor, the buttons of his ill-fitting tunic threatening to burst free from the strain of his girth. The sound of battle waged in the distance.

Zarnikorek didn't answer the slovenly king. Thousands of stalactites clung to the roof of the enormous throne room's cavernous ceiling. Between the rebels at their doorstep and the stone javelins falling from above, they had little time. Zarnikorek frantically rolled up maps and scrolls of notes strewn across the table.

"I said—*Hack!*" the king horked a cough mid-sentence. "What are you doing?"

King Sahr clawed at the little goblin's shoulder, ripping his attention away from the parchments.

Zarnikorek squeaked in fear, flinching and bracing himself for another one of the king's many bludgeoning blows. He'd always been half the orc king's height, but he was small, even for a goblin—a trait that King Sahr often exploited with bruising backhands. The little goblin trembled under the mad king's wavering gaze. The king attempted to leer at him, but his eyes darted in all directions disconcertingly.

Battle cries trumpeted outside—close enough to be on the king's landing. Wyverns roared with rage and screams of death erupted, stealing both of their attention. As if the roars had sparked a flame of courage inside his belly, a heat rose within Zarnikorek.

He opened his mouth and clamped his teeth down hard on the large orc hand that held him. King Sahr let out a horrid, wheezing screech and blinked crazily, unable to believe his abused assistant would ever lift a hand—or tooth—against him.

The little goblin stood statuesque, stunned by the act himself. The abusive king had always cowed him into submission. Where was this sudden audacity coming from?

"I'll kill you," the king sneered. "You little wyvern thorn."

The hulking orc leapt forward, and Zarnikorek's momentarily paralyzed body finally started working again. He dove to the side, scrambling on hands and feet to get away from the deranged orc king. The little goblin outpaced him, running around the throne to put some sort of barrier between them.

"I—I'm not going to die here," Zarnikorek managed to spit out.

"What?" King Sahr reared up, a disbelieving snarl twisted around his short tusks.

"I'm not going to die here," the goblin repeated, this time with a little more hardness. "I never wanted to come here. I never wanted to be your assistant." Never had such brazen boldness erupted from his lips, but his words and confidence grew as he spoke—if confidence was what the fire in his belly was called. The growing sound of battle echoed through the halls.

"Goblin and orc parents tell their children stories of the Griffin Guard monsters that hunt us down if we leave the safety of our mountain steads during the daylight. But after years of serving you, I know the truth."

King Sahr choked and coughed on a maniacal laugh that rumbled his engorged belly. "And what is that?" he asked, hardly containing his amusement at the goblin assistant's sudden and wholly unexpected boldness.

"There are monsters among us," Zarnikorek said firmly. "Monsters like y—"

A concussive explosion of light sent both of them flying. The little goblin hit his head hard on the stone. He sat up slowly, his head feeling impossibly heavy and lolling to the side. Zarnikorek blinked and blinked again, trying to focus through the blur. In the corner of the throne room, a magic mirror buzzed with life. Runes surrounding the frame glowed, and a river of magical light swirled around the frame.

No ... Zarnikorek thought. He'd seen the evil sorcerer move through the mirrors before. *Jaernok Tur ...* he shuddered at the thought of the wicked orc's name. He had to get out of there. His keen goblin eyes searched desperately for an escape. Zarnikorek knew there were several secret tunnels leading away from the throne room. He'd mapped many of them himself. But his battered brain couldn't seem to remember where they were. If only he could spot something that jogged his memory.

There! His reeling mind finally grasped the easiest of the memories: the table with his maps and notes. It stood in front of a small escape tunnel hidden beneath. He forced himself to his feet and swayed to the side, unable to control his balance.

A fierce orc hand grabbed the back of his neck, ripping him into the air. Zarnikorek clawed at the arms of King Sahr as he turned the little goblin to face him. Zarnikorek couldn't breathe. He tried to swallow, as if the act would push the orc's strong fingers away from his throat. His vision blurred even more, darkness encroaching on the edges of his sight.

The mad king blinked wildly, trying to stop the uncontrollable twitching of his eyelids. "I might be a monster"—he hacked a guttural cough—"but I'm the monster that made you."

Zarnikorek's dangling legs flailed, and he clawed at the king's solid arm that held him aloft. Something akin to a squeak escaped his mouth, but without air to give it volume, the noise choked out.

King Sahr laughed and loosened his grip slightly. "What was that?"

Zarnikorek sucked in the tiniest gasp of air, but relief flooded him. The air flowed through his body and gave his mind a brief instant of clarity. *Maybe I will die here.*

"Nothing to say then?" King Sahr sneered. Zarnikorek couldn't bring himself to answer. "Because you know it's true. A little pipsqueak like you. Even among the goblins, you're a tiny wretch. You were worthless. I gave you purpose. I gave you—" another hacking and wheezing attack cut off his words and racked the fat orc's body. He dropped Zarnikorek to the ground.

The little goblin gasped and gulped air into his lungs like he'd never breathed before in his life. He stood shakily.

"No one's leaving here today," King Sahr spat. "You're mine. You'll always be mine. Even if you somehow manage to survive this battle and I don't—*Huck!*—You'll never escape my shadow."

Zarnikorek couldn't shake the fog from his brain. His legs moved in slow motion, and he stumbled in the direction he thought his table stood. A heavy fist blasted into the back of his head, sending him sliding across the smooth stone floor. The coolness felt strangely nice on his bruised face. His long goblin ears heard yelling on the other side of the throne room, but his mind couldn't make sense of it.

He pulled his hand out from underneath his crumpled body, hoping to move his fingers in front of his face to help him regain focus, but his knuckles rapped against a table leg, shooting a dull pain through his arm. *The table* ... The uproar at the other side of the throne room grew louder, but he still couldn't make out the tumult.

Zarnikorek pulled himself farther under the table, his face squeaking along the floor. His fingers prodded against the wall until something clicked. The wall fell away, opening a tunnel before him. He dragged his scrawny frame into the hidden tunnel and kicked lethargically at the wall until he heard another click and the wall sealed behind him. Darkness surrounded him. His goblin eyes normally saw well enough in lowlight, but it was the shadow of unconsciousness that overtook him.

GHUN-RA

CHAPTER 1
GHUN-RA

One year later...

The afternoon sun warmed Zarnikorek's face as his normally green eyelids filtered pink light into his closed eyes. He breathed in the fresh summer air, crisp near the river that ran through the valley of Ghun-Ra. On the far side of the water, mountain pines grew with fervor. Aspens slipped between the evergreens, creating a beautiful canvas painted with slender white poles, contrasting the green.

"Zarnikorek," a gruff voice called nearby, jolting him from his momentary reverie.

"What can I do for you, Klon?" he asked, turning his gaze upon the orc.

His boss walked over to him, his footsteps thudding along the river dock planks. Klon's deep-green skin matched the sun-kissed shade of Zarnikorek's own.

Like most orc cities in Drelek, Ghun-Ra derived its name from the mountain in which the city was built. Most orcs, goblins, and trolls preferred to dwell within the mountain's networking tunnels that made up the interior parts of the city, but some were relegated topside or in the surrounding valleys. Farmers, fisherorcs, and livestock ranchers often lived out under the sun, their deep green skin making them easy to spot in a crowd amongst the paler green of those that dwelt within the mountain cities. Most cities had a mix of both, but there were those in Drelek on both extremes. The residents of Dak-Tahn were often jokingly referred to as "vampires" as they lived almost exclusively inside their mountain fortress. While the dwellers of Calrok were called "sun-lovers" for living out in the sun by the sea.

When Zarnikorek was young, he often wondered why his pa, a renowned goblin engineer, had chosen to live in the valley of Ghun-Ra. But after spending years in Ruk under the former king's thumb, Zarnikorek had grown rather fond of being home beneath the sun again. The fresh mountain air flowed easier through his lungs than the stifling tunnels of Ruk.

"Got a boat down the dock. From Lakjo. Has some special deliveries that need to be sorted to get to the right place," Klon relayed.

"On it," Zarnikorek replied.

He hurried down the dock toward the newly arrived river boat. A slender orc and a tall goblin who stood shoulder height to him unloaded crates and barrels from their craft. "Good day to you," Zarnikorek called as he approached.

"Well, 'ello," the taller goblin greeted him before eyeing him warily. "You must be the special delivery coordinator?"

"I am," Zarnikorek said with a reassuring nod. He readied his wooden tablet, folding the parchments and tucking them under the leather strip that held them fast. He held out his hand to receive the boater's transport parchment.

The goblin hesitated before handing it over.

Zarnikorek's face scrunched as he inspected the papers.

Special Delivery
Direct transport to:

The Wyvern's Wish
Tavern in Ghun-Ra

2 Packages
Origin: Lakjo

"Everything appears to be in order here," Zarnikorek said. *Why is the boatgoblin so hesita—*
Whump!
The slender orc dropped the large crate on the dock. Their boat danced buoyantly with relief and the orc wiped his brow. He looked at Zarnikorek and then at the taller goblin. The crate was bigger than Zarnikorek and looked to be heavier than a boulder.

"Are both packages this size?" Zarnikorek asked, looking past the crate and toward their boat.

"No," the tall goblin said with a laugh. "Oh, *'elgar* wouldn't be able to transport two of those at once."

"Right ..." Zarnikorek said, now realizing he had to get the crate over to the staging area for special deliveries.

"Uh, where can we put this thing for you?" the orc asked, a hint of concern edging his baritone words.

"Don't worry about it," Zarnikorek said with a dismissive wave. "I've got a cart. You keep unloading your other goods and I'll go get it."

The boaters shrugged and went back to unloading the heap of smaller boxes they'd transported from Lakjo.

Zarnikorek scuttled down the dock planks, running to the cart. Most dock-working orcs rarely used it; years of lifting heavy crates and sacks had made them strong and sturdy. The cart was usually reserved for rather large shipments, or on rare occasions, like this one, where special deliveries were too heavy for Zarnikorek to carry. He grabbed the cart and spun it around, wheeling it back down the dock, thudding dully from board to board.

The little goblin looked the crate over again, trying to determine how best to get it into the cart.

"You need some 'elp with that?" the tall goblin asked.

"No, I've got it," Zarnikorek said.

"Okay ..." he heard the goblin murmur.

Zarnikorek tipped the cart backward and sent the handles up high. He pulled two blocks from the back of the cart and placed them in front of the wheels. Then, he took two planks and placed them under the back edge of the cart, smiling at his own cleverness. He'd done this dozens of times before. All he had to do was push the crate far enough onto the planks and then he could leverage it onto the cart. The blocks in front of the wheels would keep it from rolling away. *Easy.*

He moved behind the crate, catching a glimpse of the two boaters watching with interest. He tried to hide his smirk. Zarnikorek lined himself up and pushed against the enormous wooden crate.

It didn't budge.

A small, disbelieving chuckle escaped his lips. He ran a green hand through his shock of dark brown hair and then laid his shoulder into the crate. Zarnikorek pushed with all his might, digging his feet into the dock below and heaving against the huge crate.

Still nothing.

"Can we—"

"Nope," Zarnikorek cut the orc off before he could finish his sentence. "Nope, it's alright. I can do this."

Zarnikorek stepped back from the crate. Normally, if he could get the crates on the planks, he could slide them along until he had enough plank revealed to leverage the crate into the cart. Then he'd be on his way. But this crate was heavier than any other he'd tried. He pressed both hands against the firm wood and pushed again, testing it to make sure he wasn't losing his mind. He rammed himself hard against the crate, but his little bones popped against the unmovable object.

Two taller figures moved past him and lifted the crate into the cart together. Zarnikorek's head fell, partly out of exhaustion and partly in defeat.

"No worries, little mate! We're glad to help," the orc said. His words were warm with generosity, but he couldn't know how "little mate" stung Zarnikorek.

"Thank you," he breathed.

"Where to?" the orc asked, taking up the cart handles.

"Oh," his companion started. "Almost forgot the other package."

He nimbly hopped into their boat, still tied to the dock. He weaved between a couple of barrels and found what he was looking for. In stark contrast to the enormous and unbelievably heavy crate, the boatgoblin passed Zarnikorek a leather wrapped package, no bigger than his hand, tied with twine. The smooth leather weighed little, and the two goblins shared amused glances at the comical difference between the two packages.

Zarnikorek led the orc along the dock until they hit the dirt path that turned toward the depot, where they stored goods until a delivery runner picked them up for further transport into the tunnelways of the Ghun-Ra. That or one of the topsiders in the valley came to pick up their wares. A corner of the depot was reserved for special deliveries, and Zarnikorek watched helplessly as the orc parked the crate.

"You can leave the crate in the cart," he said to the orc. "I'm sure the owner at *The Wyvern's Wish* is going to need to borrow it to transport that thing to his tavern."

The orc nodded.

"Thank you," Zarnikorek whispered.

"You're very welcome," the orc replied warmly. "Is *The Wyvern's Wish* in the valley or in the mountain?"

"It's here in the valley."

"Pleasant rooms and good food?" the orc asked, inclining his head as they strolled back out to the river docks.

"I've heard it's good. It's the only tavern in the valley. The rest are in the city inside the mountain. I've heard of several good ones in different caverns."

"Heard of? You've never been to any of them?"

"No," Zarnikorek replied. His gut twisted.

The orc's face scrunched and his tusks shifted from side to side as he thought. "Don't get out much, eh?" he said with a slight chuckle.

Zarnikorek's eyebrows popped up, and he nodded to the side. "No," he replied with a soft smile.

"Well, Yan and I need to rest up before heading back upriver tomorrow. We'll get some transport parchments from the dock master in the morning. Why don't you come out to the tavern with us? I'll buy you a mug of glorb for all your help."

Zarnikorek snorted a chuckle. "I think I should buy you one for your help."

The orc roared a laugh. "I wouldn't say no to that either. What do you say? This evening?"

The little goblin hesitated for a moment. He'd never been to the tavern before. Since his return to Ghun-Ra, he'd laid low, not doing much outside of work or spending time at home with his pa. He'd always told himself it was better that way. If he had to interact with anyone who knew who he was …

Just as he was about to politely decline, the orc patted a big hand on Zarnikorek's shoulder—nearly sending the little goblin off balance—and called over to his friend. "Yan! Our little mate is going to join us for a drink at the tavern tonight!"

"Excellent," the tall goblin said, stepping away from a barrel he'd just heaved onto the dock.

"Well, I …" Zarnikorek tried to say that he was just about to decline and that maybe they could try next time the duo was in Ghun-Ra. That would probably buy him a couple of weeks to come up with another excuse, but he couldn't seem to string his words together.

"Even offered to buy the first round."

"No, sir. That first round will be on us," Yan said firmly. "For all the 'elp you've been for Grahk and me."

Zarnikorek shook his head, still feeling as though he'd been utterly useless for them. But he couldn't wipe away the smile that grew on his face. None of his coworkers had ever invited him to the tavern for a round after work. Well, except for his boss. But they all knew who he was. As much as he wanted to run home and hide after work, a deep desire to spend the evening in good fellowship welled within him. Maybe he *would* join them.

"Well, if you insist," Zarnikorek finally said.

"Excellent!" Yan said again.

Zarnikorek guided them to Klon so they could record some other goods as delivered—a rather hefty crate that *tinked* with the sound of glass for one of the taverns inside the mountain, and several sacks of some unknown grains headed for a bakery within the caverns. Zarnikorek bid them farewell and moved on to help another boatorc—a single-orc operation who had a special delivery for a blacksmith in one of Ghun-Ra's market caverns.

As strange as his interaction had been with Yan and Grahk, he couldn't quell the excitement that bubbled inside him.

The musty smell of parchment filled Zarnikorek's nostrils as he breathed in. Admittedly, as the workday drew to a close, he found himself getting more and more nervous about going out to the tavern. He lit a lantern nearby. He wouldn't need it for long, but he took the last part of his daily tasks seriously.

With pious focus, he stacked his ledger parchments and double checked their order to ensure nothing had gotten out of place. The goblin swiped his fingers across the stack, pressing the parchments together to smooth them out. He was one of only a handful of orcs and goblins allowed in the docks' office, where they managed all the records of imports, exports, and passenger manifests. Ghun-Ra's river docks weren't the biggest in Drelek, but its location made it a center for trade among the orc nation. Something Zarnikorek liked.

He nodded to his stack, regarding it with warmth. The parchments might not look like much to an outsider, but to the little goblin, they were a treasure. Not in the literal sense. They contained no gilded lettering, nor did they hold some ancient and valuable wizard spell. But rather, they recorded history with great detail.

Zarnikorek admired the shelves that lined one of the office walls. Upon them rested two years' worth of records. Records for all previous years had been delivered to the Ghun-Ra library, deep within the mountain. There, the librarians condensed the information, then bundled and bound them into thick tomes to stand as records for their individual years.

Most folks would find the process tedious, but Zarnikorek looked upon the records with a sort of whimsy.

When he was in Ruk, serving King Sahr as his assistant, he'd gotten the chance to go through loads of records in the capital city's library. He'd been tasked with compiling maps for the greatest almanac the nation of Drelek had ever seen. Zarnikorek spent weeks pouring through old records to find old trade roads through the mountains and river routes that might have been forgotten in distant years. He found it fascinating to see all the different ways his people had worked to connect with each other over time. These were the records of the lives of their people, even if they seemed small or menial.

The little goblin shivered as he remembered the maps and scrolls of notes he'd had to leave behind when the rebellion descended on Ruk. He'd been so adamant about taking the documents with him, to keep them out of the wicked hands of the sorcerer who'd been manipulating the old king.

Zarnikorek shook the thought away. *Guess I don't need to worry about that anymore.*

The wooden door opened with a creak as Klon entered the office. The orc carried one of his many wooden tablets, piled high with papers. Klon held the role of river dockmaster. It was his job to ensure all operations ran smoothly. He was a good orc who cared about his work and the people with whom he interacted. That's why Zarnikorek always beat him to the office for evening wrap-up. Klon was always conversing with one boater or another, or laughing and joking with a dock worker or Ghun-Ra citizen coming to pick up a delivery before they closed for the evening. Zarnikorek always wondered how the orc was so good at interacting with everyone he met.

Klon moseyed over to a desk near Zarnikorek and set down his tablet. He'd been in and out of the office several times that day, organizing his own papers. He looked over at Zarnikorek's stack and arched an amused brow. "I think they're flat."

"What?" Zarnikorek didn't understand.

"Your papers," Klon said with a chuckle. "You'll rub the ink right off them."

"Oh!" the goblin started, not knowing how long he'd been stroking the parchments.

"You alright?" Klon asked. "Something on your mind?"

"Oh, well ..." Zarnikorek hesitated. Klon wouldn't understand. He couldn't. He was so personable. Everyone loved talking with him. How could Zarnikorek explain he was nervous about going to the tavern to have a drink with some boaters? "I just ... You've been to *The Wyvern's Wish*, right?"

"Of course," Klon said with a disbelieving laugh. "I've only invited you to go with me and the others a dozen times since you've been back."

Zarnikorek scolded himself. *Foolish.* Of course, Klon had. He'd invited the goblin many times, but Zarnikorek had always politely declined and gone home for the evening.

"Why do you ask?" Klon's face scrunched with good humor as he eyed the goblin. "You thinking to go over there tonight?"

"I was," Zarnikorek said before he could stop the words. "I mean ... I *was*, but I'm not sure."

"Well, that's perfect!" The large orc leaned to the side and reached into one of his deep apron pockets. "Lavekka wanted me to come home for supper as soon as possible tonight. My mother is visiting." He said the last part with wide eyes and an awkward smirk.

From his pocket, Klon retrieved a small leather-wrapped package tied with twine. Zarnikorek recognized it as the one

Yan and Grahk had delivered. The goblin's face must have contorted, because Klon chuckled and explained.

"Dagvek at *The Wyvern's Wish* asked me to bring this over right away when it came in. I was going to stop by tonight, but now you can take it to him. Said he'd buy my first glorb but I'm sure he'll buy one for you."

"Well, I ..." Zarnikorek hemmed. How was he going to get out of this now? "Well, I was supposed to meet some people there, but I'm not sure I'm up for it."

Klon's lips pressed together around his orcish tusks. His features squinted as he looked the little goblin over. After what felt like an hour-long appraisal, the orc spoke again, this time with a kind gentleness. "Zarni," he said. The goblin's name rang inside him. No one except his family had called him Zarni in years. When he was growing up, some other kids called him Zarni, but no one since his years-long stint under King Sahr's boot. But hearing the nickname pricked at something inside him.

"It'd be good for you to go," Klon continued. "And even though I can't go with you tonight, maybe you'll go and have some fun and invite me to the next outing, yeah?"

Zarni's mouth opened as if he were going to say something, but he wasn't sure what to say.

"Plus, aside from doing yourself a favor," Klon said with a soft chuckle, "you'd be doing me a favor. Especially with Lavekka." He added the last part with a funny look.

As much as Zarnikorek wanted to decline, run home, and have another quiet evening with his pa, something else stirred inside him. He couldn't tell what it was. Perhaps it was a sense of duty to Klon. The orc hadn't hesitated to give him his job back after years of absence. And Maker knows, he had plenty of other reasons he could have used to deny Zarnikorek. But he hadn't. He'd been nothing but kind for the last year since the goblin's return. Sure. The odd feeling probably had something to do with that. But Zarnikorek couldn't quite pin down exactly what it was.

"Alright," he said. "I'll go."

CHAPTER 2
THE WYVERN'S WISH

Warm light poured out of the tavern windows, bathing the path outside with an amber glow. A cacophony of joyful noises emanated from *The Wyvern's Wish*, giving the stout stone and wooden building a life of its own. The moon sat bright in the sky, illuminating everything the amber light didn't touch with a blue hue.

Zarnikorek stood before the tavern's front door, debating whether to go inside. *The Wyvern's Wish* seemed to buzz as the goblin's long green ears twitched, trying to garner some sort of information about what he could expect on the inside. He considered going to one of the windows to take a peek, but worried someone might see him.

Suddenly, the door swung open, forcing Zarnikorek to jump back or take a door to the nose. An orc woman held a large orc warrior upright. "Told you," she chided him as she helped him down the path and away from the tavern.

"I'll—*Hick!*—get you ... next time ..." the male orc said, his words slurring together.

"I've been drinking you under the table for years, my love," the female orc said with a laugh. "You might look big and tough, but you're just a big softy."

Zarnikorek stifled a laugh as he watched them walk away.

"You coming in, sir?" a voice asked from the doorway.

Zarnikorek flinched, realizing the question was directed at him. When he looked upon the goblin woman who stood in the doorway, his heart stuttered in his chest. He'd seen her before. *Jileva.* He'd read her name on the passenger registry when she'd first arrived in Ghun-Ra on a riverboat from Lakjo. Zarnikorek would never forget the name. Nor would he forget the first time he saw her.

Jileva had climbed off a boat and onto the docks only two weeks earlier. Zarnikorek had frozen in place. The female goblin was the prettiest he'd ever laid eyes on. Her long red hair cascaded off her head in wavy ringlets. Her big blue eyes were a piercing contrast to her olive-green skin. And strangely enough, she was no taller than Zarnikorek.

"Are you alright?" Jileva asked, concern creasing her lovely face.

"Uh ... I was ..." Zarnikorek's brain blanked. His body warmed and he couldn't think of any intelligible thing to say.

Jileva's concern morphed into an amused grin as she leaned against the open door, her arms crossed in front of her. "Do you want to come in and get some water?" she asked with a giggle, the sound music to Zarnikorek's long ears.

"Ahem," Zarnikorek cleared his throat. "I'm sorry."

"Sorry for what?" Her smile still beamed at him.

"Well, I just ..." What was he sorry about?

"What is it you've got there?" Jileva asked, nodding toward the object in his hand.

"Oh!" Zarnikorek started. The moment he'd seen her, he'd forgotten all about the leather-wrapped package. *Right!* "I'm from the river docks."

"I know," she said with another chortle. "I remember seeing you there when I arrived."

She remembers seeing me? Zarnikorek's heart began to race.

"Is that package for me?" she asked.

"Oh," he shook off his momentary daze. "I'm supposed to deliver it here. Klon, my boss, said it was urgent and to be delivered right away."

"It's for me," she said confidently, and Zarnikorek didn't question her words. "Dagvek will be glad to hear it got here so quickly. Why don't you come in and we'll get you a goblet of glorb?"

Zarnikorek rocked on his feet, trying to will them to move forward.

"Or an ale, if you'd prefer," she laughed. "We've got some stronger stuff, too."

"No," Zarnikorek said quickly, scolding his own legs internally. Finally, he forced them to move and held out the leather-bound package. Jileva took it graciously, her big blue eyes trapping Zarnikorek in their gaze. "Glorb is fine ... Thank you!" he added afterward, suddenly remembering his manners.

"Sure! Come on in," she said, leading him into *The Wyvern's Wish*.

The tavern buzzed with energy. Orcs and goblins and even a table of trolls filled the inside. The warm amber glow Zarnikorek had seen from outside poured from lanterns on the walls and hanging chandeliers made from the gathered antlers of great northern white elk.

The room spread wide, and a long bar ran the length of the back wall. Though the crowd obscured his view, he could tell that someone occupied every bar stool. Immense furs from oxen, painted and decorated in the traditional orc fashion with tribal patterns, adorned the tavern's walls.

Zarnikorek bumped into a chair. "Oops. Sorry," he said as his gaze drew upward upon a large troll.

The enormous troll looked down at him, not even seeming to have noticed. His big brow rose curiously. When he realized Zarnikorek was talking to him, he shifted and said, "No harm, little 'un. No harm."

"You better stay close to me," Jileva said, taking Zarnikorek's hand. "I've gotten pretty good at weaving through this place."

Jileva's soft hand squeezed his slightly, and warmth tingled up his arm and fluttered in his chest. She deftly navigated through the crowded room, weaving between tables and chairs filled with patrons. It surprised Zarnikorek how many people were in the tavern, though he supposed it shouldn't. *The Wyvern's Wish* was the only tavern topside. Anyone who lived within the mountain had numerous caverns with taverns to choose from, but the Ghun-Ra valley folk had to go somewhere for their glorb. And judging by all the farmers, fisherorcs, boaters, jacks, and ranchers, it looked to Zarnikorek that *The Wyvern's Wish* fit the bill.

"Jil!" someone yelled to Jileva as they neared the side of the bar.

"Yan? Grahk? What are you two doing here?" she asked. "I didn't even see you sneak in!"

"We finally got our own boat!" Yan replied. "This is our first transport to Ghun-Ra."

"Oh, and you found our friend, Zarni!" Grahk said excitedly.

There it was again. Zarni. The little goblin couldn't help but smile at the overly friendly orc.

"Oh no, you know these two troublemakers?" Jileva turned on him with mock scolding.

"We just met," Zarni said sheepishly and rubbed the back of his neck.

"Troublemakers?" Yan laughed, bringing a hand to his chest in feigned offense. A wry grin snapped across his face as he said, "Compared to you?"

Jileva laughed outright. "I'll leave you here, then," she said to Zarni. "You're in good hands with these two. Well, as good hands as any, I guess. I'll make sure someone brings over that glorb I owe you."

"And two more for his friends," Grahk said with a wink.

"You two have your own boat now. You can pay for your own glorb," she rebutted.

"Actually," Zarni said timidly. When she turned to him in surprise, he wished he could take the word back. He paused for a second as she blinked and awaited his next words. Zarni let an awkward, toothy grin split his face. "I owe them a round. I'm happy to pay for it, of course. I just—"

Jileva held up a hand and glared over at Yan and Grahk, sitting at the table and watching with bated breath. Then she turned her scowl back to Zarni, but her face soon softened. "Fine," she said with a defeated smirk. She waved the package between them. "But only because you're my hero today."

Yan and Grahk hooted and banged the table with delight as she spun and sauntered off through the crowd.

"A seat for you, sir. After that, you're *my* hero too," Grahk said, sliding a chair out for Zarni.

Zarni laughed and joined his new compatriots.

"I used to run the river route from Lakjo to the Fork with my pa," Grahk said. He scratched at his muscular forearm, his hardy frame matching his deep tone perfectly in Zarni's mind. The orc wore a sleeveless vest with a loose linen shirt underneath. Zarni hadn't done much boating, but assumed the attire kept the orc agile and cool when the sun beat down on the river.

"What's the Fork?" Zarni asked.

"Oh," Yan jumped in. "The Fork is where the rivers from Lakjo and Porak meet before coming south to Ghun-Ra. There's a small town there."

"Really small town," Grahk emphasized. He took a long swig from his mug and wiped his tusks on the back of his meaty hand. "Not even on most maps."

Zarni sat riveted by the conversation with his new acquaintances. They'd gone through so much to earn enough coin to commission the building of their own boat, which he learned they dubbed the *Helgar,* named after an ancient orc river princess.

"I wish I could visit the Fork someday," Zarni said, starry-eyed. And though he wished he could take the words back as soon as he'd said them, a whimsical longing truly pricked at his heart.

"Why don't you?" Yan said excitedly.

Grahk sat up in his chair. "Yeah! You could ride with us. The *Helgar* is a fine boat. Pah!" the orc paused for a laugh and waved his hand. "You know that. You saw her earlier today."

Nervously glancing between the two overzealous and generous boaters, Zarnikorek blinked multiple times, trying to formulate some excuse to get himself out of yet another mess. "I just mean that there are so many river ways and orcish communities that aren't on our maps, and it's fun to imagine visiting them. Surely, I couldn't actually go."

"Why not?" Grahk roared merrily. "You're good folk. Even if a bit small. You'd make a fine passenger. And the Fork isn't that far upriver. Certainly, it's a harder journey than coming downriver. But not unmanageable."

"Yeah," Yan heaped on. "You could come with us to Lakjo. And if you wanted, we could take a transport assignment for another town like Porak or Ruk."

"No!" Zarnikorek barked before he could contain himself. The mention of Ruk was too much. He couldn't go back there. He wouldn't.

Zarnikorek had been fortunate to lead a quiet life once he returned to Ghun-Ra. No one had harassed him about his connection to the fallen king, but he'd heard about others whom people had shunned for being on the wrong side of Drelek's rebellion. And *they* had just been warriors with orders. He wondered how many of them had known the truth about the king's twisted mind. How many of them knew that, in his madness, King Sahr had been manipulated by a wicked sorcerer from across the sea?

What would people say if they remembered Zarnikorek worked directly for the king?

The corners of *The Wyvern's Wish* seemed to grow closer to him. Had the place been so crowded before? How many of the orcs and goblins and trolls in the place knew who he was? How many were whispering about him right now? Zarnikorek's heart beat so hard his ears felt like they might burst.

"Zarni? Zarni? Yoohoo!" Grahk said, waving a big hand in front of the little goblin.

Zarnikorek shook out his daze.

"You alright, little mate?" Grahk asked.

"Oh, Zarni was just doing a little daydreaming about Jileva," Yan said with a wide, toothy grin. "Did you see the way he was looking at her when she was dragging him through the place?"

Every bone in Zarnikorek's body wanted to bolt out of the tavern, leaving the ruckus of the place behind. He glanced about warily, but none of the other patrons seemed to be paying him any mind.

"You should ask her to join you for a glorb one night!" Grahk said, leaning forward over the table.

"Glorb for a date? You bumble brain," Yan scolded the orc. "You even remember Jileva? She's a dragon spit. She's the kind of goblin that likes a little adventure. Zarni, you should take her on a picnic hike through the woods."

"No ... I couldn't ..." Zarnikorek tried to say.

"Sure, you could!" Yan encouraged. "Ain't no 'arm in askin'!"

Zarnikorek's normally green cheeks flushed rosy. "I was just delivering the package."

"Oh, yeah," Grahk mused over his mug before letting out a loud belch. Several orcs at a nearby table cheered his effort. He lifted his mug to them. "What was in that little package, anyway?"

As if on cue, the intentional strumming of an instrument from the corner of the tavern quieted the rambunctious patrons.

"Well, hello there!" Jileva's singsong voice rang out over them. The tavern erupted with enthusiasm. "Ah," Jileva continued. "Did you miss my singing?"

More uproarious applause.

Zarnikorek sat stunned. Jileva stood atop a box situated on a small stage in the corner of the tavern hall. Several lanterns hung around the dais, strategically placed to light the bard. The amber glow limned her with light, giving her an otherworldly presence. She was beautiful.

A thick orc finger gently pressed upward on the bottom of Zarni's chin. He hadn't realized his mouth had fallen agape. Grahk chuckled next to him.

Jileva strummed her lute, and the instrument sang out with a tune to match her beauty. Her dazzling smile shone as brightly as the sparkles in her eyes. "Well, I've missed singing to you for the last few days. A lute's not much good with broken strings, and this one is mighty special. Needed some strings I could only get from back home in Lakjo."

The package! Zarnikorek realized.

"Some old friends of mine and my new hero got them delivered today!" Jileva proclaimed, throwing Zarnikorek a wink.

Grahk and Yan waved their hands wildly, and the crowd cheered with equal enthusiasm.

An orc at the table next to them hollered, "Next round's on me!"

Another raucous uproar reverberated through the building. Zarnikorek felt the vibrations through the wooden table as he gripped it for support.

Grahk pushed at the goblin's shoulder, nearly knocking Zarnikorek out of his chair. "Wave, little mate! They think you're a hero."

Labored breaths heaved Zarnikorek's tiny frame. Everyone in *The Wyvern's Wish* looked directly at him. He held a hand up to shield his face. *A hero? If someone recognizes me ... If someone remembers ...* Zarnikorek thought he might retch.

The crowd settled as Jileva started into a song she dedicated to her new hero. But Zarnikorek couldn't hear any of the words. A barmaid, bringing drinks for the table, tapped him on the shoulder. He nearly jumped out of his skin, but instead, leapt from his chair.

And fled.

The little goblin dashed between tables and chairs, bumping into some as he went. He took the bruises as they came, too ashamed and too frightened to make eye contact with any of the other patrons. He stumbled all the way through the tavern, reaching for the door.

Zarnikorek tripped and tumbled to the stone floor. His arms shook as he pushed himself up. An orc nearby stood from his chair to help him up, but the little goblin waved him off. Hot tears stung his eyes as he tentatively glanced up to look for the door. A lone orc sat in one corner. Much of his face hid in the corner's darkness, but Zarnikorek could tell he was watching him. The orc sat unmoving, a strange aura about him.

Terrified, Zarnikorek shot to his feet again. The little goblin slammed through the doorway into the cool night, gulping at the crisp mountain air as he ran down the path toward home.

CHAPTER 3
BREAKFAST

The aroma of fresh herbs and breakfast cooking in the kitchen permeated the entire house. Zarnikorek pulled the blankets from his face and his pointed nose breathed in the intoxicating aroma. His long ears twitched, taking in the airy tune his pa hummed. Above, beautiful wooden beams weaved across the ceiling. He sighed and heaved himself upright, running his hand through his hair, and a heavy yawn escaped his lips.

As he tidied his bed, the sunlight spilled through the window, brightening the vibrant colors of the woven blanket. The summer birds sang outside almost as merrily as his pa in the kitchen. Zarnikorek basked in the warmth and joy of the morning. He remembered the years he'd spent in Ruk. How dark it had been. Brilliant goblin engineers had eventually found ways to tunnel and place reflective mirror systems to bring light into the caverns and special chambers within. But as orcs, goblins, and trolls all possess the natural ability to see in the dark caverns beneath the mountains, this sort of light was unnecessary and more ornamental in nature.

There was something about waking up to the light and hearing the happy critters singing outside that Zarnikorek loved.

"Zarni," his pa called from the kitchen. "Breakfast is almost ready."

Zarnikorek smiled and hurried out of his room. The house his pa had built wound and opened into a beautiful sitting area. It spread wide and stood tall, leaving plenty of room to entertain and breathe. Though they'd done little entertaining in the years since Zarnikorek's mother had passed. She had always been the outgoing type. Talkative, kind, and always happy to host. Zarnikorek took more after his father.

"Good morning, Pa," he said as he entered the wide-open kitchen.

Grinble slid a yellow half-circle out of a hot pan and onto a plate. "Good morning, son," he said cheerily. "I made mountain omelets. Come. Come, grab your plate."

Zarni stepped across the kitchen and grabbed both plates, each with their own yellow half-circle and a pile of cut strawberries and blue and silver griffinberries. "Smells delicious," he admitted.

Grinble followed Zarni to the table with a pitcher of berry juice. His cane clacked along, a necessary accessory after decades of backbreaking work as an engineer. As they sat, Zarni noted how lovely breakfast looked. The sun beamed through the windows, lingering on the table. The glasses glinted and the various colors of the table settings and the fresh food brought a vibrant life to the dining area. He chuckled to himself.

"What?" Grinble asked, handing a freshly poured glass of berry juice to his son.

"Oh, nothing," Zarni said. "Thank you." He took the glass and smelled the sweet, slightly tart scent. He took a sip, and the juice woke up his tongue for the morning. *Mmmm ...* "I was just thinking if you hadn't been an engineer, you might have made quite the cook."

Grinble chortled and waggled his grey eyebrows. "I doubt that very much. Your mother was always the better cook. Anything I know how to make, I learned from her." A fond smile slipped across his wrinkled face as he filled his own cup.

"You were too good an engineer, I guess," Zarni teased.

Grinble laughed. "They both take a substantial amount of attention to detail. So many details. But the funny thing is, you can't make anything beautiful without a little creativity too. Engineering or cooking. As important as the details are, creating something beautiful requires a little bit of risk."

Zarni cut a bite away from the omelet, making sure to get a bit of each of the goodies cooked into the eggs. Chopped onions, red bell peppers, sausage, eggs, and some sort of reddish-orange seasoning combined for a perfectly savory morsel. "Mmmm!"

"Good right?" Grinble said through a bite of his own. "Igrek sold me some fresh elk sausage yesterday. Perfectly seasoned."

"It's amayzinf," Zarni tried to say through another bite.

"Whafs phat nohw?"

The two started laughing, and each took a swig of their juice.

"Ma would scold us both for talking with our mouths full," Zarni said, wiping a jovial tear from his eye.

"She would have," Pa agreed. A soft grin creased his face as though he were smiling at some distant memory.

"This is just the breakfast I needed this morning," Zarni said, changing the subject. Though his mother had died several years earlier, he knew his pa had struggled with the loss, especially while Zarni was still in Ruk. Pa had steadily gotten more of himself back over the last year since Zarni's return.

"You don't seem to be in a rush to get to the docks today," Grinble said between bites.

"No ..."

"You were out late as well. You finally take Klon up on his offer to go to the tavern?"

"Not exactly. I had to stop by the tavern to deliver a special package from Lakjo. I stayed for a little while because some boaters from there invited me to have a drink with them."

"That's swell!" Grinble said, leaning forward with his eyes wide. "So glad to hear it. How'd it go? Meet any nice goblin ladies?"

"Pa," Zarni said, elongating the name with embarrassment. He wasn't sure if they'd turned rosy, but his cheeks felt warm.

"Only asking, my boy. Only asking." Grinble held up his hands in mock surrender. He scooped another bite of his omelet, but before he placed it in his mouth, a wry grin swept over his face and his brow lifted. "But did you?"

Zarni shook his head, feigning disapproval, but he knew his pa could see the smirk he tried to hide. "I actually delivered the package to a goblin woman named Jileva."

"Jileva?" his pa said with a high-pitched whistle. "Lovely girl. Ran into her at the market. Igrek told me she's the new bard at *The Wyvern's Wish*. As pretty as she is, does she have a voice to match?"

"Yes—" Zarni started to say, but he could only remember her voice vaguely in the back of his mind. He'd run out of the tavern when she'd begun singing. He cursed himself for being such a fool. A fool and a coward. He'd run away from the loveliest goblin woman he'd ever met, all because he was afraid someone would remember his association with the fallen king.

But someone had recognized him. That strange, cloaked orc in the corner ...

"Zarni?"

"What's that?" he asked as he snapped back to the conversation with his pa.

"I asked if you were going to go back to the tavern this evening? If so, I might join you."

"No. I couldn't."

"What?" Grinble asked, surprised. His forehead crinkled. "Are you alright, son?"

"I'm fine," Zarni lied.

A pregnant silence lingered between them. Grinble's lips pursed and moved from side to side. Finally, he broke the silence. "Son, I know you went through a lot, but I don't want you to let the past keep you chained. I nearly jumped out of my seat when you said you went to the tavern with some friends."

"I only met them yesterday," Zarnikorek grumbled.

"That's not the point. You put yourself out there. That's the most I've seen in all the time since your return."

"I was happy to, at first," Zarnikorek heaved through a sigh. "I loved hearing about their journey and how they became boaters and their routes and travels. It was all fascinating. I wanted to run home and add things to my notes and maps. But as soon as the attention turned on me, I quickly remembered that I couldn't let them know anything about me. I had to get out of there."

"Zarni, you can't live closed off forever. All your relationships can't be surface deep." Grinble's words were concerned, but he delivered them with a kind gentleness. "You need people you can talk with about real things. You need to get out there and experience some things."

"I *have* experienced things," Zarnikorek said. Though in truth, he was rather young when he had been whisked away to work for King Sahr, and he'd spent a large majority of his time in Ruk since. While Ruk was a hub for interesting people from all over Drelek, Zarnikorek had been granted few liberties under the thumb of the old king. "Plus"—Zarnikorek shook off his weakening argument —"I don't need anybody else. I've got you."

"Ha! You know what I mean. And I'm an old goblin. What are you going to do when I'm gone? I don't want you to grow old all alone."

"You're not going to die anytime soon," Zarnikorek bit back. Another long pause fell between them. That's what they'd thought about his mother. She had not been a particularly old goblin, and yet she'd died peacefully in the night. No other explanation than it was her time to go.

"I'm sorry," Zarni said, scratching the wild hairs on the side of his head. "I didn't mean to—"

"It's alright," Grinble said with a wave of his hand and a shake of his head. His countenance betrayed nothing more than a kind smile. "You're right. I'm not going anywhere for a long while yet. I just want to see you with more love and joy in your life. That's all I've ever wanted. What any father should want for his son. I want to see the son I knew before you were whisked off to work for that good-for-nothing, rotten king."

"I never had a lot of friends, even before that," Zarni said with a suppressed chuckle.

"No," his pa chortled in agreement. "But you smiled more. You laughed more. You engaged people. You had dreams of something different. You had more of your mother in you then. It's still there. I see it sometimes when you laugh."

"Maybe," Zarni tentatively agreed. "But I have to be careful, Pa. Not just for me, but for both of us. If I get too close to anyone and they find out I worked for King Sahr before the rebellion overthrew him, they could run us both out of Ghun-Ra."

Grinble nodded his head quietly, poking at the blue and silver griffinberries on his plate. "At some point ..." he said slowly and paused. The long breath had its intended effect as Zarni leaned in, waiting for the next words. "You're going to have to take a risk and let someone in. You can't live life on your own. We're not designed that way. You're going to need a friend."

Zarnikorek's gaze fell to his own plate. His pa was one of the greatest goblins he'd ever known. He trusted him implicitly. He sensed his pa was speaking great wisdom over him, but as much as he wanted to heed his words, fear nagged at the corner of Zarnikorek's mind.

A pang of guilt ran through Zarnikorek as he made his final notes on a parchment, where he'd sketched out a quick map of the Fork and the surrounding area. Certainly, it wasn't a perfect rendering, and if he ever got the chance to travel there, he'd fix it. Guilt weighed on him as he sat at the desk next to the large library shelves his pa had built into the sitting area, but it had nothing to do with his lackluster sketch. The pit in his stomach had everything to do with the fact he'd delayed his departure for work because he was ashamed to run into Yan and Grahk at the river docks before they embarked northward.

Zarnikorek folded the leather portfolio over his parchments, sat back in his chair, and sighed.

"That was a big sigh," Grinble called from one of the loungers across the room.

Zarnikorek peered over at his pa. The old goblin held a book up in front of himself, pretending he had not been watching his son. Zarnikorek heaved himself from his seat and walked across the room. "I'm headed to the docks," he sighed. Even if he left now and jogged the long path all the way there, the duo on the *Helgar* would be long gone by the time he arrived.

His fingers grazed the back of the couch, and his pa grabbed his hand. Zarnikorek stopped and looked down at his pa's comforting face. "It'll get better, my son."

"I hope so."

"I know so," Grinble assured him.

CHAPTER 4
SALMON SANDWICHES

"Well, now!" Klon greeted Zarnikorek with a hearty rumble. "Must have been a good night at the tavern," he teased. "New friends kept you out late?"

Zarnikorek avoided the dockmaster's gaze, instead quickly scanning the docks to see if the Helgar remained moored. No boats were lashed to the dock. The little goblin's eyes darted upriver with a hopeless glance. Nothing but slow-flowing water.

"Oh, your friends headed out early. Said they wanted to make the Fork as early as possible today. I got them set up with a cargo transport job headed to Porak. More construction materials going on to Renjak. Poor folk ..." Klon's words grew solemn.

A twinge hit Zarnikorek's cheek. He didn't like when people talked about the short-lived civil war in Drelek. He always felt that it was one step closer to someone calling him out for serving the king of the losing side and casting him out into exile. All he could say was, "Devastating."

It truly had been. Renjak had taken the worst losses of any mountain stead of Drelek. It was built half in and half on top of a wide, easily sloping mountain. When the evil sorcerer had come from across the sea, he'd gifted King Sahr a long-thought extinct dragon. King Sahr passed it to one of his generals, Gar Nargoh, and he and his wyvern squadron flew off to Renjak to test the dragon's might, targeting one of the rebel leaders that lived there with his compatriots. According to the accounts Zarnikorek had heard, the entire place had been burned to the ground. After the rebellion took Ruk captive and placed a new orc king upon the throne, nation-wide efforts had arisen to help rebuild Renjak. They needed all the help they could get.

"I'm sorry you missed your friends' departure. They seemed nice," Klon continued, changing the subject to less somber topics. "They asked after you, but I told them you don't get out to the tavern much, so you were probably still sleeping it off."

As horrible as that sounded, Zarnikorek wished it had been true. It might have felt better than the guilt that clung to his ribs. Knowing that his new acquaintances had asked after him made the pit in his stomach even heavier.

"Oh, and here's your tablet," Klon said, handing it over. Several orcs and goblins loaded their boats nearby, wiping sweat from their brows as the mountain sun beamed down on them. "I need to see to these folk. You've got an odd goblin from Calrok back at the depot. He's got a wagon-full of barrels he wants to take to Lakjo. Paying for special delivery for his barrels and himself, apparently."

"That *is* odd," Zarnikorek said, now drawn in by work. The pang of guilt lingered in his belly, but maybe he could distract himself with an odd special delivery and not feel it so sharply. "I'll go see him. Thanks."

Zarnikorek stepped off the wooden planks of the docks and turned the corner around the depot. To his surprise, he saw several orcs unloading barrels from the back of a wagon. A goblin stood nearby, watching with vested interest. Parchments fluttered in his grip, half covering his face. The deep green color of the skin on his arms marked him as a goblin who spent a lot of time topside. But Zarnikorek couldn't guess who in the valley would need to transport such a large special delivery. If anything, it was another indication of how few people he knew in the Ghun-Ra valley. A stark reminder that he'd neglected the only folk he'd spent any time with since his return to the area; and Yan and Grahk weren't even from Ghun-Ra.

That must be our special delivery goblin, he thought with a sigh.

"Hello, sir," Zarnikorek greeted the other goblin as he approached.

"Well, 'ello there!" the goblin chimed, only half-glancing up from his papers. "You must be the special delivery coordinator Klon was tellin' me about."

"I am, yes. I'm Zarnikorek."

"Nice to meet you. I'm Reglese."

The name froze Zarnikorek. He shifted his tablet up in front of his own face, hoping the goblin didn't recognize him. "Wh-What are you transporting, Mr. Reglese?" he stammered out.

Reglese looked up from his papers, the goblin's wide yellow orbs scrutinizing him. Zarnikorek pulled the tablet closer to his face, and no recognition dawned on the other goblin's face.

"I 'ave a special delivery of my proprietary glorb wine I'm taking to Lakjo."

Zarnikorek cursed his luck. There was no doubt this was the same goblin he'd met in Ruk. A few weeks before the rebellion stormed the capital city, there had been a frenzy throughout the tunnels about a new tavern that had opened in one of the lower caverns. A goblin entrepreneur claimed to have a new glorb wine that was better than any glorb in the kingdom of Drelek. Word reached King Sahr—not one to shy away from drink—and he decided he needed to taste it for himself. Zarnikorek and the old king shared a drink with an orc warrior at the tavern who later turned out to be a rebel spy. Well, the king had anyway.

"Y-You're traveling with it yourself?" Zarnikorek winced as the words came out. He had to go through the motions. He had to do his job. But he didn't want the goblin to recognize him.

"Aye," Reglese said with a nod toward the orcs, heaving barrels off the back of the wagon and hauling them toward a couple of boats moored to the river docks. "I 'ave been expanding my operations. My *Spinefish Tavern* in Calrok was so successful, I opened one in Ruk. That one was a 'uge 'it."

"Yeah—" Zarnikorek started to say, but cut his own words off. His eyes widened, and he hid behind his tablet.

Reglese said nothing for a moment, and Zarnikorek could tell the other goblin was eying him.

"Anyway, I 'ave been expanding across Drelek and even 'ave plans for the lands in the south."

"The lands in the south?" Zarnikorek couldn't help himself, lowering the tablet. A goblin expanding his glorb wine empire to the lands of men and dwarves and elves. It was ... inconceivable.

"Aye," Reglese said with a chuckle. "With the war over and all the alliances 'appening, opportunities abound, my friend."

Zarnikorek shook his head. He couldn't even imagine it. Maps of southern Tarrine flitted through his mind. How many times had he looked at those maps and thought about wandering the Nari desert to search for ancient ruins? Or sailing the warm waters to see the Paw Islands in the far south? Or even seeing the great white monolith stones that jutted up like spires from the rolling emerald hills around Whitestone?

But the orc nation of Drelek had always been at war with the peoples south of the mountains. That is, until the rebellion. Just then he realized Reglese watched him with a curious gaze.

Zarnikorek let out an involuntary squeak and lifted his tablet again.

"Wait a minute," Reglese said, placing a hand on the tablet and pressing it down to reveal Zarnikorek's face. "I know you."

"I-I don't think so," Zarnikorek stammered.

"No, I do. You were in my tavern in Ruk."

"No, don't think so," Zarnikorek said again, his heart hammering in his chest so hard he felt it in his ears. "With your tavern being so popular, I'm sure you see so many faces they all run together."

Reglese placed a finger to his lips and narrowed his eyes. A shiver ran through Zarnikorek's body. If the other goblin placed him with King Sahr ... If he realized he was connected to the old king ... A scream caught in his throat. He choked it down.

"Wait!" Reglese said. Several orcs paused and turned to the two goblins. Zarnikorek wanted to dig a hole and bury himself right there. "No, not you," Reglese waved the orcs off. They shrugged and went back to their work. Reglese took a step closer and lowered his voice so only the two of them could hear. "You used to work for King Sahr."

Dread washed over Zarnikorek; his worst nightmare was coming true.

"O', 'e was a wicked king," Reglese continued. "If I remember right, 'e swiped the mug of glorb wine right out from in front of you. You never even got a sip."

Zarnikorek blinked, a little confused. He thought back to the day they'd gone to the tavern in Ruk. King Sahr had been gluttonous. He drank fully from his own mug while all at the table waited patiently for his verdict. When he deemed the glorb wine to be delicious, the king had grabbed Zarnikorek's mug before the little goblin could lift it.

"You 'ave to try some!" Reglese said with a laugh. He slapped Zarnikorek on the shoulder and ran over to the wagon, where he grabbed a cup and filled it from a tapped barrel. "I 'ad this one tapped for the boaters for the journey. Nothing like word of mouth spreading 'ow good it is!"

Reglese shoved the glorb wine into Zarnikorek's petrified hand. He looked between the cup and the goblin, unable to comprehend what was happening. This goblin knew he worked for King Sahr. He knew Zarnikorek had been on the wrong side of the civil war. And yet ...

He stared down into the cup, the ruby liquid swirling tantalizingly.

"Well," Reglese said expectantly. "Go on."

Zarnikorek lifted the cup to his lips and took a sip. The glorb wine filled his mouth with flavor and his brows shot up. It had a full-bodied taste with significant notes of dark berry fruits. "Wow ..."

"Good, right?" Reglese said with a chuckle.

"So good."

"Now you see why I'm expanding!"

"Yeah ..." was all Zarnikorek could say as he finished the cup.

"I'm even going to take my glorb wine to Kelvur."

"Kelvur—?" Zarnikorek started. The evil sorcerer had come from that land across the sea. He'd heard the sorcerer had been defeated, but to expand a goblin enterprise there was even more unbelievable than expanding to the lands of the south.

"Aye," Reglese said, a wondrous look in his eye. "I'll be making a trip out there soon. I'll do a 'ole tour of Kelvur, setting up deals."

Zarnikorek shook his head again. Maps of Kelvur were only recently starting to circulate in Tarrine. As soon as he'd heard, he'd acquired one for his own collection. The mystery of the place titillated his mind like so many amateur cartographers. He couldn't even imagine traveling there.

"But I 'ave to get these to Renjak first. Those folk need it more than most. I 'ave a contract with the new tavern owner there. I want to get 'im set up well. Those folk need a place where they can rest and enjoy themselves after long days of rebuilding. After everything that 'appened."

A pit grew in Zarnikorek's stomach.

"Anyway," Reglese continued. "It's nice to see you again."

This caught Zarnikorek off guard. *How could that be?* Something in his heart stirred, and he pushed the emotion down. "It's good to see you too," he managed out.

"'Ow's our paperwork looking?"

"I'll help you get it all taken care of," Zarnikorek said.

"Thank you," Reglese said with another pat on the little goblin's shoulder.

Helping Reglese took a couple of hours to ensure everything was in order and accounted for—an important part of Zarnikorek's job. Once the special delivery paperwork was taken care of, he joyfully waved to the adventurous entrepreneur as the orc boaters rowed his three boats upstream. Zarnikorek still didn't understand what had transpired. He'd thought for sure that the goblin entrepreneur would have called him out as a traitor to the new king. Zarnikorek was rather happy he never had to see King Sahr again, but he'd always assumed people would label him guilty by association.

Still shaking his head in wonder, he rounded the corner of the depot to find his pa standing nearby. Grinble held a basket in his cane hand and two poles in the other. A toothy grin split his face under the wide-brimmed straw hat that provided ample shade from the high mountain sun.

"What are you doing here?" Zarni asked, delighted to see his pa.

"I thought we could have lunch together and get some fishing in," Grinble replied.

"I came to the docks so late today I wasn't planning on taking time for lunch," Zarni said with an apologetic smile.

Evidently, Klon heard him. The dockmaster walked up and nudged the little goblin with his big orc elbow. "Go on," he whispered conspiratorially. "If I had the chance to take lunch with my pa, I would take it. I miss him. The time we had was gone by too quickly."

Zarni looked at his boss with fondness. "Thank you."

"It'll be slow until later anyway, now that the morning rush is done," Klon said with a wink.

Zarni caught up with his pa and took the basket from him. The two sauntered down a path that followed the river toward one of their favorite fishing spots. The white barked aspens, pocked with eyed-shaped markings—a natural phenomenon and the result of self-pruning—watched the pair walk along, following an offshoot creek where the waters danced with delight. Enormous trout and mountain salmon frequented the area, and the peaceful meadow echoed with happy birds most of the day.

As Zarni set the basket down on the bank of the creek, he opened the top and asked, "Are we catching our lunch, or did you make us something tasty?"

"Got some smoked salmon sandwiches and some gibs in there for us."

"Wow. Someone's been busy this morning," Zarni chimed, looking over the feast. He pulled out one of the sandwiches, half-wrapped in a linen napkin. The savory and crisp fragrance wafted into his pointed nose and sent a ravenous hunger rumbling through his stomach. He handed the first sandwich over to his pa, who took it in one hand and set to work whipping his fishing line out to the perfect spot.

Zarni watched for a moment, always impressed at his pa's ability to lick the water with his fly with the perfect amount of touch in his movements. He mindlessly took a bite of his sandwich, then immediately turned his attention to the task. The sweet and savory salmon, smoked to perfection, paired beautifully with the cucumber ribbons, red onions, arugula and creamy spread. His mouth watered with satisfaction as he chewed.

"Mmm."

"Good, eh?" Grinble called back to his son through a bite of his own. If we catch any salmon, I'll have to smoke it with honey again. Oh, and I fried up the last of the gibs this morning, so keep any softbacks we catch."

Zarni looked into the basket where a small sack held a bunch of gibs, his favorite snack, and a common one among orcish communities with access to fish. The soft fish bones were fried until crispy and tasted especially good when salted and spiced just right. As Zarni shoveled the last of his sandwich into his mouth, he grabbed the bag of gibs and joined his pa at the creek side.

"Thanks for this," he said, holding the bag out to his pa so Grinble could take a few.

"Of course, my son," he said with a cheerful smile.

They fished along the banks, pulling in trout after trout, the fish apparently hungry for some early afternoon flies. The fish must have traveled a good distance downstream today to have worked up such an appetite. They fished for a long while before Zarnikorek had to head back to the docks. He set his pole over by the basket and wished his pa good fishing.

"I'll try to nab a salmon before I pack up and head home," Grinble said. "I might move out to the turn downstream. They may be biting over there."

Zarni laughed. "You do that. I'll see you tonight."

"Not going out to the tavern tonight?" Grinble asked, no judgment in his tone.

"No," Zarnikorek said. But then he laughed again. "I actually already had a drink today."

"Eh?" Grinble asked, his brow creased in confusion, but the smile never left his face.

"I'll tell you about it over dinner," Zarni said as he turned to leave.

"Fair enough," Grinble called after him.

Zarnikorek walked down the path, breathing in the crisp mountain air. He reached up to some of the low-hanging branches, letting the pine needles tickle the palm of his hand. He thought back to Reglese and how the goblin had treated him so kindly, even though he recognized his connection to King Sahr. Maybe Zarnikorek had been wrong all along. Maybe people wouldn't judge him as he thought. Or maybe enough time had passed for people to judge him less harshly than he'd anticipated. He couldn't pinpoint why, but for whatever reason, he had a hard time believing it.

As Zarnikorek strolled up to the river docks, Klon stepped away from the depot to catch him. "Just got word from the jacks that they'll be bringing in some more lumber headed for Renjak. Don't know of any special deliveries scheduled for this afternoon, so if you could help them find proper space for the lumber in the depot, that'd be great."

"Will do," Zarnikorek said, taking a parchment from the orc. "I'll add this to my tablet and be ready for them."

"Ah, you're so much better at all the organizing than me."

"Don't sell yourself short," the goblin replied, with an encouraging nod.

"Ha! Well, I don't have orcs traveling all the way from Ruk to inquire after me," Klon said.

"Wait ... What?" Zarnikorek asked, stunned. His heart started beating faster again.

"Oh, yeah. While you were gone to lunch with your pa, an orc from Ruk came by the depot looking for you. Asked about you by name. He was very interested in your work. I showed him how skilled you are and how diligent you are with all your paperwork. Seemed pleased to see it."

"What orc? Who? Why?" Zarnikorek couldn't string together a full sentence. His mind was racing, and the incessant beating of his heart pounded in his temples. He scratched at the dark brown hair just above his ear.

"He didn't say," Klon said with a shrug. His dark green lips pursed between his tusks. "He was tall, wore a cloak. Maybe a mage or something. Had that magic way about him, you know?"

An orc mage from Ruk ... looking for me? Zarnikorek's mind reeled. Who was this orc? What did he want with Zarnikorek? He'd been so careful to lie low. Now, some mage from Ruk was looking for him? On the same day he'd run into Reglese, who had recognized him. Could this be some sort of coincidence?

A flash of a memory sparked in his brain—a vision of the cloaked orc in *The Wyvern's Wish* the night before. The one who'd watched him disconcertingly as Zarnikorek had fled. Could it be the same orc?

Just then, several trolls ambled down the street toward the depot. Each of the enormous trolls carried long logs over their muscular shoulders. The jacks had arrived. As disturbed as Zarnikorek was about this new revelation, he had work to do. He watched the trolls stroll toward the depot and prayed that the terror in his heart wasn't reflected in his eyes.

CHAPTER 5
A SURPRISE VISITOR

Zarnikorek rushed through his walk home from the river docks. He paused occasionally, glancing about at one noise or another. The forested road that led to his house provided ample hiding places for an orc mage to lurk in the shadows. But the only eyes that seemed to be watching him were those of the ever-vigilant aspens. Their leering eyes made him shiver as they swayed in the evening breeze. Their rustling leaves created a continuous noise that—to Zarnikorek's worried mind—could cover the movements of a stealthy stalker.

Thus, Zarnikorek scuttled home as quickly as his short legs could carry him.

As he approached the beautifully designed wood and stone cabin his pa had built, he noted the amber glow of lanterns through the windows. Visions of his pa cooking away happily while an orc mage crept up behind him with ill intent soured Zarnikorek's stomach. His legs slowed as his long, pointed ears picked up the muted tones of speaking from inside the house. *Someone is here!* It took every ounce of courage Zarnikorek could muster to force his feet forward again.

He grabbed the door handle, his ear twitching in an attempt to hear the conversation inside the house. But the house was built sturdy. He couldn't make out any of the words his pa spoke.

Zarnikorek's chin quivered as he forcefully held his shaking hands still on the door handle. He gulped down a breath, only now realizing he'd been holding it. Someone was in his house with his pa, the only person in the world Zarnikorek had left. He couldn't leave his pa in there to fend for himself.

"Ow!" he heard his pa yelp, as a pan clattered to the paved stone floor.

Before he knew it, Zarnikorek burst through the door and into the kitchen. His hands raised before him, ready to fight whoever was attacking his pa. But the scene before him was not what he'd expected.

Grinble sucked one of his fingers as a pan sizzled on the floor. Hot oil dripped over the side, staining one of the paved stones. "Ooh, that burned," Grinble said, shaking his hand and blowing on it. Zarnikorek watched his pa in confusion, his balled fists lowering slightly.

Grinble caught sight of him and said, "Oh, Zarni! I was just getting the pan ready to fry up some more gibs for you."

"Pa ..." Zarnikorek huffed. "I thought you were ... There was ... You were talking to ..." He couldn't seem to string together the story his mind had fabricated about some villainous intruder with nefarious motives.

"Oh, yes," Grinble said, retrieving the pan from the floor with a thick rag. "Master Deklahn, this is my son, Zarnikorek."

Zarnikorek turned to find the cloaked mage standing in the hallway. The little goblin's green face paled as his gaze traveled up the tall orc. Standing in the entryway with him, Zarnikorek saw exactly what Klon had mentioned. There was a strange way about the orc mage. Ordinarily tall and a little lean for an orc, he stood with his hood swept back revealing a kind smile around his tusks. Yet, there was some quality about the orc that Zarnikorek could only explain as magical.

"W-who are you?" Zarnikorek stammered, taking an involuntary step backward.

"Zarni," his pa said, his tone laced with confused scolding.

"It's alright," the tall orc said, holding a dismissive hand up. His posture softened, and he spoke to Zarnikorek directly. "My name is Deklahn. I'm the mage adviser to King Genjak."

"King Genjak?" Zarnikorek parroted. His chest heaved with labored breathing as his heart quickened impossibly further. "We don't want any trouble. I've done nothing wrong. All I've done is my job with diligence and care. I-I hardly talk to anyone. I don't even go to the tavern and engage with people."

"Except last night," Deklahn said with a slight smile.

"Well, yes," Zarnikorek backtracked. "But that was the first time I've been there since my return to Ghun-Ra. I just met with some boaters from Lakjo. They invited me out. We weren't talking about anything nefarious."

"No," Deklahn said, his eyebrows raising and his lips forming a smirk around his tusks. "I expect not."

"Truly," Zarnikorek continued. For the life of him, he couldn't understand why he kept talking. He was normally so quiet. "My pa and I are loyal citizens of Drelek. We don't want any trouble."

Deklahn held up his hands in surrender. "I believe you. And I don't mean to bring any trouble down upon you."

The way he said the words made Zarnikorek believe him. He gulped to settle himself, but the act didn't ease his curiosity. "But ... if you're not here to bring condemnation upon me ... why are you here?"

Deklahn's smirk broke into a smile. "I bring you a quest from King Genjak himself."

"A quest?" Zarnikorek said the word as if it were from some ancient and foreign language.

Deklahn chuckled. "Yes, a quest."

It took every ounce of self-control for Zarnikorek not to burst into a volley of questions. His pa had been particularly firm on them eating supper while it was fresh and saving any talk of quests for evening tea. Zarnikorek watched his pa host as masterfully as his mother used to. Grinble asked questions and listened with genuine interest. It wasn't difficult. Because they had never before hosted a master orc mage, and because Deklahn advised the new king, he instantly became one of the most interesting people to ever dine at their table.

"And that's why the king is still traveling from town to town. Not everyone in Drelek was even aware of King Sahr's devious plans. Many of them don't understand why we have a new king," Deklahn said before cutting another bite of trout for himself.

Zarnikorek scoffed. Grinble looked at his son and Zarnikorek quickly explained his reaction. "Not everyone had to live with him every day," he grumbled.

He looked at his plate. He'd devoured his dinner, trying to get to evening tea as fast as possible. Zarnikorek could hardly wait to learn more about this so-called quest. His pa and the mage ate painstakingly slowly, enjoying the spread—a trout fillet for each of them, plus an arugula salad tossed with bacon, beetroot, bread, almonds and a wine vinegar dressing. As he watched them finish their meals, he wished he'd savored it more.

"That's true," Deklahn said. "There may be no one in all of Drelek who experienced his wickedness like you did."

Zarnikorek sat, stunned. He always figured everyone assumed he was just as culpable as the nasty king.

"I've had some time in Ruk to look over your maps and notes," Deklahn continued. "And your pa was kind enough to show me some of the ones you've got here. They're rather impressive."

Zarnikorek flushed. "I—well ... King Sahr knew I had a mind for such things. And when the sorcerer from Kelvur came, he wanted an extensive atlas put together for his own reference. I didn't really want to help the sorcerer. It was easy to see he was twisting the king for some other game. I just didn't know what. But ... but I was afraid."

Deklahn nodded thoughtfully and placed his fork on his plate. "I never met Jaernok Tur myself, but I remember when my old gar, Gar Zotar, came back to Lakjo after meeting the sorcerer for the first time. He was shaken. It's the whole reason he helped form and lead the rebellion."

"It wasn't just the sorcerer ..." Zarnikorek said, his words barely above a whisper. "If I didn't do what King Sahr wanted ..." The words halted in his throat. Tears welled in his eyes.

Grinble grabbed his son's shoulder and squeezed, tears dripping from his own eyes. The older goblin's throat bobbed as he swallowed down the pain of shame and regret. "I never should have let him take you. How could I have known he'd lay his hands on you? I would have liked a chance to put mine on him," his pa growled with an anger Zarnikorek had never seen in him before.

"King Sahr was an abusive king. I am sorry you had to take his madness and wrath upon yourself," Deklahn said.

The tears that burbled to the surface spilled out over Zarnikorek's cheeks. He didn't understand why the orc mage was being so kind to him, but his compassion was genuine. Zarnikorek didn't know how he knew, but he did.

"What is this quest?" Zarnikorek said at length.

Deklahn's empathetic concern shifted to a warm smile. "Everything is changing. Now that Drelek has a new king—a better king"—he paused to assure the little goblin—"and the sorcerer of Kelvur is defeated, our world is changing. We have new friends and new allies and new opportunities to grow into being a part of the rest of Tarrine. If we can establish our new relationships with the peoples of the south, we'll no longer be isolated to the Drelek Mountains. Imagine orcs and goblins and dwarves and men and elves and trolls all living side by side."

Grinble let out an inadvertent laugh. "Sorry," he apologized quickly. "It just reminds me of something my pa used to talk about when I was just a mite. I never thought it would actually happen. But my pa was a dreamer."

Zarnikorek squinted at his pa. Grinble had never told him that. He knew his grandpa had been a traveler. He'd even been a part of an expedition to the Chartok Tundra, a place that was still mysterious and largely unknown to their people even to that day.

Deklahn's face crinkled with mirth. "That dream is closer than ever before."

Zarnikorek shook his head, drawing back to the conversation. "But how does that involve me?" he asked. "What could I possibly do to help with that?"

The orc mage adjusted himself and leaned in across the table. "After reviewing the maps and notes you left in the castle of Ruk, we knew we had to find you. Someone among the castle staff remembered when they'd originally brought you to Ruk. Said they'd heard gossip that you were from Ghun-Ra. I asked about you in the mountain tunnels, but none could give me any information. So, I went to *The Wyvern's Wish* last night and, to my fortune, you were there."

"Maker bless," Grinble breathed out. "Zarni, what are the chances? The first time you go to the tavern since being home and it's the same night he's looking for you there."

Zarnikorek could hardly believe it himself. "Why ... why didn't you stop me when I was leaving?"

One corner of Deklahn's mouth fell. "You didn't seem to be in the mood for talking. Looked as though you were having a difficult night."

Zarnikorek blushed. He had been.

"You seemed to be in a hurry to leave, and now that I knew you were here in the valley, I figured I could try to connect with you today."

"How did you know I worked at the river docks?"

"I asked your friends," Deklahn said.

Friends, Zarni thought. A pang of guilt sat bitterly in his mouth.

"They seemed a little worried about you. They weren't sure why you left so quickly. Assumed you were getting up early for work today, but thought it odd you didn't even say goodnight."

Zarnikorek's cheek twitched. Now, he felt terrible. "Well, what can I do for the king?" he asked, ready to change the subject.

"Like I said, I'm not here to heap any trouble on you, but maybe a dash of adventure," Deklahn said.

"Adventure?" Grinble echoed, sitting up.

"Yes. You see, we want to establish trade roads with the folks of the south. I've got personal connections in Galium."

"Galium? The dwarven city?" Grinble asked, a hint of nervousness lacing his words.

"Yes," Deklahn said with an amused nod. "Galium has a rather well-established wagon depot and trade routes that run all the way to Crossdin on the coast of the Tandal Sea, Hillstop to the east, and even Loralith, the city of elves, in Elderwood Forest."

Zarnikorek's face contorted as he wondered what in Finlestia King Genjak could want him to do. "I don't understand."

"We're hoping that you would accompany one of Galium's exceptional wagoners and forge a new trade route between Drelek and the people of the south. A joint venture between our peoples."

Zarnikorek's eyes bulged and his stomach dropped. "Me? You want me to go to Galium?"

"Yes," Deklahn said, trying to hide his amusement. "That and then help map a reasonable route to establish a trade road for wagoners between us and Galium."

"I can't do that," Zarnikorek said, his heart pounding and his mind racing.

"Why not?" Deklahn asked, though his face never lost its kindness.

"I'm not ... I just ... Well, look at me." Zarnikorek stood, his height still shorter than the seated orc mage. "Look how small I am. I stopped growing years ago. This is all you're going to get. I'm no mountain of an orc warrior." He held up his scrawny arm and flexed. "I'm not covered in muscle. I'm small even for a goblin."

The orc mage suppressed a laugh. "You know," he said slowly. "After everything that's happened over the last year, I've learned some things from some friends of mine. It doesn't matter how small you are or how small you think your role is, anyone can do something that changes the course of the future."

Zarnikorek gulped. His emotions churned within him. The weight of the mage's words hit him like a mighty war hammer. Could he really change the course of the future? Even with his past?

"No," Zarnikorek said. "No ... I can't."

"Zarni," Grinble said softly next to him.

"I can't," Zarnikorek repeated. "I'm sorry you came all this way looking for me. Surely, this is a terrible disappointment. But I'm no ambassador. I'm hardly an amateur cartographer. I might be good at organizing and logisticizing things. But I can't do what you're asking. I just can't."

Deklahn's gaze dropped to his plate, and he rose from his seat. "I think you're probably far more capable than you believe yourself to be," he said as he stepped around the table. "I know this is a lot, but I'd ask you to do me a personal favor."

Zarnikorek could hardly meet the orc mage's gaze. "I ... Uh ..."

Deklahn held a hand up, indicating that the little goblin didn't need to say anything. "King Genjak expects a pigeon from me in the next couple of days. I leave for Galium tomorrow. It took me a few more days to find you than I expected since you weren't inside the mountain.

"Think on it tonight. Discuss it with your pa. Don't make your choice right now. I'll be at *The Wyvern's Wish* in the morning for breakfast, but then I'll need to head out. Come and join me for breakfast after you've thought it through, and tell me your answer, then."

"I—" Zarnikorek said, but his pa cut him off.

"He'll be there," Grinble said.

Zarnikorek nearly choked but said nothing.

Deklahn looked between the two goblins for a moment and then nodded. "Thank you for dinner. It was delicious."

"Of course," Grinble said. "Come back another time and I'll make you some honey-glazed salmon."

Deklahn smirked and said, "I might just have to take you up on that."

Zarnikorek stood frozen in the dining area as his pa saw the orc mage out. His hands tingled, and he felt like he wasn't even inside his own body. He couldn't go on a quest to Galium. A dwarven city? Was the king mad? No ... he'd seen a mad king up close. King Sahr would never have even considered such an extravagant notion. He was too busy batting Zarnikorek around for not catering to his ever-shifting whims. Zarnikorek could never get anything right. Every time he did something the king asked, King Sahr's mind would change before he could complete the task.

"Useless!" the king would spit at him as he swung a backhand to collide with his face. He always fell short.

How could Zarnikorek possibly go on a quest for a new king? He couldn't. Could he?

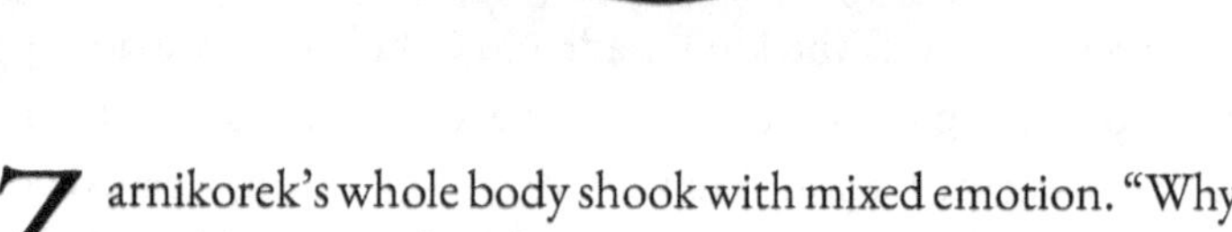

Zarnikorek's whole body shook with mixed emotion. "Why would you say that?"

"What?" Grinble asked, a surprising edge to his voice.

"Why would you tell him I'll meet him tomorrow morning at *The Wyvern's Wish*?"

"Because you will," his pa said sternly.

"I can't go on this quest," Zarnikorek stated. He shook his head as his eyes narrowed. What was his pa thinking?

"You can. And you should," Grinble said, gathering plates from the table to clean up.

Zarnikorek's roiling emotions burbled over. "Grizzlefoot," he cursed. "Pa, have you lost your mind?"

Grinble placed the plates on a long stone counter and turned to face him with a heavy sigh. "Son, you've been stuck for so long. Burdened by the weight of the coals that wretched king heaped upon you."

"That's precisely why I can't go, Pa," Zarnikorek pleaded with his pa to understand. "I'll forever be marked as the fallen king's assistant. And if the wrong person should find out ..."

"Zarni," Grinble said, leaning on the butcher block island in the middle of the kitchen—closer to his son. "Don't you see? This is your opportunity. Of all the folks of Drelek, who would want to exile all of King Sahr's old compatriots more than the new king? And yet he asked you to be a part of this new venture for our nation?"

Zarnikorek paused, biting his lip as he pondered his pa's words. There was some logic to what the old engineer said. But ... "What if that's the whole plan? Send me on this impossible quest to get rid of me?" As soon as the words came out, he wished he could reach out, grab them, and force them back down his gullet.

"Zarni." His pa's creased brow and pressed lips spoke volumes. "That doesn't make any sense, and you know it. Why would he request this task of you? How often did King Sahr ever ask you if you would do something? Never! Now, you have a king who offers you the opportunity to do something great. When have you ever had that freedom?"

"I have the freedom to say 'no.'"

"But why would you? Think what you could be a part of. This could be your chance to get unstuck."

Zarnikorek's will to fight waned. He *had* been stuck for so long. He remembered when he'd first been brought to Ruk to work for King Sahr. The king's madness had not been so evident in the early days. Zarnikorek had thought he really had the opportunity to make a difference for his people. But everything had grown sour shortly afterward as Zarnikorek learned what kind of selfish king he served. And no matter what he did, the king had never been satisfied.

A sudden shiver slithered up his spine as a terrifying prospect pricked his mind. "And what if I fail?"

Grinble stepped around the wooden island and embraced his son. Tears spilled from Zarni's eyes as he pressed his face into his pa's shoulder. It didn't matter how old he got, his pa's hug always had a way of piercing through the fog and getting to the heart of the matter. "If you fail, I will love you, anyway. Because that's what a pa does. But a pa also doesn't want his son to miss the greatest opportunities of his life."

Zarni didn't know what to say, so he merely stood in his pa's embrace, breathing in the moment.

"You have more of your mother's heart in you than you think. Brave and open. Fierce and determined. Loyal and kind. You've just lost sight of it." Grinble placed his hands on both of Zarni's shoulders and pushed him out where he could look his son in the eyes. "But you also have my short stature and that logical brain. So, let me talk to that part of you for just a minute.

"Son, this may be the best opportunity you ever get to finally put that past behind you. By taking on this quest, you'll be showing loyalty to the new king of our nation. And by completing this quest, you'll have established something for Drelek that we've never seen before. You'll be changing the course of history forever. You'll be changing the very maps you love so much. This may be the very thing you were created to do."

Grinble's words resonated within him. His pa had always been a faithful goblin, something that had carried him through hard times. Could his pa be right? What if this was Zarnikorek's moment? The greatest thing he might ever do? A creeping black web of doubt crawled into the corner of his mind.

Grinble continued. "You can't be so worried about what folks will remember from your past that you don't consider what they could remember from your future."

Zarni blinked several times, dripping the tears away. His pa was right. This was an extraordinary opportunity for him to not only put his past behind him, but also write a new narrative for his life. If he could do that, perhaps he wouldn't live in constant fear and worry and doubt. Perhaps he could even forge some genuine relationships—like his pa said he should—without worrying about trusting the wrong people with his past. Maybe he could even pursue a romantic relationship ... his mind flitted to Jileva at the tavern, standing with confidence in the lantern lights. Perhaps ...

But could he really? Who was he to go on such a quest?

And yet, King Genjak had sent his closest mage adviser to find *him*.

Zarnikorek absentmindedly started washing the dishes, but Grinble stepped in. "I'll take care of these," he said. "You've got a lot to think about, and I want you to make the right decision. I can clean almost as well as I cook." Grinble smirked and winked at his son.

Zarnikorek responded with a bobbing nod and strode through the living area. His fingers tapped at the desk as he walked by, and a parchment crinkled. His gaze dropped to the parchment. Upon it, he had drawn the makeshift map of the Fork. Delight rolled up from his belly, warming his heart. How intrigued he had been. How fascinated by the prospect of seeing a new place. And now, here he was, terrified and very much considering declining the greatest offer he'd ever gotten to do just that.

Zarni gulped the fear and anxiety back, holding on to the warmth of that momentary excitement. His heart hammered in his chest as water splashed over pans in the kitchen. His pa would expect an answer in the morning, and so would Master Deklahn. Zarni's heart pounded against his little ribs. He couldn't help feeling he would be up all night thinking about it, even though he already knew his answer.

After sleepless hours of rolling in his bed, Zarni had gotten up and readied a bag. He rolled and packed clothing, only to remove items to roll and pack others. He may have stuffed the bag seventeen times, but the goblin couldn't make up his mind. It was only when he'd tucked the last, and most significant item inside, that he was able to lay his head down and sleep. Packing clothing was one thing, but packing his portfolio and parchments sealed the deal. Several times, he'd considered throwing the bag into the creek on the way to *The Wyvern's Wish* the next morning. But he'd never even consider it with his portfolio in there.

He woke to the summer sunlight and birdsong pouring through his window. Strangely, Zarni couldn't remember the last time he'd slept so well. He swung himself out of bed and stretched his arms up high. A jovial bounce accompanied his step until the lack of a bag near his door frame halted him. He could have sworn he'd packed it in the night.

Had it all been a dream? Had he really been asked to go on a quest for King Genjak? Had there even been a mage in his house the night before?

A sadness washed over him. As terrifying as the dream had been, it had also been exciting and had stirred something in him he'd thought long gone.

Zarni shook his head as he hurriedly grabbed a tunic. He stopped short, realizing that he only had one left. *No, it couldn't have been a dream.* But where was his bag? He rushed to dress, his arms wrestling with the fabric and his brown hair popping through the hole.

Grinble sat at the table, cheerily eating his breakfast as Zarni rounded the corner. The younger goblin noted his bag next to the front door and tried to recall if he'd placed it there late in the night. He could have sworn he'd placed it by his bedroom door.

"Good morning," he said to his pa. "Breakfast smells delicious."

"Thank you," Grinble said, and with a wan smile he added, "I'm just finishing up."

The older goblin scooped his last bite and gobbled it down. It was then that Zarni realized there was no breakfast set out for him.

"On your way to *The Wyvern's Wish* for your breakfast?" Grinble asked, a glint in his eye.

"Seems I won't be having breakfast here," Zarni said with a humored huff.

"Not today," Grinble chimed.

It was then that the reality of Zarni's word choice struck home. He might not have breakfast here for a long time. The shift in his pa's countenance told him that the realization had just dawned on Grinble as well. He tossed the empty plate on the counter and rushed to Zarni, his cane clacking on the stone floor.

Zarni met him, unable to hold back.

They embraced each other—a hug entirely different from the one they shared the night before.

"Pa," Zarni blubbered.

"I'll be fine," Grinble croaked through his own tears. "You're going to be great. I'll miss you, my son. Never doubt that. But I'll be here when you get back to celebrate your great accomplishments."

"You'll be all alone again," Zarni said, pulling away to look at his pa.

"But this time I know you're coming back," Grinble said. He sniffed and wiped his face with his sleeve.

Zarnikorek bit at his lip and shook his head. "How are you so confident?"

"Because you're my son, and I know you. I've known you since you were small enough for me to swaddle in my arms. And *I* know you've got more in you than even *you* know."

"I'm afraid," Zarnikorek admitted, his head and shoulders drooping.

"You are brave," Grinble said, lifting his son's chin.

"I don't know ..." the younger goblin's words came out a whisper.

His pa wore a compassionate smile. "You know what my pa told me about his expedition to the Chartok Tundra?" Zarnikorek pursed his lips and shook his head. "He told me he was scared out of his mind to go. Being brave doesn't mean you're not scared. Being brave means you rise to the challenge in spite of fear. My pa didn't know what lay on the path before him, but he went anyway. Not because he was some glorious hero, but because he didn't know who he was, and he wanted to find out.

"You spent so long being told who you were by a mad king that I think you started to believe him," Grinble paused, his pointed teeth grinding together at the thought. He inhaled through his long nose and let the breath out through his mouth. "I don't know much about this new king, no more than you do. But I'm more afraid, my son, that you don't even know yourself."

Zarnikorek nodded solemnly.

Grinble placed a hand on his son's chest, like he used to when he spoke blessings over him before bed when he was little. "I pray this journey helps you to see everything I see inside of you."

Zarni sniffed, choking back the emotion that threatened to erupt from within.

He nodded to the door and said, "Suppose I ought to get going. I take it you placed my bag by the door?"

"I did," Grinble said. "Woke up early. When I came to check on you, I saw your bag and got right to work."

"Oh?" Zarni's brow crinkled.

"Made as many gibs as we had fish spines. For you to take on the journey."

"I thought breakfast smelled extra good this morning."

"Yes," Grinble said with a chortle. "I also put your grandpa's compass in your bag as well. It's nothing special, but I figured if you ever get lost, it could help you get home."

"Thanks, Pa."

The two stood in the entryway for a long moment. Neither of them spoke. No words were needed. They simply appreciated one another.

After a moment, though, Grinble snapped to and shooed his son out the door. "Off you go now!" he said. "Don't want to miss your meeting."

Zarni hustled along the dirt path that led away from their house. "Oh, wait!" he said, turning around. "I have to tell Klon."

"Don't worry about that!" Grinble called. "I'll go see him today and explain everything."

Zarni nodded to his pa and a prickling sensation rolled across his nose. Pa nodded back, and Zarni took his leave.

Approaching *The Wyvern's Wish* in the morning seemed far less daunting than when it had been bursting at the seams with patrons. Zarnikorek's hesitation to cross the threshold welled for different reasons this time around. He wiggled from side to side, trying to shake out his nerves. Then he heaved out several quick breaths, grabbed the door handle, and whipped the door open. An orc on the other side jumped, his hand outstretched as if he were about to grab the handle on the other side.

"Oh, sorry!" Zarnikorek apologized quickly.

"It's alright," the orc said, clutching his chest. "Just startled me, is all. I'm glad you came. I was just about to give up and leave."

Suddenly, Zarnikorek realized it was Master Deklahn. For whatever reason, he'd expected to find the orc mage brooding in the corner of the tavern like he'd seen him the first time. He snickered at the thought.

"Oh, sorry," Zarni said again. "I was up late packing my bag." He pointed a thumb over his shoulder.

"I can see that," Deklahn said. "Looks like you're ready to go."

"Well ..." Zarnikorek hemmed. He inclined his head to peer into the tavern past the orc. He glanced about, but didn't see Jileva anywhere within. *Of course she wouldn't be here,* he thought. *She was likely up late singing and entertaining the patrons.*

"Well ..." Deklahn returned the dangling word.

"Oh, right," Zarnikorek snapped back to the conversation at hand. "Mind if I get some breakfast to go? *The Wyvern's*

Wish has the best poppy seed muffins and Pa didn't make any breakfast to share."

Deklahn smirked. "Your pa is a wise goblin."

"Hehe, yeah," Zarnikorek said sheepishly.

"I actually grabbed an extra one for the flight, but you can have it," Deklahn said.

"The flight?" Zarnikorek asked, his eyes widening.

Deklahn's smirk grew into a wide grin around his small tusks. "Have you ever ridden a wyvern?"

Zarnikorek gripped the mage's cloak, holding tightly so he wouldn't plummet down the long, long way to the mountains below. The wyvern's smooth, scaly skin rubbed against his legs where his breeches had ridden up but it didn't bother him too much. The wind in his eyes, however, had formed tears the moment they took to the sky. Luckily, Zarni had his goggles—passed down to him from his grandpa. He didn't normally use them, but he'd packed with an adventure in mind, and knew he might find cause. After all, unexpected things were on the horizon, and he knew not what would come his way. *Better to be prepared,* he'd thought. And he was glad to have them now.

As they flew high above the Drelek Mountains, tears welled in his eyes for an entirely different reason. He had never seen the world from this vantage. The sight of the high mountain peaks far below, like giant rows of teeth capped with white snow, moved him to tears of wonder as they glided over.

"Have you ever seen the like?" Zarni wondered aloud.

In front of him, Deklahn laughed, his shoulders rolling as he turned to reply, "It is a sight you never get used to."

"I imagine not," Zarni said. For truly, it was unlike any other view he'd witnessed.

After a long while, Gloh, Deklahn's wyvern, spread her leathery wings wide, bringing the group into a descent, and gracefully glided toward an alpine lake high among the mountains. Zarni had seen several on their trip thus far, and each one seemed just as beautiful as the last. The water was incredibly clear, bluer than any blue he'd ever seen. *Finlestia truly is a marvelous place,* he thought.

The stark reminder that the world was so big, and he was so small, tied a knot in his stomach.

"We're going to land down here," Deklahn said, pointing over to the alpine lake as they approached. "I've stopped here before with the rest of the riders of Renjak during a patrol. We'll let Gloh get some water and hydrate. We can take a break and stretch our legs. There may even be some food to forage while we're here." And with a wink over his shoulder, he added, "Just a little snack."

Zarnikorek patted Deklahn on the shoulder in acknowledgment. He wouldn't mind stretching his legs a bit.

As they landed, Deklahn slid himself off of Gloh's back and ran his hand along her long neck until he reached the wyvern's head. He patted her on the snout as she clicked and cooed at him lovingly. Zarni slipped off the wyvern a little less gracefully than Deklahn had, but managed to stay upright as he hit the ground. He adjusted his satchel over his shoulder and straightened.

"I'm going to step over here," Deklahn said. "I'm looking for a couple of roots for a potion I've been working on. Hopefully, I can find some around the water here."

"Sure," Zarni said. "Maybe I can find some mushrooms we can eat later."

"Maybe," Deklahn affirmed. "Just don't go wandering too far. Don't know what creatures call this area home."

Zarni laughed, but as he turned to walk down what appeared to be a game trail, he realized that there must be animals that lived in the area. A natural bowl surrounded by mountain peaks formed the alpine lake, and although the area was well-treed and likely had things to forage, Zarni hesitated. If he got lost, he didn't want to have to spend a night or two by himself while Deklahn searched for him. Or even worse, he didn't want to run into any of the Drelek Mountains' numerous dangerous predators. He thought maybe he'd rather stick with Deklahn, but when he turned around again, the orc mage had already disappeared into the woods.

Alright, Zarnikorek thought to himself. And aloud, he reenforced, "I can do this."

Zarnikorek followed the game trail, the easiest access for him and his short stature to make it through the forest. Along the way, his long, green goblin ears bristled as he listened for sounds—snaps of twigs and rustling of bushes—but nothing seemed to pop out at him, and no creature loped into view. Instead, the sun flitted through the branches of the high-altitude evergreens and warmed his nose against the crisp mountain air.

"What a lovely place," he thought aloud as he strode through the mountain bowl forest. To his left, he spotted a tree, well shaded and giving life to a large swathe of fungi. Rather thick and meaty, the fungi made Zarnikorek's eyes bulge with excitement.

He unslung the satchel from his shoulder and set it next to a nearby tree, then picked and broke off chunks of the thick, golden-brown mushrooms. He inhaled the nutty scent, breathing it in, knowing that these would make great snacks for the rest of their flight. For a moment, he thought of Galium and how it was going to be the first city he ever visited that wasn't an orc or goblin dwelling. He wondered about the dwarves that lived there, previously considered to be the orc nation's greatest enemy. And now he and an orc mage were making their way there to discuss peaceful matters with the king of the dwarven people. Would they welcome them? Did they really have beards so long they got underfoot? Would they be as fearsome and unforgiving as all the stories say? A lump grew in his throat as he considered the implications. He was such a small goblin in such a wide world, and a monumental task lay before him.

A rustle in a bush nearby caught his attention. Zarnikorek swerved to inspect what manner of creature might be lurking in the shadows. With so many emotions roiling within him, his nerves got the better of him, and he jumped more than he would like to admit.

"H-hello?" Zarnikorek called out, his voice shaky. "D-Deklahn? Is that you?"

No answer.

"Uh … mountain creature?" he called, even shakier.

No answer.

His eyes slowly pulled away from the bush to inspect the rest of the surrounding forest, just in case his pursuer had silently moved away from its spot in order to flank him.

"Um, okay … If you're out there, I'm friendly. So, you can come out …"

Suddenly, a horned marten hopped out of the bush. Its big black eyes shone as they inspected the goblin. The creature's round furry ears twitched thoughtfully, and the horn that protruded from its head was not grotesque, but rather becoming for the small, weasel-like creature. Other than a lighter patch that ran across his chest, all of his fur was chestnut brown. The creature was adorable.

"Well, hello there," Zarni said to the horned marten. "Would you like some gibs?" he asked as he knelt and opened his satchel that rested nearby. "Here! My pa makes some of the best gibs I've ever tasted. You'll love them," he continued. He remembered reading a while back that horned martens regularly partook in nuts, berries, and plants, but enjoyed some meat occasionally when they could get themselves fish or bugs.

Zarni pulled the wrapped gibs out of his satchel and plucked one of the fish spines from the wrappings. The scent of the salt and seasoning made Zarni's own mouth water.

Zarni put the first one into his mouth slowly, making sure that the horned marten saw him eat it. He nodded toward the critter, hoping to convey it was safe for consumption. He plucked another one from the wrappings and held it out. The creature's nose twitched curiously. It scampered closer, grabbing the gib from the goblin's hand and scuttling away. Zarni chuckled and tossed another gib into his own mouth, before wrapping up the rest of them to put back in the bag.

What a cute little creature, Zarni thought to himself. Though when it stood on its hind legs, it was half as tall as he was. "See you next time," he said. He threw the wrapped gibs back into his bag.

Before he turned back to the mushrooms, the horned marten reappeared from another bush. The adorable creature neither spoke nor moved, but Zarni could tell it was looking for more of his pa's famed gibs. At least famed for the two of them.

"Sorry, pal," Zarni said. "No more gibs for now. I've got a long journey ahead, so I really should ration them."

Zarni turned back to the mushrooms, and when he glanced back over his shoulder, the horned marten was gone. Zarni smirked and shrugged to himself.

He continued to gather the mushrooms, tossing them into his satchel until the thing was overflowing. He snacked on a couple as well, but stopped in a hurry when Deklahn called out his name.

"Zarni! Zarnikorek! Are you ready to go?"

"One second!" Zarni hollered back and threw the last handfuls of mushrooms into his satchel without looking. He flipped the top closed and heaved it onto his shoulder. He hadn't realized how many mushrooms he'd gathered. Nonetheless, he shouldered the extra weight and hurried to meet Deklahn.

"Did you find anything good?" Deklahn asked.

"I found some good mushrooms." Zarni still had a large one in his hand and passed it over to the mage. "I think I may have grabbed too many."

"Ah, that's alright." Deklahn chuckled, eyeing the little goblin's satchel. "Gloh can handle the extra weight."

Zarni didn't doubt it.

The wyvern stood much larger than the two of them. Nowhere near the size of the wyvern's four-legged and fire-breathing cousin, the dragon. But Gloh still drew awe from the little goblin.

They climbed atop Gloh's back, Deklahn situating himself in the saddle and Zarnikorek just behind. Gloh reared back, lifting her head high before her wide wings stretched out and flapped, propelling them into the air. Onward they flew to Galium.

GALIUM

CHAPTER 8
A TRAITOR'S MAP

As they crested the front range of the Drelek Mountains, the south seemed to open up and sprawl as far as the eye could see. The goggles pressed into Zarnikorek's face as his eyes widened, staring in disbelief at the city of Galium down below. The city center clung close to the mountains, while farmlands and rolling hills dotted with doors and windows spread away from the city. Parts of the castle walls that surrounded the city looked new or rebuilt as they approached, contrasting to the older parts that had survived the Battle of Galium a year prior.

The castle of Galium erupted straight out of the side of the mountain. Its front jutted out of the rock to form a straight face before the other walls and towers angled and connected to the mountain. Much of the castle's footprint lay inside of the mountain, dwarves being talented engineers, on equal standing even with the greatest of goblins.

Zarnikorek thought his pa would love to see this place. Even his untrained eye found the blocky yet intricate and ancient dwarven masonry rather astounding. Deklahn heeled Gloh, and she brought them into a glide. The wyvern turned and shifted her wings, so they descended smoothly toward the front of the castle.

Many stairs led up to a stone pad where garvawk warriors from Galium lined the walkway, standing firm and proud, awaiting their arrival. Beside each of the dwarven warriors sat a stone garvawk—great panther-like creatures with huge bat-like wings furled in on top of themselves. The creatures, as Zarnikorek understood, were bonded with their dwarven warriors through a magical spell denoted upon their shoulders with an etched rune, and each warrior knew a secret phrase that unleashed the garvawk from its stone form, making the creature a formidable ally for the warrior.

"Did they know we were coming?" Zarnikorek asked. Deklahn chuckled, the orc mage obviously knowing something the goblin didn't. He reached into his cloak, rooting around for something in one of his myriad pockets, and produced a small abalone shell. The sea greens and blues of the shell shimmered in the evening sunlight.

"I have ways of communicating with the archmage of Galium. We're rather good friends, actually."

"A magic shell?" the goblin asked further.

"A Shell of Callencia. It lets us communicate at vast distances. It's rather difficult magic. There are only a few in all of Finlestia."

"Wow ..." Zarnikorek said, genuinely impressed. The arcane object was a stark reminder how special Deklahn was. *What am I even doing here?* the little goblin thought. He squeezed tighter to the orc mage's robes.

One garvawk warrior strode between the others and their regal stone creatures. His long brown beard brushed the front of his armor with every step. As Gloh put her feet down on the ground and planted her wings to hold herself up, Deklahn slid from her back with ease and met the garvawk warrior with a jovial embrace.

"Deklahn, long time no see," the dwarven warrior said.

"Lotmeag, it's good to see you. How are you, my old friend?"

"I can't complain," Lotmeag said. "Though I'll admit, I'm looking for an excuse to get back to Calrok to try some more orcish cuisine. I don't suppose you brought any yerself?"

"No, no. Not this time," Deklahn said with a chuckle. The mage must have seen the confusion on Zarnikorek's face, because he said, "Foredwarf Lotmeag had a rather extensive adventure with one of my fellow orc mages, Smarlo. The foredwarf grew something of a taste for orcish cuisine."

"Really like those omelets," Lotmeag grumbled thoughtfully. "Got the castle staff making them now. Though, we've only recently gotten back and are setting up a *glendon* team to capture a new garvawk. We'll be stuck here for a time while we train the new member."

"A stout and hardy dwarf from the warhog cavalries?"

"Aye, only the best of the best," Lotmeag said with a nod. "Nevertheless, next time I come to visit, ye'll have to share a new dish with me. I rather like orcish cooking." He said the last part conspiratorially toward Zarnikorek before he shrugged sheepishly and popped his brow.

"It's a deal," Deklahn managed to agree through another chortle. The orc mage patted the dwarven warrior on the shoulder and Zarnikorek got the sneaking suspicion that Deklahn was well-liked among the dwarven people.

"What's a *glendon* team?" the little goblin asked, before he could tamp his curiosity.

"Now, who do we have here?" Lotmeag asked Deklahn.

"Ah, yes, this is Zarni. He is the one I mentioned to Argus the last time I called from the Shell of Callencia."

"Right. Right. He mentioned ye were bringing a goblin. This is the one that's good with maps, huh?"

"Judging by all the maps and notes we found at the castle of Ruk, he's rather talented."

Zarnikorek's green cheeks rosed, and he scratched at the side of his head bashfully.

"Well, I like to draw. And I like maps. And I'm pretty good with logistics," he said, stumbling over his own thoughts.

"Don't be so shy," Deklahn said. "I've seen your work. I think you're going to do great on this quest."

"Ah, yes, the quest. King Thygram is up in the meeting chamber right now, awaiting us. I'm not sure if Master Argus will be there, but I imagine he knows ye're coming. The king wanted us out here to welcome ye. As ye know, some people are still a little nervous with the idea of a wyvern flying into Galium."

"That is understandable," Deklahn said, a hint of sadness lacing his words. "An unfortunate side effect of our past conflict."

"Wyverns are dragon cousins. The city is still recovering from the dragon's wrath," Lotmeag said to Zarnikorek to explain. "People will get used to it, I think."

His words surprised Zarnikorek. He hadn't considered that the dwarves and their people might also be having a difficult time transitioning into a state of alliance.

"Well, let me show ye up to the meeting room. I'm happy to take ye up there. Are ye good with stairs, Master Zarni?"

Zarnikorek shrugged and said, "I've got two legs. I can manage."

"Well, great. Let's take yer bags," Lotmeag said, turning to one of his warriors. "They'll get them to yer rooms so ye don't have to worry about them."

They handed their bags over and followed Lotmeag toward the castle entrance. "Now, a *glendon* team is a group we put together to go capture a wild garvawk to bring it into the fold for a new warrior to bond with. It's a dangerous type of mission, but the only way we can get new garvawks. I, myself, have been on a few teams. Like the first *glendon* team I ever led myself for a new garvawk warrior named Felton. See, he was ..."

Lotmeag's words faded away as Zarnikorek stared up at the castle jutting out from the mountain before them. His eyes followed the distinct dwarven architecture rising high above to where the king of Galium awaited his arrival. The knot in his stomach grew tighter.

He was about to meet the king of the dwarves.

There was no doubt in Zarnikorek's mind who was king. King Thygram Markensteel wore regal golden armor embedded with rare gems and minerals. His burly beard hung just below his belly. And though his height placed him somewhere taller than Zarnikorek and shorter than Deklahn, he stood with an undeniable presence. The king had a serious air to him, but to Zarnikorek's surprise, he greeted the goblin with warmth, and the castle staff had prepared a fine meal for them to share.

Zarnikorek, still nervous and unable to believe he was really there, had been content to sit quietly at the feast while the others talked.

They'd run into Argus Azulekor, the archmage of Galium and the king's closest adviser, while they ascended the many stairs to the meeting chamber at the top of the tower. Deklahn had quickly embraced the overloaded dwarven mage and taken some of the parchments and scrolls he carried. Now, the old mage's materials spanned the wide stone table around which the group stood.

Argus scratched at his long white beard as he gathered his thoughts and looked over all the elements. "Ah!" he started. He snatched a specific map and flattened it, while all the others leaned in to see what had excited the old dwarf. The table rose to neck height for him, so Zarnikorek scooted around the table, close to the mage, so he could see better.

Argus shifted the map toward the little goblin and gave him a quick wink. Embroidered silver stars sparkled curiously on the mage's long blue cloak as he shifted. "This map here is of greater Tarrine."

Zarnikorek's brow furrowed as he noted numerous cities in the far south that their own maps in Drelek did not have marked. The world was even bigger than they knew. The thought only made him feel that much smaller.

"As you can see here," Argus said, placing a thick dwarven finger on the map next to the city of Crossdin in the west. "We have a wagon route from Crossdin to Galium, and even Galium to Hill Stop. And then you can see this one here." He jabbed his finger at Whitestone, north of Whitestone Forest, but south of the Drelek Mountains. "Whitestone has routes to Hill Stop as well. And they've been establishing a route between the newer joint city of Kane Harbor. But because they're busy with that, we thought it would be wiser to establish the route with one of our experienced wagoners from here in Galium."

"I'm sure, eventually, it would make sense to do a wagon route from Kane Harbor to Calrok, but currently, using ships on the Gant Sea just works better," Deklahn said.

"Correct," Argus affirmed like a proud teacher to his pupil.

Zarnikorek scratched at his dark brown hair. Something about the maps on the table emboldened him. There was a simplicity to maps. Maps, he understood. "But with no established roads ..." he paused for a moment, unsure whether to continue. A quick nod from Deklahn encouraged him. "It will be difficult to cross the front range of the mountains. Our ancestors built the cities in specific places to make it harder for our enemies to reach."

"Right, you are," the dwarf mage said with an approving nod.

King Thygram spoke up. "That is one of the biggest problems. Ghun-Ra is already a central city for Drelek, but south of Drelek, we have many trade centers. The difficulty will be connecting them."

"I have a feeling Hill Stop will grow a lot bigger in the coming years," Argus said with a smirk.

Zarnikorek eyed the old dwarf. Was he some sort of seer, able to see the future? The moment of wonder passed quickly as the little goblin inspected the map. "Hill Stop sits directly south of Ghun-Ra, following the Palori River. Many roads are built along natural waterways. It seems logical enough that a new trade route between them would follow the river."

"Very good," Argus said, and Zarnikorek warmed under the old dwarf's praise.

"But if I recall, the mountains in that area are particularly treacherous terrain," Zarnikorek added. "And the Palori River is full of boulders and dangerous rapids as you get farther into the mountains. That would rule out boater trade. A wagon route might be the only option."

"That's why you're here," King Thygram said. Nervousness washed over the little goblin as the king addressed him directly. Zarnikorek felt as though he was not worthy of the king's attention. "Show him the other map, Argus."

"Ah, yes!" the old mage chimed as though he'd been waiting for that moment. He rifled through a stack of parchments on the table and pulled one free. It was an old map, weathered and browned by the years. As Argus laid it on the table, Zarnikorek was struck by its crudeness, but even more so by the fact that it was marked in old orcish.

"Is this what I think it is?" Deklahn asked, leaning over the stone table to get a better look.

"Aye," Argus said with a chortle. "This is the map of Koris."

"Wow ..." Deklahn whispered.

Zarnikorek stared at the map intently, not sure why the orc mage was so impressed. But as he scanned the parchment, he realized it was a map that indicated some mountain pass to the ancient city of Ghun-Ra. "Wait ... Is this ..."

"The Traitor's Map," Deklahn finished the goblin's thought. "It has long been held as a myth among our people. None believing that one of our own would turn against the kingdom."

"Aye," Argus nodded quietly, knowing what this meant to the two of them. "You see, it was this very map that led the allied army to Ghun-Ra in the last days of the Second Great Black War."

Zarnikorek racked his brain, remembering the historical texts his pa had on the great war. The battle at Ghun-Ra had been a loss for the peoples south of Drelek. The city had repelled their siege. However, there had been a secret campaign of misinformation by the enemies. The battle at Ghun-Ra was merely a distraction for other smaller and stealthier missions that led to the end of the war. Though it had been a loss for the elves, dwarves, and men, the battle had been a key cog in their strategy to end the war.

"This map was drawn by Koris himself," Argus said with a fond smile.

"Koris ..." Deklahn whispered, rolling the name around on his tongue.

"Aye," the dwarf mage affirmed. "Did you not know the name?"

"No," Deklahn answered. "Like I said, that story has fallen to the way of myth among our people."

"Well," Argus said. "We have a rather detailed account of him in the secret annals. Most of our people know nothing of him, either. But the scribe of the records seemed rather fond of him. Paints a picture of Koris as a brave and honorable orc."

"I should like to see that sometime if you don't mind," the orc mage said.

"Of course."

"But," King Thygram cut in, "we were hoping that with your help, Mister Zarnikorek, we could rediscover some of the ancient route and potentially use it as a starting place for our new wagon route."

"Yes," Argus said quickly, getting back on topic.

Zarnikorek stared at the map, a tear welling in his eye. *Koris.* He'd never heard the name. The orc had played such a pivotal role in ending a tragic and bloody war, and Zarnikorek had never even heard the name. A conflict waged within him. On one hand, this was the Traitor's Map. While crude, it may be one of the greatest artifacts he'd ever seen in his life. The very object an orc had used to betray his people to end a war. On the other, it seemed to the goblin that he was doing exactly what Koris had attempted to do. He was building a bridge between his people and their former enemies. Perhaps Koris had done it in a different way, but it made Zarnikorek wonder, *How will history remember me? Will they?*

"I'll do it. Of course," Zarnikorek said with a gulp. "But I will need a skilled wagoner. The only wyperience I have with wagons is when I would travel with King S—"

Zarnikorek's words choked off. His heart pounded and a warm flush rolled over his little body. His long green ears burned. The others stared at him for a moment, as if they expected him to continue. But when he didn't, the foredwarf of the garvawk warriors saved him.

"Well ..." Lotmeag said slowly. "We should be able to get ye a good wagoner for the journey. My own brother-in-law is a wagoner, so they know me around the depot. I'll take ye over there in the morning to talk to the wagon master before he calls the hauls for the day."

"Excellent," King Thygram agreed. He placed a thick hand on Zarnikorek's little shoulder. His serious face softened. His eyes gazed at the goblin with ... *Is that respect?* Zarnikorek wondered. "Go get some rest for tonight. You have a long journey ahead, but I have no doubt you will make all of us very proud. Go in honor and glory."

Zarnikorek whispered the well-known dwarven phrase back, "For honor and glory."

The king excused himself, seemingly happy with the plan. Argus reached out and stopped Zarnikorek before Lotmeag led him to his room.

"Here," Argus said, placing the folded Traitor's Map into the goblin's hand. He chuckled and something glinted in the old dwarf's eye. "How interesting that a piece of ancient history will play a role in making history yet again."

Zarnikorek took the map and squeezed it in his hands.

CHAPTER 9
GIBS

Zarnikorek rolled over in his bed again. It was not an uncomfortable bed, and the dwarves had given him a rather cozy guest room in which to sleep. However, rest evaded him. What was he doing here? Him. Of all the goblins and orcs they could have chosen, King Genjak chose him?

For the hundredth time that night, he started thinking about how treacherous the journey might be. He couldn't beat back the notion that it would be an easy way for the new orc king to eliminate him. But Deklahn had assured the goblin that the king's interest in him was pure. And though he'd only known the mage for a couple of days, he'd come to trust him. Even more so after seeing how much the dwarves seemed to like the mage. As sad as it was, Deklahn might be the closest thing to a friend Zarnikorek had.

The little goblin sighed and sat up in his bed. He rolled his shoulders and shivered after a couple of relieving pops and cracks. The map lay securely on his satchel. He considered lighting a candle to study it some more.

Until it moved ...

Zarnikorek blinked and rubbed his eyes. He peered hard at the map, wondering if he was so tired he was seeing things.

Again, the map moved.

No... Wait ...

His satchel moved.

The map slipped off his satchel as it bucked to the side.

Suddenly, a mushroom popped out of the opening and skittered across the floor. Zarnikorek gripped the blanket and drew it up to his chin. His normally green skin blanched. What was happening? Some sort of dwarven assassin? *Wait*, he thought, *I'm a guest here, and everyone I've interacted with in Galium is excited about the alliance. Why would they send an assassin? More likely it's a ghost.* The thought did nothing to ease the tension in Zarnikorek's gut. Bile crept up his throat. He might be sick before the ghost killed him.

Another mushroom popped out and bounced away from the bag.

The satchel lurched and fell over, spilling more of the mushrooms. Zarnikorek squeaked.

His satchel flipped and toppled, sending even more mushrooms scattering. Zarnikorek squeezed his eyes shut in terror. He had to be dreaming. This couldn't be real.

He peered through his squinted eyes. His satchel laid sprawled open, surrounded by mushrooms. It was then that he noticed his pouch of gibs torn to bits and empty.

What in Finlestia ...

A furry, horned head popped up over the side of the bed. Zarnikorek jumped back, holding the blanket tight.

"You!" he managed out. "You ..." Frankly, Zarnikorek didn't know what to say. His heart thudded so hard in his chest he could barely breathe.

Suddenly, laughter burbled up from within, the only reaction that his body could muster. Zarnikorek laughed so hard, tears welled from his eyes, streaming down his cheeks.

Adorable black eyes blinked as the horned marten pulled itself up onto the comfy bed. It tilted its head to the side and twitched its round ears. Something akin to a cooing purr came out of the creature as it padded on the bed toward Zarnikorek. It turned in circles for a moment, seemingly testing the spot. The creature laid down and snuggled next to the goblin. Its body heaved with a little snore.

Utterly confused and unable to gather his wits, Zarnikorek rubbed his eyes and shook his head.

"I see you ate all my gibs," he finally said.

The creature didn't respond. He merely slept cozily pressed up against the goblin.

After a long while, Zarnikorek finally laid himself back down and placed a gentle hand on the furry marten. The goblin found the cozy creature was rather comforting to him. "Alright, Gibs," he said to the little thing. "I guess we can sort this out tomorrow when we're not so tired."

Zarnikorek closed his eyes, feeling the soft breathing of the horned marten curled up next to him. In short order, they were both snoring.

CHAPTER 10
THE WAGON DEPOT

Lotmeag Kandersaw woke Zarnikorek early. The poor goblin groaned when he realized the sun hadn't even risen. Thankfully, the foredwarf took him by the castle kitchen to enjoy an omelet before they headed to the wagon depot. It wasn't quite the same as the omelets he and his pa made, but the spinach and bacon wrapped in eggs and sprinkled with a seasoning Zarnikorek had never tried before hit the spot.

They arrived at the wagon depot at the same time as several wagoners. Zarnikorek found the place oddly comforting. It reminded him of the docks warehouse back in Ghun-Ra. The wagon depot was an enormous wooden structure with several offshoots. Stalls for wagons branched off to one side, with through stalls where horses could rest. Workers and wagon loaders were already going over the goods that needed to be transported out that day.

A burly human stood high above many of the workers, which included sturdy dwarves and other humans—even some beanpole teenagers. His salt and pepper beard was respectable for a human living among dwarves, and the air with which he stood among them and shuffled through the parchments on his wooden tablet helped Zarnikorek pinpoint the man as the wagon master of the depot.

The man glanced up toward Lotmeag and Zarnikorek as they approached. He did a second take, and his already serious face grew grave in the dim dawn light. Lotmeag waved to the man before pulling Zarnikorek to the side. The human nodded curtly and shot a finger in the air to indicate he would join them momentarily.

"Best we go back here to wait," Lotmeag whispered to the goblin.

"He didn't look too pleased ..." Zarnikorek said slowly.

"Sham never looks pleased," Lotmeag said with a chuckle. "I've told him he shouldn't be so dour. Humans don't live so long as dwarves. They should spend their shorter lives with a smile on their faces. Dwarves have lots more time to be dour and then joyful and then whatever else they want to be."

Zarnikorek chuckled along, but he was pretty sure it was just his nervousness coming out. But as the foredwarf's words sunk in, he paused. Goblins were even shorter lived than humans. The oldest goblin of record was the notorious Blinjetka. She was notorious, of course, for her rather ill temper and her red root addiction. But because she lived to 79 years old, a good 20 years longer than the average goblin, many had attempted to follow in her footsteps. Red root, however, addles the mind with visions and sent most into madness without any obvious effect on longevity.

Thinking on such things made him wonder what attitude would define his life at the end of his days. Fear? Cowardice?

The wooden door behind them shut suddenly.

"Foredwarf Lotmeag," Sham grumbled.

"Ah, Wagon Master Sham, it's good to see ye and h—"

"What is this?" the wagon master cut the dwarf off.

"Special assignment from the king," the dwarf growled back, dropping all pretense of cordialness. He clearly didn't like being cut off.

"I don't have time for this," Sham said quickly, rifling through the parchments on his tablet. "I've got forty wagoners waiting in the other room. All these transports need to go out today."

"Ye have time for yer king's commands," Lotmeag said sternly.

Sham heaved a long sigh and wrinkled his nose. His jaw tightened, and he spoke through clenched teeth. "What does my king wish of me? And why have you brought this goblin into my depot?"

"*This goblin*," Lotmeag emphasized, "is the goblin hand-picked to help establish a new wagon route between our people and the city of Ghun-Ra."

Sham pushed air through his lips in disbelief.

"*And,*" Lotmeag continued, as Zarnikorek, getting rather uncomfortable, slowly inched behind the dwarf. "This goblin has a name. Zarni, please meet the wagon master of Galium. I promise, his logistical acumen far outweighs his manners."

Lotmeag turned and ushered Zarnikorek forward. The goblin mustered all his might to keep his body from visibly shaking. He reached his hand high above himself. Sham grunted and enveloped the goblin's small hand with his own.

"Pleased to meet you," Zarnikorek squeaked.

"Fine. Fine. What is the assignment, then?" Sham shifted, pulling a parchment from the bottom of his stack and scribbling on it.

"Special transport assignment for King Thygram Markensteel. To be paid in full by his lordship. Single transport of one goblin passenger, Zarnikorek. From Galium to

Ghun-Ra, by way of Hill Stop. Will require a rather experienced wagoner. Terrain will be rough and the trip through wild country. Not for the faint of heart."

"Fine," Sham said and brushed past them. "Stay hidden here. I'll bring the wagoner back after all transports have been called."

"Aye, that will be sufficient. We can discuss the details with them thoroughly."

Sham grunted and turned to leave.

"Oh, and Sham," Lotmeag called.

The hurried man stopped, but didn't turn back.

"Make sure ye get us one of yer finest."

Sham's body didn't seem to make any motion of acknowledgment, but Zarnikorek judged by the pause that the man had heard the foredwarf. The wagon master disappeared through the doorway.

"Come," Lotmeag beckoned the goblin. "We can watch the proceedings from here."

Zarnikorek followed the dwarf around a wall. They stopped in a walkway where they remained out of sight, but could clearly see the gathering. "Is he always like that or does he just really hate goblins?" he asked before he could bottle up the question.

Lotmeag grunted a suppressed laugh. "I told ye he was dour. It's not just ye. He's always grumpy. Maybe the grumpiest human I've ever met. Probably because he has to work with my brother-in-law." The dwarf's shoulders bobbed several times as he chuckled to himself.

"Is your brother-in-law grumpy too?"

"Stones, no!" Lotmeag whispered. "Quite the opposite. He's so full of joy he's bursting with it. Got so much, it comes out of him in an overabundance of words. And if ye couldn't tell, Sham doesn't conversate so well."

"Here!" someone called from the crowd, gathering their attention.

Zarnikorek watched for a moment, picking up on the proceedings. Sham stood on a small platform as depot workers waited nearby. Sham called out each transport as he went through the parchments. All of them seemed to be for some various good or another. Three sacks of seed. Four barrels of mead. Five crates of linens. And onward.

"Ye see," Lotmeag whispered. "The wagoners are only allowed to say 'here' to claim a haul. If they say anything else, they're passed over for the next person to say 'here.' That was one of the hardest things for my brother-in-law to get when he started wagoning. He's way too talkative. But he's been good at it for years now."

"I see." Zarnikorek watched the proceedings with interest. They'd have to adopt some of the methods in Ghun-Ra as well to make it easier for wagoners getting transports there.

"Sham usually does all the goods hauls before he calls any goods and passenger transports. Then after that, it's the passengers only."

"I suppose certain wagoners have wagons better equipped for passengers than—"

"Hang on," Lotmeag paused him. "Sorry to interrupt ye, but it looks like Sham's about to call our transport."

With the heavy sigh, long pause, and the glare Sham shot over at them, Zarnikorek guessed the dwarf to be right. The man's face shifted from disdain to a rather curious expression of mirth.

"What are ye ..." Lotmeag mumbled under his breath.

Quickly, Sham turned to the gathered wagoners and called out, "This next transport is a special one. It comes as a special assignment from the king and requires the best among us. It's a passenger transport and we'll need to show our best hospitality on this one. We'll need a wagoner who prides themselves on a 'comfortable journey experience.'" The way the wagon master said the words gave Zarnikorek pause. They were almost … mocking.

"No, no, no …" Lotmeag grumbled under his breath.

Several of the wagoners chuckled and many of them turned to a halfling standing toward the front of the gathering. He was half the height of a human and shorter than his dwarven compatriots. Maybe even as short as Zarnikorek. His wavy, dirty-blond hair curled on top of his head and he pulled at his suspenders with a prideful smile that gripped a pipe with ease. It appeared that the wagon master could be speaking of no one else.

"It will require much bravery as well. A single passenger transport from here to Ghun-Ra."

Murmured whispers rippled through the crowd of wagoners. The halfling wagoner's eyes went wide. His face contorted momentarily as he seemed to be considering the matter. After a long moment, the depot went quiet, as if the very air had been sucked out of the place.

"Don't ye do it," Lotmeag whispered.

Zarnikorek glanced at the dwarf, who seemed very invested in this strange moment.

"Here!" broke the silence.

"Boehlen's Beard!" Lotmeag cursed.

The whispers erupted again, and Sham shot a smug glance over at the pair before he continued to the other transports.

CHAPTER 11
DOUBTS

Round and round they went, the dwarf and the halfling arguing over the quest.

"Nope!" Lotmeag blurted for maybe the hundredth time. "It's not happening. Anybody but ye. Yer not going."

"It's my transport," the halfling said with a sigh and a tired smile. "I'd wager there's not a better wagoner in all of Galium to accomplish this task. No one has the comfortable journey experience I try to give my passengers." He turned to Zarnikorek with an assuring look.

"Tobin," Lotmeag growled. "Yer not going."

The halfling chuckled as though he pitied his brother-in-law for not understanding. "I have to go."

"That doesn't make any sense," Lotmeag barked.

The door opened and Argus Azulekor slipped into the room, his blue cloak swishing behind him. "Excuse me," he said politely. "What have I missed?"

"Oh, perfect," Lotmeag said excitedly. "Master Argus, talk some sense into Tobin. Tell him he is not going on this quest. Someone who can fight should go."

"I can fight," Tobin said. The statement came out with a little more fire than anything Zarnikorek had yet seen while listening to the argument. "I have my crossbow. Finest crafted in all of

Galium. Dead bull's eye every time. Probably the straightest shooter in all of Tarrine, I'd wager."

"We need someone stronger. Maybe a former warrior. Someone bigger," Lotmeag said.

The room fell silent.

"Bigger ..." Tobin whispered. Something in the short response from the halfling seemed to cut Lotmeag.

"I'm sorry," the foredwarf said, turning his attention to Zarnikorek. "I didn't mean bigger. I just meant ... ye know ... I just want ye to be protected. I just ..."

"Worry for your brother," Argus put in kindly.

"No," Zarnikorek said quietly. "He's right. Who am I to go on this quest? I'm a nobody."

"Nobody is a nobody," the old mage said, turning toward the goblin.

"But I'm just ... this is so big. And I'm just so small."

A kind smile pressed the mage's lips together. "I have been studying some recently rediscovered texts from the elven library of Loralith. Funny, elves live so long they forget things over the centuries." He paused to shake his head at some humorous memory. "Anyway, did you know that when the Maker was creating the world, he created thirteen seeds smaller than any we see in Finlestia today? And it was from those initial seeds, the smallest of all, that he created the First Trees of every land of Finlestia. And we recently rediscovered the First Tree of Tarrine in the Nari Desert. It is larger than a mountain. A whole city of people live in the tree and its roots."

Tears welled in Zarnikorek's eyes as he let his mind dream of the place. A knobby dwarven hand landed on the goblin's shoulder and the mage looked him straight in the eye.

"Even small things can have great impact on the world. Just like a small deed can impact one person and lead to more small deeds that ripple into a thousand. This task may seem large, but it will require many small acts of courage, and I think you have more in you than you know."

"As do I," Lotmeag added with a nod. "Forgive me for sowing doubt."

Argus's brows popped as if he was awaiting Zarnikorek's answer before he continued. The goblin wanted to yell. He wanted to cry. Zarnikorek wanted to tell them there was some sort of mistake. He couldn't do this. But then the halfling said something that sounded to him as a promise.

"And I'll be right there by your side," Tobin said.

"Tobin ..." Lotmeag started, but changed course with the hard glance he got from Argus.

Zarnikorek let the silence between them linger for a moment longer, but finally said, "I forgive you. I'm sorry for letting my doubts show."

"You are among friends, Zarni. Friends are there to help you shoulder your doubts. And if you can't share your doubts with your friends, then whom?"

Argus gave the goblin a pat on the shoulder and a wink.

"Tobin," Lotmeag started, softer this time. "What about Lenor and Button and baby Bandix?"

Tobin smiled. "You know they'll be alright while I'm gone. Lenor is the best dwarven woman in all of Galium. You know that."

"Aye, but what if ye get lost or injured or can't make it home?"

"Just as much as it's my job to get Mister Zarnikorek there safe, it's his job to get us there without getting us too lost." The halfling paused and gave the goblin a wink. "Plus, he looks pretty tough to me. We'll take care of each other."

Zarnikorek wasn't sure he agreed with the halfling that he looked tough, but the way he said it filled the goblin with a quiet confidence.

"I hear ye, but we could get another wagoner. Any other wagoner. Argus, help me out here."

The old dwarf mage stroked his long white beard thoughtfully.

"I have to do this," Tobin said. And with the short answer, Zarnikorek wondered what the halfling was holding back. Lotmeag had said the halfling was overly talkative, even zealous with his words, but Zarnikorek had not seen such in the conversation.

"But why?" Lotmeag pleaded.

A long silence stretched through the room again.

Argus's eyes narrowed as he searched the halfling. Tobin scuffed his feet on the wooden floor. "Mister Tobin," the mage said, his tone gentle. "Why do you need to do this?"

"I'm not like you, Lotmeag," he said, turning his answer on his brother-in-law. "I'm not the foredwarf of the garvawk warriors. I'm not one of Galium's elite force. When the dragon came with the Drelek army to destroy the city, I was one of the wagoners charged with shuttling civilians out of the city and taking them to Crossdin. I wasn't even here when the city was attacked."

"Oh, Tobin," Lotmeag said, his stance softening. "That's nothing to be ashamed of. You played a pivotal role in protecting people. Keeping them safe."

"But many of my friends fought for this city. Some died. Even more of my friends went on to fight across the Gant Sea in the dangerous lands of Kelvur. Risking everything for a future hope. Why shouldn't I assume some risk to see that vision through when they've already given so much? Why should I give any less effort?"

Lotmeag's beard wobbled from side to side as he adjusted his clenched jaw. Zarnikorek hadn't known the dwarf long, but it was obvious the foredwarf was fighting to hold back his emotions. A mixture of pride and sorrow and understanding squeaked through his defensive countenance.

"I ..." Lotmeag choked out.

"Understand the feeling," Argus offered.

Lotmeag merely nodded. And at that moment, Zarnikorek saw the foredwarf in a new light. The goblin had no idea what the warrior had experienced over time, but he could tell that Lotmeag had done everything he could to hold honor at the forefront of his life. And though the dwarf wasn't much taller than he, Zarnikorek thought him monumental.

Tobin walked up to his brother-in-law and wrapped him in a hug. Lotmeag hugged him back, but shortly pushed him away. "Alright, alright. Enough of that now. We'll make sure to get ye all the supplies ye need to make this quest possible. But ye better not get lost. Not that I doubt Mister Zarni, but I don't want my niece and nephew to grow up without a father. Lenor would kill me."

"You should probably come to dinner tonight to help explain all of this," Tobin said with a smirk.

"Oh, no ye don't," Lotmeag said, taking another step back. "I'll come for dinner, but ye got yerself into this. Ye can explain it to her."

Tobin chuckled. "Fair enough. Zarni, will you join my family for the evening? Lenor is quite the cook, I tell you. I wagered a friend of mine from the Garome district that she's the best in all Galium. He said his aunt was the best cook. Though admittedly, Aunt Cleary makes a mean gumbo. Just enough kick to make your ears sweat." Zarni parted his lips and took a breath as though he were about to answer, but the halfling kept going. "But don't worry, if you don't like spicy, most of Lenor's dishes are pretty tame. But it'd be good for you to meet Button and our new addition, Bandix, as well. I'm sure the whole family will love you. I—"

"That'll be lovely," Master Argus cut the halfling off. He smiled at the goblin. "Won't it?"

"Uh, yes. Of course," Zarni managed out.

"But before you leave to acquire supplies for the journey, I brought something for you I think may ease everyone's minds." With a swish of his blue cloak, Argus retrieved a crystal orb from his pocket. The sphere was larger than his palm, but not so cumbersome that it required two hands to hold. Everyone in the room took an involuntary step toward the mage to see what gift he bore.

"This is a stello glass," he said with some air of awe. "It's a rather beautiful artifact. There are others, and I have known some ship's captains in the south seas to use them to navigate by night. Though the most skilled sailors do not need them, mind you."

Zarnikorek leaned closer, marveling at the object.

"What does it do?" Tobin asked.

"It's imbued with an ancient magic that identifies constellations in the night sky. Many known to us today, but many forgotten over the centuries. It's a remarkable tool." Argus handed it to the halfling carefully. "Should you get lost on your journey, perhaps it will help you."

"Thank you, Master Argus," Tobin whispered, apparently too moved by the gift to string more words together.

"Of course," the mage replied and gathered Zarni and Tobin before him, placing a hand on each of their shoulders. "This journey will be difficult, but I believe both of you will come out the other end of this stronger. There can be no courage in the absence of fear. Embrace it. However, do not let fear waver your steps. For you two embark on one of the greatest journeys of our time. To build bridges for generations to come. To see the vision of a future hope come to fruition. Go now. For honor and glory."

Tobin clutched the orb to his chest and gave the old mage a respectful bob of his head. Zarni copied the motion, not knowing what else to do. But when he looked back, the old dwarf gave him a quick wink, and any doubt in his mind melted away.

CHAPTER 12
THE HALFLING'S HOME

Zarni shoveled another bite of roasted potatoes into his mouth. The savory seasoning burst with flavor as he moaned with delight. The truth was, he was stuffed. But Lenor had made a delicious dinner with broccoli cutlets, onion chips, bell pepper chunks, cubed potatoes, and sausage slices.

When they'd arrived at Tobin's home, Zarni was blown away by the summer flowers that coated the hill in which the home was built. A rainbow of summer colors filled his eyes as the sun descended for the evening. Even before they stepped through the door, he could smell the meal Lenor had been preparing for them. But when they walked through the front door that led straight into the hill and their home, Zarni realized just how hungry he'd gotten.

He poked at the last potato cube on his plate. Speckled with seasoning, it tempted his tongue with one more bite of savory goodness, but the little goblin could eat no more.

"All done with that, Mister Zarni?" Lenor asked as she came to grab his plate.

"Oh, please. Let me," the goblin replied, standing to his feet and carrying his plate to the washing basin.

"I'll take that," Tobin said, placing another plate on the counter to the side to await drying. "My wife cooks like a queen, so I try to wash the dishes when I'm home." The halfling gave the goblin a wink before his face contorted. "Though I suppose queens don't usually cook. I'd wager they've got all sorts of kitchen staff to take care of such things. Dishwashers and chefs and bakers. All sorts."

"That's probably true," Zarni agreed. "Can I dry these?"

"Sure, sure!" Tobin said, swinging a towel from his shoulder. "I normally wouldn't let a guest do such a thing, but I figure anything we can do together to practice a little bit of teamwork is a good thing. We're partners on this endeavor after all. Mind you, I've wagoned with an old mentor of mine for years. Georl. Creaky old dwarf. Ears worse than a prickly bean hog. And his eyes are greying. But he's still out there wagoning. Says he doesn't want to retire because he likes the traveling to visit his daughter in Crossdin." The halfling paused to laugh over something he found humorous. "Well, he doesn't actually say all that much. He mostly just grunts nowadays, but you can tell that's why he keeps going."

"Roar!" Cackling laughter erupted, following Lotmeag's faux cry from the sitting room. Zarni glanced toward the sitting area where Tobin's daughter jumped on her uncle's back as though she stood triumphantly over a slain dragon. In quick order, Lotmeag came back to life, and the two were rolling in another bout of wrestling, laughing the whole time.

Tobin snorted a chuckle. "Button loves her uncle. Lotmeag is quite the warrior. You know, before he became the foredwarf of the garvawk warriors, he'd only led one *glendon* team. That's where they go on a mission to capture a new garvawk to bring into their ranks."

"I heard that," Zarni said quickly. He smirked as he got the words in during a rare breath for the halfling. He guessed this was what Lotmeag had meant about Tobin being zealous with his words.

"Oh, sure. Sure. I suppose Lotmeag told you all about that. It's a very fine thing, actually. I have a friend in the Garome District who used to be a garvawk warrior. They always pick the best of the best from the warhog cavalry to join the ranks of the garvawk warriors. But he got injured in the Battle of Galium."

Zarnikorek didn't respond. A weight fell in his stomach. What could he say? It was his old king who commanded the attack on the dwarven city. The little goblin hadn't done it, but he couldn't help but feel guilty over the matter.

"... now, she has this amazing herbs and tea shop." Snapping back to the conversation, Zarnikorek wasn't sure what he'd missed. "Speaking of, we should take some herbs and seasoning for our trip. No sense in cooking bland food on the road, I'd say. Lenor can head over to the shop and restock when we leave. I'd wager there's not—"

"Oh!" Lenor's startled outburst froze everyone in the house. Tobin and Zarnikorek swiveled to see the dwarven woman. She clutched at the swaddled baby Bandix, his tuft of blond hair sticking out from the wrap, as she stared at something near the front door. Lotmeag's chest heaved, his boulders of shoulders tensed, and his legs planted in a fighter's stance. Button dangled from his back; her little arms wrapped around the dwarven warrior's thick neck.

"Well, hello there," Lenor said as she knelt.

Zarni and Tobin moseyed closer to see what could have startled the halfling's wife. As they did, Zarni blushed. A long furry creature with a horn atop his head purred and nuzzled against the dwarven woman's leg.

"I didn't know you were bringing along a pet," Tobin said. "He's adorable. Look at those black eyes and that little button nose. Ha! Button, you see this. He's got a little button nose."

Lotmeag let the little girl down slowly and she scampered toward her mother to get a closer look at the horned marten. "Pretty kitty."

"It's a horned marten," Zarni said with a chuckle. "And in truth, I didn't know he was coming along either."

"What's his name?" Lenor asked as she scratched the creature behind the ears. The horned marten maneuvered its head, positioning for more and more pets, relishing in her attention.

"Well, I call him Gibs. Since he ate all my gibs out of my bag."

"Gibs is pretty kitty," Button said.

The others laughed.

"What are gibs?" Lenor asked. "Can I make some more for you before you two leave?"

"Oh, I don't know," Zarni said. "They're a snack really. You take flexible fish bones, season them, and fry them up to make them crispy and crunchy."

"Never heard of something like that. And I've spent a good bit of time in Crossdin by the Tandal Sea," Tobin said, stroking his chin as he placed an empty pipe in his mouth and chewed on it thoughtfully.

"It's probably more of a goblin snack. My pa makes them often with fish we catch in the river in the Ghun-Ra valley."

"Sounds nice," Lenor said. "I'm not sure we can make some before you two leave. Not sure we'd be able to get the fish bones."

"That's alright, love," Tobin offered. "Perhaps it's something they make in Hill Stop since they're on the Palori River. We can ask around when we go through there. I know I'd sure like to try some gibs. They sound interesting. And Maker knows, I'm not too picky when it comes to good eating." The halfling laughed and patted his round belly.

It took some doing to successfully get Button down for bed—a task Zarni found to be rather entertaining. The little girl came up with every excuse under the hill to stay up. First, she needed a drink. Then she had "forgotten" to give everyone hugs. Then she'd "forgotten" to give everyone kisses. Even Zarni got goodnight loves from the sweet girl. Then she'd forgotten to pet the "pretty kitty."

Lotmeag explained to the goblin that she did this circus routine every time he visited. The warrior's eyes glinted mischievously, knowing that he'd been the cause of riling her up. That is, until Lenor told the foredwarf it was his turn to put the girl to bed. He'd gone into the other room sometime earlier while the others each found a cozy wingback chair in the sitting room and warmed the hearth. As Lenor came back from checking on the status of her brother's mission, she shook her head and whispered, "They're both asleep."

Zarni chuckled into his steaming mug of chamomile tea. Tobin had scooped a generous helping of honey into the mug, but it wasn't over-sweet. The halfling placed a mug on a side table next to his wife's favorite chair and snuck a quick biscuit from the jar.

"Tobin Keeland ..." Lenor whispered a mock scolding.

The halfling quickly shoved the biscuit into his mouth before replacing his pipe. His lips curled around the pipe in a sheepish grin as he winked at Zarni. The goblin smirked and held his drink with both hands in front of his face, breathing in the comforting steam. The wingback chair was designed for dwarves, so it was just big enough to surround the goblin like a nest with the throw pillow wedged on one side of him and the quietly snoring horned marten on the other.

Lenor's head angled to the side as she sat. Her brown hair, braided into a net with stone beads, draped over her shoulder. "Well, don't you look cozy?"

The brightness in the dwarf's eyes. The cheer with which her husband drank his tea in between puffs of his now lit pipe. The rhythmic rise and fall of the little furry body curled next to him. The warm glow of the fire in the hearth. All of it. He was cozy. Zarni thought it strange how much he felt at home. The little goblin hadn't expected anything like this on the quest.

"I am cozy. Thank you," he replied. "You have been a wonderful hostess. I cannot thank you enough. I wasn't sure what to expect on this trip, but your generosity and warm welcome have been more than I could have hoped for."

"You are very welcome," she said as she blew on her hot tea. She turned her gaze to her husband. With an amused pop of her brow, she said, "He has a habit of bringing folks home."

Tobin chuckled, his teeth gripping the wooden pipe. "Last year, I brought home a crew from Crossdin. Well, they weren't from Crossdin. They just landed there, coming in from the Tandal Sea. They were out there in a tiny little river boat. Nearly drowned, they did. But they were a crew of heroes. A deep gnome and a dwarf. Turned out the dwarf was a clan prince." Tobin's face lit up as he told the story. "And they had two humans with them. One was from the Griffin Guard of Whitestone!"

"Whitestone?" Zarni repeated, trying to make sense of it. "Whitestone is all the way on the other side of Tarrine. How did the guardian end up in the Tandal Sea with such a ragtag crew?"

"Well, that's just it," Tobin sat up excitedly, leaning forward with fervor. "He was part of a griffin squadron that was lost in a skirmish with some wyvern riders of Drelek. But that was back before the truce, you see. He was the only survivor. But then this huntsman and his family healed him up. And they went on this wild adventure. But—"

"But that is a story for another time," Lenor interrupted her husband. Zarni smiled as he took another sip. He'd have to get that story out of the halfling another time, but the goblin imagined the dwarven woman wanted to chat more about the journey ahead. "Why is it that Lotmeag can't go with ye?"

"Ah, yes," Tobin said. "They're preparing to head out on another *glendon,* as you know. And with all the changes the garvawk warriors have gone through in the last year, he needs to be here to lead them. Says they are also in the middle of gearing up for a joint training deployment to Crossdin with the 3rd Warhog Cavalry. Lots going on for them. I remember when he got to lead his first *glendon* team. He was so—"

"That all seems reasonable," Lenor said, cutting him off again. Tobin didn't seem to notice or show any offense whatsoever. Zarni was starting to piece together that the only way to get a word in edge-wise with the halfling might be to cut him off mid-sentence. That, at least, appeared to be the tactic his loved ones used. Zarnikorek wasn't sure how comfortable he was with the notion, but he was about to spend a lot of time with the halfling, and their journey would require good communication.

"You plan to blaze a trail north from Hill Stop then?" She directed the question to Zarnikorek.

"Yes, Ma'am," he affirmed politely. "It should be the easiest route. There is already a road that runs north from Hill Stop. There are plenty of farms north of the town until you hit the mountains. From there, our challenge really starts. We've got an ancient map used during the Second Great Black War. It led the allied peoples north through the mountains to the valley of Ghun-Ra. If we can rediscover the route they took, it may make for a good wagon route."

"Seems reasonable," she said with a soft nod. "And what sort of dangers do you expect?"

"Well," Zarni hemmed. "To be honest, we're not really sure. Certainly, there are wild creatures in the mountains."

"None that *Meldonna* can't handle, my love," Tobin assured her.

"*Meldonna?*" Zarni inquired.

"My crossbow," Tobin said, sitting up again with excitement. "I bought it from a weaponsmith in the Castle District. Said it was his finest work and there's likely not another crossbow in all of Tarrine its equal. Said—"

"Save some conversation for your trip," Lenor said with a huff and a smile. She turned on Zarnikorek with a genuine inquiry playing on her face. After a long pause, she voiced it. "You will take care of my husband?"

Zarni glanced at Tobin, who smiled and nodded to the goblin. He remembered the halfling's own words to Lotmeag about them protecting each other. "I will," he assured her. "We're a team. We'll look out for each other. And my hope is that we won't even need to use any weapons. That would be ideal, anyway."

"Well, that's all I needed to hear," she said with a nod of her own.

As they lounged in the sitting room, enjoying the evening fire in the hearth, a thought pricked at Zarnikorek's heart. This loving family, made up of peoples who were so recently enemies of his own people, had welcomed him with open arms and generous hearts. Even more so, this family trusted him with their world—their father and husband. Zarni didn't know how to explain it, but the dwarven woman's confidence in him was breaking something down deep within him.

CHAPTER 13
GREGORY

A tall human woman waved to Tobin and Zarnikorek as they approached. "Hello there ..." A wide-brimmed hat sat atop her head, providing ample shade from the morning sun that bathed the ranch with warmth. The distinct smell of livestock singed Zarnikorek's nose hairs, but he wasn't quite sure what combination of animals expelled the pungent aroma. The woman's bright-blue eyes contrasted her slightly confused face. Zarnikorek figured the rancher had never seen a goblin in person before.

"Good morning!" Tobin greeted her, but removed his pipe to continue. "Miss Calli, I'd wager?"

"That's a bet you'd win," the woman said. As she approached, Zarni's neck craned backward so he could look up to her face. He was surprised that this human woman was so much taller than he and Tobin. Most human women were shorter than human men, but just like orc women, they were usually taller than goblins—or at least, most goblins. Especially one his size.

Suddenly, Zarnikorek realized she was eyeing him.

"Uh, hello," he stammered.

"Hello."

"I'm Zarnikorek."

"Nice to meet you," she said. Though the words came out with a hint of confusion, she did seem to mean it.

"And I'm Tobin Keeland. Wagoner of Galium. Renowned for my comfortable journey experience for my passengers. I'd wager there's none more renowned for it." He said with a chuckle as he replanted his pipe in his mouth.

"I see," she said with a smirk. "What can I do for such a renowned wagoner and his ... compatriot?"

"Ah, yes," Tobin said. "The kings of Galium and Drelek have commissioned Zarni and me for an expedition to chart a new wagon route for trade between our peoples."

"I see ..." Calli replied, though her eyes narrowed and she bit at her lip contemplatively. "And what can I do for you?"

"Calli!" a rough voice hollered from a barn nearby.

The rancher heaved a heavy sigh and rolled her eyes. "What is it, Glin?"

A dwarf in a similarly wide-brimmed hat rounded out of the barn, stomping his boots on the dirt path. "That's it!" he barked. "I can't take it anymore. If I have to work with that creature for one more day, I'm going to ... I'm going to ... Well, I don't even know what I'm going to do. He's the most stubborn ..." the dwarf grumbled incoherently as he wiped and scooped some sort of wet feed from his long beard. "The most aloof beast ... thinks he's the king of the ranch ..."

"Glin," Calli said more firmly, startling the dwarf from his own commiserations. "We've got visitors."

"Oh!" Glin said, shaking the goop from his hands. "Pleased to meet ye. Glin Stelchin, ranch hand ..." The end of his sentence elongated as he realized a goblin stood before him.

"These two were just about to tell me how we could be of service to them," Calli said through a clenched smile.

"Ah yes," Tobin said. But he cocked his head and pointed to his chin. "You got a little something right there."

"Right here?" the dwarf poked at his beard, smearing more of the feed into the hairs.

"Right there," Tobin tried to clarify.

"Right here?" The dwarf smudged more into his beard.

"No. No. Right th—"

"What can we do for you?" Calli's forced demeanor finally snapped. She pressed an apologetic smile together and widened her eyes toward Zarnikorek. The goblin issued his own sympathetic smile and shrugged.

"Right, sorry," the halfling said. "As we're heading into unknown mountainous terrain, we thought it best not to use my horses to pull the wagon. Thought it better to acquire a sturdy boulder goat for the journey, and I've been told that you have the best boulder goats in the area."

"Aye, that we do," Glin said with pride.

"Very good! Very good," the halfling said excitedly. "I'm sure you'll be able to help us then. We're going to need the biggest and strongest and bravest boulder goat you've got."

"Oh, you don't want—" A sharp elbow jab from Glin cut Calli's words off.

"The biggest and strongest you say?" the dwarf asked.

"Yes. He's going to have a full wagon to pull. Figured a boulder goat would be more agile and sturdier for the rough terrain we're most certain to encounter."

"Aye, that makes sense," Glin agreed, an odd glint in his eye. "I've got just the beast for you. Come this way. He's quite the brute. The biggest and strongest of all the boulder goats on our ranch. He'd be able to haul a fishing ship up the side of a mountain."

"Yes! Yes," Tobin said, pulling his pipe out of his mouth as he nearly skipped after the dwarf.

Zarnikorek followed along quietly, content to let Tobin take the lead on this particular transaction. The ranchers didn't seem all that keen on his presence. He couldn't blame them, of course. He imagined that when the orcish people of Ghun-Ra first started seeing wagoners from different lands arriving in their own city, it would take them some time to grow accustomed to their presence as well. Plus, Zarnikorek knew little of wagoning. He assumed Tobin would know better what kind of hauling beast was best for their endeavor.

"Wow! Isn't he a right beauty?" Zarni heard Tobin say before the goblin turned the corner into the barn. But once he did, he couldn't deny the halfling's awe.

Looming tall above them, even taller than Calli, stood a massive boulder goat. Thick white fur covered the creature's great muscular legs and ran all the way to his hoofed feet. Zarnikorek had never seen a goat like this. It stood tall in the front with a regal mane of fur around its neck like a lion. The creature's beard grew into a thick mane and twisted into three braids tied with red bands. Atop its head were two enormous curved, golden-brown horns. Its beard wobbled from side to side as it chewed on something and stared at them. Zarnikorek couldn't help feeling that the beast was looking down on them as if they weren't worthy of being in his presence.

"He's majestic! He's glorious! How much for him?" Tobin could hardly contain his mirth.

"Gregory?" Glin scoffed. "You can have this bloke for free. I'll even—"

This time it was Glin's words that got cut off by a sharp elbow from Calli.

"What Glin meant to say is that we can offer a harness for free with the purchase of our finest boulder goat. You said the kings of Galium and Drelek are sponsoring this venture? I assume they are funding all your requisitions?"

Zarnikorek watched as the words sunk in for the dwarf. The ranch hand's eyes widened, and he nodded greedily.

"Yes, ma'am. I've got full permission to acquire whatever we need for the journey. We're happy to pay whatever price for this marvelous creature."

Zarnikorek watched as the halfling scooped up a bucket full of feed. Another bucket lay on the ground nearby with grain splattered out around it.

"No, wait!" Glin tried to stop the halfling, but Tobin reached out to stroke the creature's regal mane.

Everyone froze. Tension paralyzed everyone except Tobin.

But nothing happened.

The halfling pet the boulder goat and it continued to stand there. Chewing. Either totally oblivious to the halfling, or simply caring so little for him that he didn't feel the need to acknowledge his existence.

Glin and Calli shared a confused look. Zarnikorek was starting to get the feeling that this was not the ranch's best boulder goat.

"Well ..." Glin said slowly. "It seems he likes you."

Zarnikorek wasn't so sure.

"I love him!" Tobin said. "We'll take him."

"Good," Calli agreed, though she still looked confused by the whole encounter. "I'm sure we can put together some good ... royal prices for you."

"That would be wonderful," Tobin said. "You know, I've feasted with King Thygram before. He's the nicest king you'll ever meet. Although, I suppose Zarni's new king must be pretty nice too. At least nicer than the old one. But anyway, I don't know what royal prices are, but I'm sure thankful you two are so thoughtful."

Zarnikorek didn't know what royal prices were either, nor did he know the going rates for a hauling animal. But for some reason, he had a feeling the king was about to part ways with a significant sum of coin.

CHAPTER 14
THE ROAD TO HILL STOP

T he wagon rolled along the well-trodden route to Hill Stop without any trouble. Gregory pulled the transport along with little effort. Zarnikorek had watched as Tobin adorned the boulder goat with his harness and connected an intricate leather strap system to attach the brute to the wagon. Tobin narrated his actions the whole way. At one point, Zarni regretted asking to learn how to prepare the wagon, but he figured he should know how to do some of the practical work. It would be an even longer journey if he didn't know how to lend a hand. But, as they drove onward through the rolling green hills accented by the backdrop of the immense and majestic Drelek Mountains, it was easy going. *I could get used to this,* Zarni thought.

"Hello, Marnia!" Tobin shouted and waved from the driver's bench as another wagon rolled by in the opposite direction.

Zarnikorek stood in the back of the wagon, holding the railing between him and the halfling in the front. Tobin had concocted a sort of nest in the back of the wagon between the barrels and sacks of supplies they needed for the voyage. He bade the goblin to "take it easy," and "get as comfortable as possible." But after a few hours of pouring over the Traitor's Map and catching only parts of the halfling's never-ending stream of words, he'd begun to feel guilty; like he wasn't bringing enough to the table in this partnership.

So, he stood and leaned on the railing so he could hear the halfling at the very least. Tobin had proved to have no shortage of words, but more interestingly, Zarnikorek noted that he never seemed to have a negative thing to say. The pure joy the halfling exuded baffled the goblin.

"Hello there, Tobin!" Marnia responded. She sat tall on her driver's seat, her wagon drawn by a rather lanky horse. "How fairs the road?"

"Well. Very well!" Tobin said through his grin, his pipe bobbing on his lips.

That was another thing Zarni noticed. Even though the halfling always seemed to be talking, he also always seemed to have something in his mouth. Usually it was his pipe, lit or otherwise. But snacks frequently passed his lips as well. Homemade jerky, scones, biscuits, berries, and dried fruits. Zarni smiled at the carefree halfling. By contrast, he himself worried about everything. Zarnikorek wished he were more like Tobin.

Marnia's wagon slowed, and she eyed the halfling's new hauling beast. And then his passenger. "You've got ... quite the transport today ..."

"Yes! On a quest for King Thygram himself. This is Zarni!" The halfling introduced the goblin with fervor as he proclaimed their special mission. Zarnikorek slunk behind the railing, leaving only his eyes and uncooperative brown hair visible. When the woman's eyes didn't leave him, he waved awkwardly. To his surprise, she smiled and waved back.

"Shy one, eh?"

"Doesn't talk so much," Tobin admitted. Zarnikorek almost argued that Tobin didn't leave much room for anyone else to get words in. Instead, he stifled a laugh. "But you know me,"

Tobin giggled and continued. "I've got enough words to hold a conversation for the both of us from Galium to Hill Stop."

"Aye. That you do," the woman agreed with a laugh of her own. She leaned forward on her bench to meet Zarni's gaze. "Don't let him have all the words. You cut him off. I can't tell you how many times we've been around the fire, and he asks a question, but you can't get an answer in without stopping him."

Tobin's shoulders bobbed in amusement.

"Will do," Zarnikorek said tentatively.

"Good. Well, easy roads to you. I'm back in Galium for a few days this week."

"Oh nice, visiting the family? We won't be back to Galium for a while. After a short stop in Hill Stop to chat with the wagon master, we'll be blazing a new trail north to Ghun-Ra."

"Ah," Marnia responded, as though everything about the strangeness of Tobin's wagon made a lot more sense. She snapped her reins and put her wagon back into motion. Zarnikorek initially thought it quite rude, but quickly understood that the woman knew the halfling well, and likely knew that if she didn't cut off the conversation, they'd be stuck there all day. "Well, easy roads to you."

"Easy roads!" Tobin said as he snapped his reins and Gregory's muscular legs carried them forward. "Always loved Marnia. Lovely woman. Tough though. She always has a Castle Brick set with her. Careful getting into a match with her around the campfire. She'll leave your coin purse a little lighter, I'll tell you. But I know a few old dwarven ladies in the Garome District that'll play the tunic right off your back!" He paused to laugh and swivel his pipe to the other side of his mouth. "You ever play Castle Brick? It's quite the game depending on who your opponents are. I'd wager—"

"I haven't," Zarni cut in. A pang of regret stung him. He hated to interrupt. But Tobin didn't seem offended in the least.

"Oh, no? Perhaps while we're in Hill Stop we can play a match at the tavern. I'd wager there will be several games going at the *Hop Stop*. You know, they have some fine ale over there, but I'm a bit partial to mead. And the best mead is in Galium, of course. No one would deny that. Although, I suppose I've never had goblin mead. But I think I heard goblins prefer glorb. Isn't that right? I mean, they wouldn't have that in Hill Stop. I'd wager that'll be something that spreads as the wagon route is established though. Imagine all the things we'll ..."

Zarni grinned. It would take some time to get used to conversing with the halfling, but the goblin couldn't deny he was jolly good company.

As evening approached, they rolled over a hill and into a gully where several rounds of wagons were parked in circles. Inviting campfires blazed in the middle of the wagon circles and people of all kinds sat around the fires. As Tobin steered them toward one of the circles that had space for another wagon, Zarnikorek's stomach clenched.

The halfling had mentioned earlier that they were going to stop the night at the route's regular wagon stop. According to Tobin, it was located semi-centrally between Galium and Hill Stop, and wagoners from both cities often stopped there for rest unless they had urgent transport that required them to haul overnight.

Zarnikorek considered asking Tobin to push onward overnight to make better time to Hill Stop, but his logical mind won over. Starting the journey by pushing too hard on the "easy part" wouldn't do them any favors if they reached the difficult parts utterly exhausted.

"Can I help with anything?" Zarnikorek asked as they came to a stop. Helping would prolong the inevitable interactions he'd have with the other wagoners already sitting around the fire. He dreaded the looks they'd give him. Plus, he wasn't sure how they'd react. Would they be wary and distrusting? Would they begrudge his very presence in their midst?

"Sure!" Tobin said cheerfully. He stood on the platform that made up the driver's box. The halfling twisted his trunk, managing a couple of cracks as he sighed with relief. "Ah. This new seat cushion does wonders, but I should really stand up more often while we drive. Don't need an achy back for the long haul. Usually don't drive more than a couple of days. But this trip is going to be a long one. Got to stay spry and limber. Never know what's going to cross our path." He laughed to himself and patted the red fabric that upholstered the driver's seat.

"Want to unhook Gregory, and I can take care of setting up the beds for this evening so you can see how it's done? Another good thing to know how to do. We're going to need good sleep. Lenor always says your body needs good rest, so it remembers which way is upright in the morning. And I know just the way to set up the bedding. It'll take—"

"I'm happy to unhook Gregory," Zarni cut in, still with a hair of hesitation.

"Right you are. Right you are," Tobin said, climbing over the railing into the back of the wagon. "I'll try to slow down after I ask a question. Bad habit, I know."

The halfling cleared his throat and stared at Zarni for a long moment with what looked to be a pained expression. The goblin realized it was taking all the self-control the halfling had to leave the silence between them, allowing for Zarni to respond. But the goblin wasn't really sure what to say. His hand brushed against something furry and he realized Gibs lay curled up in a ball on a supply sack next to him. Zarni ran his fingers along the curve of the little creature, and without opening his eyes, the horned marten's hind end raised high to take in all the scratches. "Do we have anything for Gibs to eat?" Zarni asked, knowing they did, but wanting to relieve Tobin of his silent pain.

"Yes! Of course," the halfling breathed enthusiastically, as if he'd been holding his breath just to keep the words in long enough for the goblin to respond. "I'll get him a bite while I'm preparing the bed rolls. And I'll set up a feed bag for Gregory and hang it on one of the back posts of the wagon for him to have easy access."

Zarni nodded and climbed out of the back of the wagon. As he strode around, a small furry head popped over the side. Two sleepy eyes blinked at him. Apparently, Zarni had woken Gibs, and the horned marten yawned curiously.

As Zarni rounded to the front of the wagon, he spoke to the massive boulder goat. "Hey Gregory," he cooed. "Let's get you unhooked for the night." But as he reached for the leather straps, the boulder goat lumbered sideways to get away from him.

"Easy there, boy. I just want to get you unhooked."

But as Zarni stepped toward the brute, Gregory puffed several annoyed bursts of air through his nostrils and skipped back in the other direction.

"Whoa!" Zarnikorek said, raising his hands. "I'm trying to help you get unhooked so you can get some rest."

Gregory snorted and popped his bearded chin high as if he couldn't even stand the sight of the goblin.

"Come on, pal." Zarnikorek shifted tactics. "We've got a long journey ahead. This isn't the last time we'll have to work together. Let me get you unhooked."

As Zarnikorek moved forward, hesitation in his steps, the boulder goat let out a scream that tore through the night. It stomped its hooves and reared up, scaring Zarnikorek as he dove away. From his vantage on his rear, the goblin saw the boulder goat in a much less regal light.

Laughter floated into the goblin's long, green ears. He turned over his shoulder to see all the wagoners around the campfire watching with wide grins. *Great first impression*, Zarnikorek scolded himself. *Instead of looking at me like some monster, they see me as a jester.*

A large hand hovered above his head. As the goblin followed the rippling arm attached to the hand, he found it belonged to an enormous human man. Dark hair framed his face with a haircut that could only have been done at home or by a blind barber. His beard was scraggly and opened around his mouth, revealing a toothy smile that contained a few more gaps than teeth.

"Come on, now," the large man said. "Let's get you up on your feet. Not going to do much wagon work on your hind end—" The man paused, his face contorting before he bellowed a laugh. "Actually, on your hind end in the driver's box is where a lot of wagoning happens."

Around the campfire, other wagoners chuckled along with their compatriot's humorous remark.

"Right you are, Lengard. Right you are," Tobin said as he rounded the wagon, having just finished hanging Gregory's feed bag.

Zarnikorek placed his tiny hand in the big man's, and Lengard hoisted him up. The goblin's feet left the ground for a moment before he landed upright. "There you go, now. Looks like you've got yourself a stubborn boulder goat there."

"No," Tobin said, elongating the word and cooing at the big beast. He stepped closer to Gregory and the boulder goat stood firmly in place as the halfling showered him with affection. "He's just the most majestic boulder goat in all of Finlestia. Look at his beard. Have you ever seen the like? He's sturdy and strong. He's got horns like a king's crown."

Zarnikorek watched, mouth agape, as the halfling unhooked the boulder goat as if it were the easiest task in the world. Gregory stood straight as a statue. His chin jutted skyward, as if he couldn't be bothered to look at the only servant worthy of unhooking his leathers.

"That boulder goat has got a real attitude problem," Lengard grumbled next to Zarnikorek.

"I ..." Zarnikorek didn't even know what to say. He merely shook his head.

"Thinks he's the king of all boulder goats. Only two ways to get that goat under control. Treat him like a king—as Tobin's so unabashedly demonstrating. But I don't really like that method. Right now, it's a one-way road. You give him everything he needs. He pulls the wagon because he thinks it proves how strong he is. How he's stronger than the horses and other boulder goats. Stubbornness is close to determined, but not the same. It can keep him going through a storm, but not to help you, just to prove he can. You don't need him stubborn. You *need* his loyalty."

Zarnikorek looked up to the mountain of a man standing next to him. "And how do we get that?"

"You show him you're the king in the relationship. You're the wagon master. Not him."

"I don't know ..." Zarnikorek said slowly.

"Nothing to know," Lengard grunted. "Animal that stubborn, it's about proving you're more determined than he is. Showing him you won't back down."

"There we go," Tobin said, clapping his hands together to dust them off as he joined Zarnikorek and Lengard. "All set for the evening. What do we have cooking around the fire tonight?"

"I only just arrived, but Sora was just preparing some sausage for the group."

"There's plenty," a woman called from the campfire.

"Wonderful," Tobin said. "Just wonderful. Now you can meet some of the other wagoners and get to know what the wagoner life is like! Come on. I'll introduce you to everyone. We don't always get to share a circle because we don't always end up at the wagon stop on the same nights. And I don't always take transports to Hill Stop. A lot of times I'll go west to Crossdin instead. And some of these folks are from Hill Stop and they take transports out east to Whitestone. So, you can see how we don't always run into each other on the road. But it's sure nice when we do. I'd wager it's one of the best parts of wagoning. Running into good folk and ..."

Nervousness tried to rear its ugly head within Zarnikorek's gut, but as he followed Tobin and Lengard to meet the others, a strange sense of peace washed over him.

As the duo lay in their bedrolls in the back of the wagon, Gibs snuggled up tight next to Zarni. The goblin couldn't help but stare into the night sky with awe. He'd seen the stars before, of course. But that summer night, in the back of the wagon, with adventure before them, the sky seemed to explode with the little pinpricks of light. It was as if the Maker was giving him some sort of sign. Finlestia was full of possibilities.

The fact that the other wagoners had happily welcomed him around their campfire only bolstered the feeling. He'd been surprised by their attitudes. They'd been so easygoing and even curious about the quest. Tobin happily shared everything in painstaking detail, but many of them wanted to hear from Zarni, interested in his culture and his home. As he shared, the thought of a new wagon route to Ghun-Ra grew more and more exciting. Several of the wagoners from Hill Stop expressed how interested they were in taking the opportunity to haul between their town and the orc city. Zarni realized that even among the wagoners, he was playing a major role in this quest. He was an emissary for his people.

A shooting star dashed across the sky, burning a searing line of light.

"Did you see that one?" Tobin asked. Zarni had thought him already asleep, but apparently the halfling was also enjoying the view.

"Beautiful," Zarni whispered back.

"Aye," the halfling uttered.

Zarni grinned. Either the halfling was half asleep, or he was so in awe of the night sky he could barely string words together.

"Thank you for introducing me to some of your friends," Zarni whispered.

"Of course. That's part of wagoning. Good people on the road. All of them just trying to make an honest living for their families. If you think about it, isn't that what we're all trying to do? That kind of thing brings people together, I'd wager. You'll never see a wagoner broken down for long. Either they pick themselves up and get back on the road, or another one comes along to help."

"That's pretty amazing," Zarni said. "It thrills me that such good people are excited about what we're trying to do."

"Aye," the halfling said. "It takes good folk to do good work that changes the world for the better. We might be doing some good work to get things started, but it'll be other good folk who keep it going for generations to come."

Tobin's words struck the goblin. For all the halfling's words, there were some wise ones among them.

He's a dreamer, Zarni thought with a smirk. And then another thought struck him. He turned over and rustled between their bags.

"You alright?" Tobin whispered. "Your bed not comfy enough? I've got more blankets rolled in the corner. I just didn't want you to be too hot tonight. Figure we'll need the extra blankets in the mountains, but not down here among the hills."

"No," Zarni said. "The bed is fine. I just wanted to grab ... this." He held up a cloth bag that swung heavily from his grasp. "May I?"

"Oh, good idea," Tobin said, now sounding a bit more energetic.

Zarni slid the orb from the cloth bag in which Tobin had placed the artifact to protect it. His green hands held the stello glass up high. He angled it just right and peered through. Instantly, ethereal blue lines and script appeared to hover in the heavens. Zarni pulled it away from his view and saw only the stars above. "Wow," he said as he moved the stello glass back in front of his vision. A strange blue glow highlighted specific stars and traced magical lines to other stars. The orb pointed out constellations Zarni knew, and many he didn't. Each one marked with a script and a symbol.

"You've got to see this," the goblin said, handing the orb to the halfling.

"Well, I'll be ..." Tobin whispered. And this time Zarni knew the halfling's speechlessness was a side effect of his awe.

The two took turns with the stello glass long into the night. Whispering over constellations they knew and sharing about the ones the other didn't recognize. A myriad of constellations were unrecognized by either of them, but each seemed content with the magnificent mystery of the orb.

Eventually, their excitement gave way to exhaustion. Tobin fell asleep first. And Zarni was sure of it this time. The halfling snored like a plains bear, but the noise didn't keep him up. It wasn't long before he too drifted into promising dreams of the future.

HILL STOP

CHAPTER 15
CASTLE BRICK

Zarnikorek knew the *Wyvern's Wish* was an oddity among the taverns in Ghun-Ra, being built in the valley rather than inside one of the mountain caverns. What he didn't realize was how similar it made the place to taverns south of Drelek. *Hop Stop* bustled with activity as Tobin and Zarnikorek entered the building.

Wooden beams rose high above to support the roof, and iron fixtures bore lanterns that illuminated the place in an amber glow. Patrons laughed and talked all around the place while a bard sang from a small stage in the corner. Zarnikorek's ears twitched and adjusted, attempting to recognize the song.

Even in the face of giants
Tally Lomern's love did triumph
She would not let him go
Never would she do so

Though Finlestia embattled
Their two hearts were never rattled
Two stones forever true
No evil could break through

If love were a

Safer game
Would we ever play?
And would we face
This daring fate
If we would not be changed?

Zarnikorek didn't recognize the love ballad, but a flush rosed his cheeks. *If Jileva were singing the song, the whole tavern would be silently soaking it in,* he thought. He scratched his hair and adjusted the goggles resting on his forehead. *That's one difference between the taverns,* he thought, trying to shift his line of thinking. But it wasn't the first time he'd caught himself thinking about the beautiful goblin bard.

"I'll be right back," Tobin said quickly.

Zarnikorek's eyes widened in horror and he nearly reached out to snatch the halfling's cloak.

Tobin laughed at the goblin's expression. "It'll be alright. I'll only be a minute, and I'll get us some food and beverages."

Zarnikorek's heart pounded so hard he felt it in his ears. "You can't ... I can't ..."

"You can," the halfling chuckled. "No doubting yourself, now. Look. Right over there. That's Dirk and Gram. They're friends. And here, take some coin." Tobin paused and counted out a handful of coins. Before Zarnikorek could protest, the halfling shoved the money into the goblin's hands and said, "Looks like they're teaching some guardians how to play Castle Brick. Prefect time for you to learn."

"But ..." was all Zarnikorek could say before the halfling sped off through the crowded tavern toward the bar. The goblin's stomach soured as he turned to find Dirk and Gram. The two dwarves sat at a table, boisterously laughing and hurling good-natured insults at each other. Two men in sleek metal armor sat at the table with them, each quietly pondering the game bricks in front of them. Several men and women in similar griffin-adorned armor gathered round, watching the game and chatting amongst themselves.

Zarnikorek gulped, hoping it would carry courage all the way down to his immobile feet.

"You alright there?" someone asked next to him.

Zarnikorek turned to find a fair gnome woman who was just as short as he. Her large eyes were as golden as the hair that fell in ringlets over her shoulder. Even her fair skin seemed to have a golden hue. He'd never met a gnome, and never expected to. The gnomish population of Tarrine was not believed to be very large. But then again, they tended to be jovial peoples that kept to themselves in vast forests where they could be easily concealed. Even harder to find were the deep gnomes who lived underground. There were gnomish cities, but few people of other races lived among them.

"You alright?" she asked again, her shining smile brightening the place.

"Oh, uh ..." Zarnikorek hemmed. "My, uh ... friend ..." Was Tobin his friend? Zarnikorek figured he was as close to a friend as Deklahn had been. *Why am I over-complicating this?* "He said I should join Dirk and Gram to learn how to play Castle Brick."

"Oh, yeah. Come on over here," she said, wrapping his arm and pulling him toward the table.

Raucous laughter burst from everyone at the table as one of the miniature brick towers on the table fell and scattered. "No!" one of the armored men cried and held his head in his hands.

"No points for you!" one of the dwarves said.

"You're killing us," the other man said to his dismayed comrade.

"I'm sorry."

"Hey boys," the gnome said. "This is ... this is ... Actually, I didn't catch your name sweety."

"Zarnikorek," he choked out. *Why is my mouth so dry?*

"I'm Dirk," one of the dwarves said. "And this is me brother, Gram. Though sometimes I wish he weren't!"

Everyone laughed as Gram punched his brother, and they started to wrestle, rolling out of their chairs and onto the floor. The two grappled and maneuvered until Gram was sitting atop Dirk with a red face and a wide smile. "And who is Zarnikorek?" he said as others cheered the dwarf's victory. Dirk popped his head out to look at the goblin as well. His smile was just as wide as his brother's.

"Uh, well. Tobin. You know Tobin?"

"Ye're Tobin's friend? Well, why didn't ye start with that!"

"Any friend of Tobin's is a friend of ours!" Dirk said as he muscled himself out from under his brother's weight.

"Where is Tobin? Is he here?" Gram asked, looking about.

"He is," Zarnikorek shifted. Looking around as well. "He said he needed to talk to the barkeep about something and I should come and learn how to play Castle Brick."

"Ye've never played?" Dirk roared.

"Come, come!" Gram said. "Take me seat. These Griffin Guard types might be mighty warriors, but they're an easy mark in Castle Brick!"

"Hey ..." the pair of guardians said in unison. Their armored friends laughed.

The dwarven game of Castle Brick turned out to make a lot of sense to Zarni's logical side. The game accommodated up to four players. Each player got their own set of twenty bricks with their color on the back. Zarni got green when he took over Gram's spot, a happy coincidence, as green was his favorite color. The other side of the brick was split into two colors—one of his own color, green, and one of the other three colors. That is, except for five bricks which contained double greens.

Zarni quickly learned the mechanics. It was a stacking game where the four players competed to get the most squares of their own color built into three different towers. But they had to be careful not to play too many of one of their opponents' colors into the tower, lest they give the tower away. A die was rolled for each tower, determining its value, and they took turns placing their bricks on top of the towers to grow them. If someone knocked over the tower, none of that player's colors counted for that tower at the end of the round.

The game was played in rounds until a player hit a certain number for victory. Zarnikorek scrutinized the other players while Gram coached him along through the first round. The second round, Gram started saying things like, "Wow, nice move," and "That was clever."

By the third round, both Zarni and Dirk were in position to cross the victory number, but Zarni had to make sure he got more points than the dwarf this round. He realized that Dirk needed the tower with the most points to win, but the two guardians were also vying for that tower.

When Gram realized Zarni's strategy to take the second highest valued tower without much competition, the dwarf grabbed him by both shoulders and shook him with enthusiastic delight. Zarni's bones rattled, but he couldn't help smiling as well.

"Oh, no ..." Dirk muttered as he placed another brick on a tower and realized what was happening too late.

Tobin leaned over the table, stuffing a huge bite of ham into his mouth. "Uh oh," he said through a mouthful.

Several of the guardians around the table leaned in as well.

"Oh, no ..." Dirk grumbled again, now resigned to the inevitable.

The players at the table laid their last bricks. Each tower was demolished so color squares could be counted. Gram only got halfway through counting the tower Zarni had claimed before grabbing the goblin's hand and raising it high. "Zarni wins! Taught my brother a new trick, he did! Plays like a natural, he does! This round's on me!"

The surrounding members of the Griffin Guard cheered.

"You don't have any coin," Dirk said, his tone defeated.

"Oh, right! This round's on Dirk!"

The cheering recommenced.

For the rest of the evening, they played Castle Brick and shared merriment. Bellies were filled and hearts were warmed. Fellowship was had by all.

At one point, the guardians convinced the bard to play "Rise of the Griffin Guard" and taught Zarni the words.

Oh, come take to the sky
For fair winds and fair nigh'
We will rise as the Griffin Guard

Over mountains and seas
Against all enemies
We will rise as the Griffin Guard

Fly away, fly away
Ours is vict'ry this day
We will rise as the Griffin Guard

We will rise as the Griffin Guard!

Zarni couldn't remember the last time he'd had this much fun. It made him think of Grahk and Yan, who had been so kind to invite him out to *The Wyvern's Wish*. And that made him think of Jileva again. The whole scenario got him thinking. If these people, who were enemies of goblins for centuries, were willing to befriend him, maybe—just maybe—his own people could, too.

CHAPTER 16
NORTHWARD

Zarni and Tobin set out from Hill Stop early the next morning. They rolled northward along the road that followed the Palori River. The morning was warm, and the dawn painted the sky pink. They'd gotten good rest at the *Hop Stop*, and the goblin had been pleasantly surprised at how warm the people had been. Another farmer nodded to them as they drove by. Zarni smirked and lifted a brow. He supposed a large majority of the people south of Drelek had surprised him in one way or another. Maybe he should start expecting the unexpected.

The hills rose toward the front range, and Gregory drove his legs with power and an even cadence, clearly not hindered by the rolling hills. As they came toward the last farm along the road before they forged onward into the mountains, Zarni's stomach fluttered. On one hand, he was excited. They were about to do something no one had done in hundreds of years. On the other hand, there was an air of safety in this place where farmers faithfully went about their work, producing the food that people needed.

Zarnikorek's elbows slid along the railing as Tobin turned the wagon toward the last farm. "We need to make a quick stop here," the halfling said. "I've got a surprise for you. Well, I hope I've got a surprise for you," he added with a chuckle.

"Could be a moot stop. But this is our last chance to get some, anyway. There's nothing between here and Ghun-Ra for us. I'd wager—"

"Get what?" Zarni asked, not quite sure what the halfling was talking about.

"You'll see," Tobin said, trying to hide his excitement, but his tone giving it away. "I was asking the barkeep back at the *Hop Stop* if she knew of anyone who—Oh, hello there!" Tobin cut himself off and waved to a woman who appeared from around a barn with a couple of buckets in hand.

"Hullo," the woman said, her face scrunched. "What can I do for you?"

"Ah, mighty kind of you to ask," Tobin said as he climbed down from the driver's box. "You see, we're on a quest for the kings of Galium and Drelek. We're in need of a particular supply. And I've been told you may be the only one around who can help us. Or at least, that's my hope. I was chatting with Kendri at the *Hop Stop*, and she mentioned you make something called kips. And we've got a hard journey ahead and my friend here—" Tobin turned to find Zarni but nearly jumped out of his skin when he found the goblin standing right next to him. The halfling clutched at his chest, and Zarni placed a hand on Tobin's back to steady him.

The woman took the momentary pause in the halfling's stream of words to respond. "Aye. I've just made a batch. Not many folks in Hill Stop looking for kips. But we like 'em just fine. Come on into the house. I'll pack some up for you."

"Thank you! Much obliged!" Tobin basically sang.

"What are kips?" Zarni whispered as he caught up to the halfling, who was more than excited to enter the farmer's home.

And in an eerily short response, he replied, "You'll see."

An outrageous laugh burst from Zarni's lips, startling Helenda, the woman who stood at the kitchen counter, wrapping gibs into a cloth. "You make gibs?"

"These are kips, dearie," she said with a sympathetic smile, as though Zarni had mistakenly heard her.

"Oh, sorry," the goblin said, shaking his head. "We call them gibs in Ghun-Ra. How do you know how to make these? May I?"

"Of course," she said, sliding one across the counter for him. He sniffed it but quickly popped the savory fishbone crisp into his mouth and chomped away. The salty, seasoned crisp hit his tongue and, to his surprise, tasted almost exactly like the gibs his pa made. "Mhmm," was all Zarni could say.

"Good, eh?"

"So good," Zarni said.

"Not many folks are interested in them around these parts. It's an old family recipe. My husband's great great great ... well, I'm not so good with counting greats, but one of his great grandmother's long ago learned the recipe ... from an orc." Helenda whispered the last part conspiratorially, but perked up when she realized, the pair likely wouldn't think such a thing as scandalous as many of the nearby farmers.

"Really?" Zarni asked excitedly. "What was the orc's name?"

"Don't know," the woman said, pursing her lips as she placed more gibs into the cloth. "Story goes, she didn't tell anyone his name because he was some sort of spy or something from Drelek. This was way back during the Second Great Black War, mind you."

Zarni and Tobin shared a glance as the halfling requested to try a gib, himself.

"That had to be Koris. Right?" the goblin mused.

"Maybe," Tobin said, licking his lips and nodding appraisingly at the gibs. "Better wrap an extra batch for us, if you please."

"Aye," the woman said, her slender shoulders bobbing as she chuckled. "Not many of your kind among the northern farmers, but never met a halfling who didn't like my kips."

Tobin chuckled and slapped his belly. "As you can see, Ma'am, I'm a pretty happy eater."

"Seems you two are an interesting pair," she said, turning the conversation on them. A hunger glinted in her eye, as though she'd been starved for some good gossip for a while.

"Too true. Too true," Tobin offered without hesitation. "As Zarni has said, we are following the trail of an orc that may just be the same one your many-times-great grandmother may have encountered. We've been tasked with marking out a new wagon route between Hill Stop and Ghun-Ra."

"We've been hearing tale of new alliance initiatives popping up," she responded with a nod, slowing her work, clearly prolonging their stay just to keep the conversation going. "Even heard about a couple of griffin guardians learning to ride wyvern. Did you ever think such a thing could happen?"

Zarni had heard the same. Their peoples had rallied together out of necessity to protect all the lands of Tarrine from the wicked sorcerer that had infiltrated them from across the sea. There had been many joint missions during what was now being referred to as the War of the Stones.

"... though, knowing how good my friend Zarni here is, I don't know how I ever doubted such things could happen." Zarni caught the end of Tobin's response. "This new wagon route will open up trade for our peoples like Tarrine has never seen before. Maybe gibs—pardon me—kips," Tobin corrected himself for the woman's benefit, laughing at his own flub. "Maybe they'll become a regular snack for our peoples too. You could be on the forefront of an entrepreneurial empire!"

Zarni smirked. He might have a lot of words, but Tobin did seem to have a way about building others up.

"As grateful as I am for you supplying us with these," Zarni said, picking up one of the tied cloths, heavily dangling with the weight of all the gibs, "We must get back to our quest. We've got a long trail ahead, even if we don't run into anything unknown."

"Yes, yes," Tobin agreed. He inhaled deeply as though he were about to start another long stream of words, but the woman cut him off.

"Be watching out for the wild sorcerer now!"

"The what?" Zarnikorek asked, glancing toward Tobin. The halfling shrugged, each hand bobbing a cloth loaded down with gibs.

"The wild sorcerer. Folks say he's ancient as a wizard and crazy as a loon. Been known to turn folks into mountain mules. Heard a while back, some of the boys from Hill Stop thought they'd be brave and go into the mountains to prove their courage." She leaned over the counter, fixing each of them with disconcerting eye contact. "Only three of them made it back. Story goes, the rest were turned into mountain mules and spend their days eating high valley grass and braying the day away."

"That can't be true ..." Zarnikorek said through a gulp. Then he turned to Tobin. "Can it?"

The halfling chewed on his unlit pipe thoughtfully. "Not sure I could say one way or another. I've never heard the tale myself. I think—"

"It's true, dearies," the woman said, her eyes wild.

When her stare became almost unbearable, she popped straight up and said, "Or at least that's how Linda says it." She smiled at them with a twinkle in her eye that suggested they'd never been discussing such dire and terrifying things.

Tobin and the woman started to laugh, and Zarni chuckled nervously along, not really sure he understood the humor in the moment. Regardless, the scenario felt a lot lighter suddenly. Perhaps the woman had merely been teasing them.

She walked them out of the house and back toward their wagon. Gibs's furry head popped up over the side of the wagon, his black eyes blinking wide and his nose twitching excitedly.

"Good nose, that one," Tobin whispered. "We'll have to tuck these into a barrel so he can't eat them all."

Zarni chuckled. "He can share a few of mine. But I'm not letting him eat all of them again."

They loaded up and Tobin clicked at their boulder goat. Gregory lurched the wagon forward, headed northward toward the immense and majestic Drelek Mountains that now filled their vision. Zarnikorek took one last look back at the farm. Helenda stood at the gate, watching them roll away. And if the goblin wasn't mistaken, she fixed him with another one of her wild-eyed stares, worry etched on her face. Zarnikorek strained his eyes to see her, and he could have sworn her lips mouthed the word, "Beware."

CHAPTER 17
DETOUR

For several hours that day, the Palori River burbled peacefully next to them. Birds sang their summer songs, and wildflowers sprouted up in meadows between forested tracts of land. The nearer they drew to the mountains, the rockier the soil, making much of the land in the front range difficult or even impossible to farm. Not to mention for hundreds of years, the people of the south had been wary of the orcs who inhabited the Drelek mountains. Zarni knew there weren't any orcs living in the mountains this far down. But certainly, the people of the south didn't know that.

Zarni leaned over the railing on the front of the wagon, holding the Traitor's Map out in front of himself. He eyed the map, then lowered it. Eyed it again, then lowered it. His lips pursed and his brow crinkled. He thought following the trail of an army would be easier. He'd expected to spot more signs of them. But everywhere he looked, the mountain grasses and trees had grown over, covering any trace that the army had ever existed at all. *What did you expect?* he wondered to himself. *It's been hundreds of years.*

"You keep looking at that map like something's going to change on it," Tobin said as he lit his pipe. "To me, it looks like we follow the Palori River almost the whole way to Ghun-Ra. I'd wager—" Tobin stopped himself, some internal conflict warring within. "I'd wager that would make the most efficient route. Wouldn't you say?"

Zarni popped a brow at the halfling, who bit at his now lit pipe. The goblin's face softened. Tobin was really trying hard to communicate better with him without monologuing. "Well, I've been wondering about that. See, where we live in Ghun-Ra, the source of the Palori is on the other side of a mountain. The river in our valley comes from the north for us. This map is crude, but I'm not sure it makes a whole lot of sense to follow the Palori all the way to the end. To my knowledge, there's no access to the Ghun-Ra valley from there."

"Perhaps there's a secret tunnel? How neat would that be? I don't know a single wagon route that has a tunnel. This one could be the first."

"I'm not sure ..." Zarni mumbled, getting lost in his own thoughts.

"I'm just excited to meet some of your other friends."

A sharp laugh escaped Zarni's lips. Tobin glanced over his shoulder and side-eyed the goblin, clearly wondering what he'd said that was so funny. Zarnikorek turned away. He hadn't meant to react. His insides turned, matching the tumultuous rapids that now raged against the boulders in the river they followed.

"You must know loads of interesting folk," the halfling continued. "I'd wager you're quite the talk of the city with you being on this mission for the king."

"I don't know about that ..." Zarnikorek said. He really hoped not.

"Oh, I'd wager they're preparing a celebration in your name right now! Your friends must have been really excited about you being selected by the new king for such a quest."

"Yeah ..." Zarnikorek huffed.

Tobin turned on the driver's bench and eyed the goblin. "You alright?" he asked, immediately gulping down the sentence that was ready to follow the question.

Zarnikorek appreciated the halfling's effort, but what could he say? How could Tobin possibly understand that he was a nobody and had no friends? The halfling was so outgoing and became fast friends with everyone he met. Not for the first time, Zarnikorek wished he were more like Tobin.

"Zarni?"

The halfling's deliberate insistence snapped the goblin back to the present.

"Ah, well …" he hemmed. "I'm not quite as popular as you."

"What?" the halfling balked. "You're the most interesting goblin I've ever met! Well, you're the only goblin I've ever met." He paused to laugh. "I can't believe you're not friends with just about everyone in Ghun-Ra."

"Well, it's a big city," Zarni said with a laugh of his own. "Do you know everyone in Galium?"

"Well, that's fair." Tobin's belly rolled as he chuckled. "I just mean, you're nice and smart and good company. Wanted to be your friend the instant I met you. I don't see why anyone *wouldn't* want to be friends with you."

The sentiment warmed Zarni's heart, but he was pretty sure the halfling thought that about everyone he met. He thought back to the ranchers who'd sold them Gregory. They didn't seem to be of the highest integrity, but Tobin had been overjoyed to make their acquaintance. A smirk tugged at the corner of his mouth.

"I may have *started* to make some new friends recently," he said, thinking of Grahk and Yan. "They invited me to *The Wyvern's Wish.*"

"Oh nice! Very nice. Is that the local tavern there in Ghun-Ra?"

"It is. It was the first time I'd been there since I returned to Ghun-Ra. The glorb is good. There's an excitement about the place," Zarni said. "Especially when Jileva sings."

"Jileva, eh?" Tobin inquired, waggling his brows. Zarni hadn't realized he'd said her name with whimsy, but apparently the halfling had caught it. "A lady goblin friend?"

"I ... Well ... She ..." Zarnikorek stammered. Heat rose to his cheeks, and he turned toward the raging river to hide his blush.

Tobin chuckled to himself. "You know, when I first met Lenor, I was smitten. I could hardly think of anything else. I'd spend all day thinking about when I was going to get to see her again. Funniest thing, I was a halfling, and she was a very desirable dwarven woman. Good family, you see. With her brother, a garvawk warrior. He wasn't the foredwarf at the time, but everyone knows the garvawk warriors in Galium.

"Anyway, she had the brawniest and beardiest dwarves from all over the city lining up to take her out on a date. And here I was, an upstart wagoner with nary a hair on his chin. Though, I still don't have any hair on my chin—never grows more than stubble—but I'd just finished apprenticing with Georl. My old wagon master. He was good friends with Lenor's father for decades before he passed. That's how I got my first introduction to her.

"Anyway, I made quite the fool of myself. I couldn't wait to see her again and had stopped along the road to pick summer flowers for her. I gathered them up and went to see her. Caught her just as she was preparing to leave her house to meet with a suitor for a date in the city. She looked so pretty at the top of the stairs. My heart nearly leapt out of my chest." Tobin's words came out with a fond softness.

"Anyway, I ran up the stairs to see her and tripped, launching the summer flowers and scattering them all over her." The halfling laughed and slapped his knee. "She knelt down and checked me out. And we spent half the night chatting while I picked flowers and stems and leaves out of her hair. She missed her date that night, but I think you might agree, it worked out quite right."

Zarni laughed. He hadn't heard the story while he was visiting with Tobin's family. The goblin thought back to the day they'd departed. How sweet it was to see Lenor, with baby Bandix wrapped up on her chest, and Button waving to them as they rolled away. How little Button had run to the highest point of the hill to wave as long as possible before they disappeared from sight. The moment had touched him. As much as he loved his pa, he wanted something like that. He wanted a family of his own someday. He'd thought that dream impossible, though. But was it?

"Have you taken Jileva on a date yet?" Tobin asked, emphasizing the pretty goblin's name.

"Oh ... well ..." Zarnikorek hemmed again. "I couldn't. I don't think she'd want to go on a date with me."

Tobin stared back at him for a long moment. "You know," Tobin said, slowly. "There's this one thing about good friends that isn't always comfortable, but is necessary."

Zarnikorek wasn't sure where the halfling was going with this.

"Friends are the ones who can say the hard things others wouldn't." Surprisingly, the halfling let the sentence linger between them for a moment, making Zarnikorek wonder what exactly he was getting at. "Can I say something that might be hard for you to hear?"

Zarnikorek's throat bobbed. Now he really had no idea where the halfling was going with this. "Sure," he managed to reply.

"We haven't been friends all that long, but I've noticed you say 'you can't' a lot. You shouldn't talk yourself down before you even try things. I'd wager you're far more capable than you give yourself credit for."

As Tobin's words came out, a short burst of guilt exploded in Zarnikorek's chest, but it quickly dissolved into gratitude. He couldn't remember the last time he had a friend who would say such a deeply personal and yet genuinely kind thing to him. Maybe he never had. For whatever reason, it disarmed him.

"You know," Zarni started slowly. "I was on the wrong side of the war. Not by choice, mind you. I'd been working for King Sahr for a number of years. Most of them were horrible. But I was stuck. I didn't have any other options. Regardless, I was in the employ of the fallen king. That left me in a rather bad spot when the ashes finally settled. It's hard to make friends when everyone sees you as the enemy."

Tobin jutted his chin thoughtfully, taking a long draw on his pipe. "So, the others treat you like an outcast or a traitor ..."

Zarni nodded, but switched to shaking his head. "Actually, they don't ..." he said with an odd realization. "Now that I think about it, no one has mistreated me."

"No?" Tobin asked. "I'm not sure I understand."

Zarni shook his head and scratched his brown hair, adjusting his grandpa's goggles. "I'm a fool."

"I think you're rather bright," Tobin countered.

"No. That's not what I mean." Zarni took a long breath to gather his words. "Tobin, you're right."

"I've been known to be right on occasion," the halfling said through a chuckle.

"I mean, you're right about me standing in my own way. I expected everyone we met south of Drelek to hate me as a monster. Hate me as one of the enemy. But everyone has been so kind and welcoming."

"When you assume what others will think of you, you isolate yourself and never give them the chance to surprise you with their kindness."

"Though not everyone exudes kindness ..." Zarni said slowly. "We really ought to talk about those two ranchers who sold Gregory to you."

"What's wrong with Gregory? He's the king of all boulder goats!" Tobin proclaimed. Gregory's chin popped and Zarni swore the wagon started moving slightly faster.

"Alright, alright," the goblin said, waving his hands in front of him in surrender.

"And besides, that's not the point."

"You're right," Zarni agreed.

"There I go again."

Zarni smirked. "The point is that I've been getting in my own way for far too long. If I'm ever going to have a family like yours, I'm going to have to start letting people in."

"Right you are! Look at us, both right!"

A long silence stretched between them while Tobin drove the wagon onward. The Palori River roared as raging waters slammed against ever-growing boulders.

"You got all that from what I said?" Tobin asked with a cheeky grin.

"Yeah. I guess you're rather bright, yourself," Zarni said, rolling his eyes, though he couldn't help but smile himself.

Tobin shifted in his seat, sitting taller in faux pride. "So, you'll ask Jileva on a date when we get to Ghun-Ra?"

"One step at a time," Zarni said. But in truth, he wrestled inside. His stomach fluttered at the mere thought of it.

"No, no, no …" Zarnikorek grumbled. He'd climbed over the front railing of the wagon to sit on the driver's bench and show Tobin the map. "There is no marking whatsoever denoting any kind of canyon here."

"Well, it's not a very detailed map," Tobin said, pulling his pipe from his mouth and pointing the end at the map as a whole.

They'd driven northward along the Palori River until they could go no farther. The map's lines continued to follow the river. Or so it seemed. But there was no way their wagon could continue through the canyon northward. Zarnikorek thought an army on foot could. Potentially. It would leave all the soldiers soaked, which would not be ideal for an army. And who knew how deep the river got farther into the canyon?

"There's no way the allied army went through here," he ruminated.

"Doesn't seem likely," Tobin agreed.

The halfling climbed down from the driver's box and pressed his hands into his back. With a groan, he extended his belly, then heaved a sigh as his back cracked. He raised his elbows and swiveled from side to side, before walking around the wagon, looking for some sort of sign.

Zarnikorek's eyes flitted between the map and the canyon ahead with no understanding. A little furry head appeared over the railing behind him. The horned marten let out a big yawn, clearly confused as to why the wagon that so lovingly swayed him to sleep had stopped. Gibs gently butted his head against Zarni's.

"Careful with that thing," Zarni said, petting the creature around its singular horn. Gibs hadn't hurt him. He was just wary of the horn.

"It's getting pretty late," Tobin said, walking back toward the wagon. "Might be a good spot to camp out for the night, anyway. Maybe make supper. Then we can make some tea around the campfire."

Gibs butted Zarni again. "Alright, alright," he said. The horned marten could obviously tell he was stressed. "Fair enough. It gets too much darker, we won't be able to see the map soon, anyway."

"And it's been a long day," Tobin added. "It'll do us good to eat something and get a good night's rest. Start fresh in the morning."

Zarni smirked. The halfling had snacked almost the entire day. He couldn't imagine still being hungry. But Lenor had warned the goblin that's how the halfling traveled. That's why she packed extra snacks and goodies for them.

Tobin drove the wagon away from the river and parked it near a dramatic granite rock face. He offered to let Zarni unhook Gregory, but the goblin politely declined, not sure if he was ready to take on the stubborn boulder goat when he was in such a discouraged mood himself. Though, as Tobin joined him around the fire, Zarnikorek felt guilty for not even trying. *I've got to stop telling myself I can't before I even try.*

Tobin sizzled some sausage and potatoes in a skillet and they ate their fill, Gibs happily nibbled on the bits Zarni shared, and not long into the night, the exhaustion of travel and the relaxing sound of the river nearby had all of them snoring in the back of the wagon.

CHAPTER 18
BUMP IN THE NIGHT

Zarnikorek woke in the middle of the night. The moon rested high in the night sky, bathing the rocks and trees in a silvery glow. Zarnikorek sat up and looked through the railing of the wagon. The mountains appeared as black silhouettes that scarred the deep navy of the sky. The sight took Zarni's breath away.

Zarnikorek wasn't sure what had awakened him, but since he was up, he decided to grab the stello glass from its bag. He lifted it high and looked through the orb, quickly identifying several of the constellations he knew, before moving on to the ones he didn't. The ancient constellations were numerous. Teklahn, Bovak, Nolar, Mavro, and more. How interesting they all were. He had never been an astronomer by any means, but there was something about them that drew his interest. He'd have to show the stello glass to his pa when he got home. Zarni knew he'd love it.

A moment of homesickness washed over him. His stomach clenched as he thought of his pa all alone. Hopefully, he was enjoying some time with friends while Zarni was away. He didn't want him to grow sick with loneliness.

Zarni smiled to himself. *I certainly won't grow sick with loneli—*

The thought evaporated as he looked at Tobin's empty bedroll. Zarnikorek jumped to his feet in the back of the wagon. "Tobin?" He prodded the covers with his green toes.

Nothing.

It was then that he realized Gibs was gone, too. "Gibs? Tobin?" he called, looking out over the area surrounding the wagon.

A large mound of fur expanded and contracted on the ground nearby. Gregory was still here. *Great,* Zarnikorek thought.

He dressed quickly and crawled out of the back of the wagon. "Tobin? Gibs?" he called again.

Pow! Crack!

Zarnikorek dove to the ground as explosions rang out through the night, lighting the trees with orange and purple and green lights. *What in Finlestia?*

"Tobin?" he called in an urgent whisper, wanting to find his friend, but not wanting to draw the attention of whatever ...

The mad sorcerer!

Zarnikorek's eyes widened in realization. Maybe Helenda's gossip hadn't been so far-fetched after all!

Maker, help us ... Zarnikorek prayed silently.

What if the sorcerer had stolen his friends right out of their beds? What horrific things might the sorcerer do to them? What if he turned them into mountain mules? What would Zarnikorek tell Lenor and Button and baby Bandix? What would he tell Lotmeag?

Zarnikorek gulped, trying to get his shaking body back under control. *Think. Think,* the goblin scolded himself. He couldn't do nothing, but what could he do against a mad sorcerer? He was just a regular old goblin. Not even that. He was a *small* goblin. *I can't do any—*

He cut the thought off with a growl. "I have to do something," he whispered to himself. The mere act of speaking the words aloud, even though it was a whisper, seemed to encourage him.

What am I doing?

"I don't know, but we can't sit by and do nothing."

Zarni pushed himself up from the ground and hustled over to Gregory's snoring form.

"Gregory, get up," he said hurriedly.

The boulder goat opened one eye to see who dared wake him at such an unholy hour. Realizing it was Zarni, Gregory let out a derisive snort and laid his head back down.

Zarni pressed both hands on the boulder goat's shoulder and heaved his weight to shake the creature. "Tobin and Gibs are gone, and I have to go find them. And if I do, we might need a quick getaway. You need to wake up and be ready."

The boulder goat opened both of his eyes, condescension evident on his face.

Boom! Zzak!

"Look at me," Zarni growled, grabbing the goat by the horns and looking him squarely in the eyes. That seemed to get his attention. "I don't have time to play games with you. The one that treats you like a king might be in grave danger, and I need you to be ready to get us out of here in a hurry. So, you're going to get up right now, and let me get you hooked up as fast as possible so I can go help our friends."

Gregory pulled his horns from the goblin's grasp and rose. His glaring eyes never left Zarni's, but the goblin stared right back. *I don't have time to fight you ...* he thought, willing the stubborn creature to understand. The boulder goat eyed him for another moment, before puffing out an annoyed breath and lifting his chin as if to say, *"Whatever."*

"Thank you," Zarni growled through clenched teeth and readied the boulder goat's harness. He fumbled with the straps in his haste and wished he'd taken the chance to practice before they'd had supper. He cursed himself as he accomplished the task, but managed to get the boulder goat hooked up and ready to go. "Yes!" he whispered triumphantly. He wasn't sure, but he thought Gregory rolled his eyes at his elation. *Whatever,* Zarni thought. "You stay here. Don't go anywhere without us. Be ready for anything," he instructed firmly.

Gregory gave another annoyed huff, seemingly acknowledging the goblin's orders.

Good enough, Zarni thought.

He patted his pocket, making sure he had the Traitor's Map. He could mark it as he ran toward the direction from which he'd heard the explosions. *The explosions ...* he thought. Was he really doing this? What was he even doing? He didn't know. But what he did know was he couldn't let his friends get turned into mountain mules.

The morning had grown later than Zarni expected. Of course, he didn't know how long he'd hurried through the high mountain pines, following the lights and sounds of explosions. But eventually, he'd caught sight of the mad sorcerer.

Though he wasn't really sure what he'd expected, Zarni knew it wasn't what he discovered. The dwarven sorcerer sported a thick red beard only partially tamed by a few golden rings. Though he couldn't make out the color of one of the dwarf's eyes, the other socket glowed golden-yellow through the night. On one hand, the sorcerer wore a gauntlet that elicited yellow light from the knuckles. Glowing, emerald crystals adorned the wooden staff he raised high. Though, if Zarni was seeing things right, the gnarled staff seemed broken into pieces and held together by the ethereal green magic the sorcerer wielded.

Crack! Bang!

After finding him, Zarni followed the mad sorcerer, careful to stay hidden behind pines. He hadn't caught sight of Tobin or Gibs, but knew in his gut that if he followed the sorcerer long enough, he'd find them.

As the sun began to kiss the morning sky, not quite dawning upon Finlestia, the sorcerer led Zarni to a building that could only be the eccentric dwarf's home. He couldn't quite wrap his head around the shape of the building, as it appeared to be a sort of octagon of logs with various other shapes shooting off the central building in all directions. Several of the offshoots rose into oddly shaped towers, peaked with pointed roof caps.

The dwarven sorcerer looked about, and Zarni ducked behind the pine from which he'd been watching. The sorcerer grunted and nodded, seemingly proud of what he'd accomplished, though Zarni had seen nothing but a crazed dwarf running around a mountain forest at night, shooting colorful ethereal fireworks into the sky.

As Zarni peeked around the trunk of the pine, he glimpsed the door closing behind the dwarf's purple cloak. He watched the strange house for a long time, trying to see something through the oddly shaped windows. Unfortunately, they betrayed nothing of the interior, likely covered in dust on the inside and reflecting the pre-dawn light in an infuriating way.

Zarni squinted, tensing his body to give his eyes every ounce of effort he could.

Just then, something grabbed his arm.

"Ah!" Zarni cried out and threw himself sideways into the duff of the forest floor. Whatever gripped his arm held fast. He jumped and wiggled, trying to free himself. But nothing freed him.

He rolled over in a panic and finally saw what held him. Gibs blinked his black eyes, and his head lolled from side to side. The poor horned marten had been shaken dizzy.

"Gibs!" Zarni barely whispered, utterly out of breath. His heart hammered in his chest so hard, his ears tingled. "You just about scared me out of my skin. Where in Finlestia have you been all night? I thought the sorcerer captured you. And where is Tobin?"

The little horned marten turned his face toward the sorcerer's strange cabin.

"That's what I was worried about. Is he in th—"

Zarni's words choked off as fear gripped him once more. Standing only ten paces away, the mad sorcerer held his staff high. His golden eye locked on Zarni and Gibs.

CHAPTER 19
A MAD SORCERER

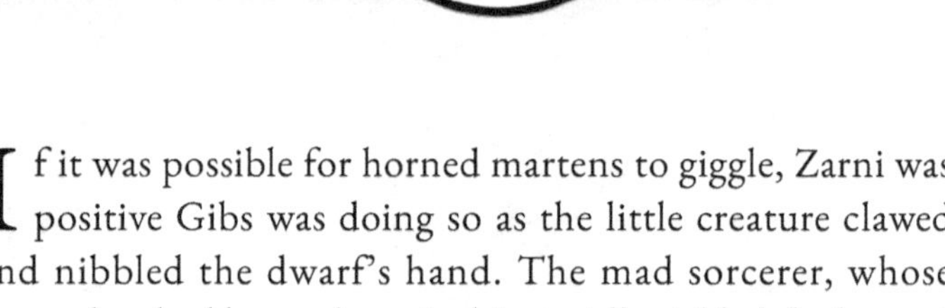

If it was possible for horned martens to giggle, Zarni was positive Gibs was doing so as the little creature clawed and nibbled the dwarf's hand. The mad sorcerer, whose name they had learned was Jorbinan, idly tickled the horned marten on the counter as he flipped yet more flapjacks on the skillet.

The warm scent of cinnamon and vanilla filled the cottage. As tasty as the flapjacks were, Zarni had already eaten four, and wouldn't be able to finish the one on his plate; let alone any more of the stack on the serving dish that rested in the center of the table. Tobin didn't seem to have any problems, having eaten half a dozen and angling his fork to maneuver another one to his own plate.

Zarni shook his head, still not sure how they'd ended up eating breakfast with the very *"mad sorcerer"* they were warned to avoid. When he'd turned around to find the dwarf staring at him outside the cabin, he had nearly wet himself. He'd had a flash of uninvited imagination, showing his trembling green legs bursting with fur and grotesquely contorting before his body convulsed and hunched and he turned into a mountain mule. Instead, Jorbinan had asked him who he was. And the only thing Zarni could think in the moment was to tell the dwarf the truth. At the mention of "the halfling," a wild smile split the dwarf's mangy red beard, and he roared an unnaturally long laugh.

"Come in, come in! He sleeps within."

Though Zarni had hesitated and required a little more coaxing, the dwarf had eventually opened the front door and revealed Tobin standing just inside with his eyes closed. The dwarf snapped in front of the halfling's nose, and Tobin had awoken as though he'd had the most restful sleep of his life. Now, they were eating flapjacks at the mad sorcerer's table.

"Jorbinan, tell me what happened to Tobin again."

"Snapplers," the mad sorcerer said with a shiver. "Jorbinan clears snapplers with firepops. Firepops are strong magic. Play tricks on sleepy eyes. Makes short ones walk and talk in sleep."

"Right ..." Zarni and Tobin shared a glance. The goblin had pieced together that whatever magic the dwarf had conducted affected halflings in a strange way. "And you don't remember anything?"

"I just remember waking up here in this lovely home and you were here, and these delicious flapjacks," Tobin said as he stuffed another big bite into his mouth. "Doesn't hurt my feelings. I'd like to get this recipe from you too, Jorbinan. If you don't mind, that is."

"Jorbinan can do this." He chuckled and bent his face down to blow raspberries on the horned marten's furry belly. Gibs grappled happily with the dwarf's beard. Zarni cringed, afraid the creature might claw Jorbinan's face. But the dwarf didn't seem to mind.

"And you use ... firepops?" Zarni used the sorcerer's word for the magical fireworks he'd seen Jorbinan using all night. "To clear the snapplers?"

"Snapplers," the dwarf said with another shiver. "Yes. Jorbinan does this."

"What are snapplers?" Tobin asked between bites.

"I don't know," Zarni admitted. "I didn't see anything else out there with us." He lowered his voice to whisper, "I'm not sure there was anything."

"Snapplers ..." Jorbinan paused to shiver. "Monsters. Little monsters. Faery foes. Mock Jorbinan. Mock Zarni. Mock Tobin. Mock Milirore love. Mock—"

"Snapplers mock people? Mock everyone?"

"Snapplers"—another shiver—"do this."

Zarni and Tobin shared a look that suggested neither of them was sure of the validity of the sorcerer's information. Jorbinan's mind seemed to be as chaotic as the inside of his home. Scattered objects littered the floors and every piece of furniture with a flat surface. The only surface not covered was the table, and Zarni assumed that was because the dwarf used the table every day. Decades of neglect left thick layers of dust on many of the random objects, as if the dwarf had shelved them and forgotten they existed.

On a side table nearby, Zarni noted a glass orb balanced on a stack of thick, leather tomes. Beside those, some metal contraption, the purpose of which the goblin couldn't even venture a guess, sat on an artfully scrolled wooden box, inside which, who knew? All of that together pinned down a leather strap that drooped over the edge of the side table holding a dangling, oiled leather bag. And that was just one of the myriad piles. The house, which shot off in multiple directions from the dining area, was full of such mounds of trinkets and mysterious miscellany.

Jorbinan brought the flapjacks to the table, Gibs clinging to his arm with glee. The dwarf flopped the last of the flapjacks on the serving plate before dishing some onto a plate for himself and an extra plate, which he set at the last remaining empty seat.

"Are we expecting more company?" Zarni asked.

"Oh, yay! Are we?" Tobin asked through a mouthful.

"Milirore love visits orcs. But Jorbinan does this. Milirore love might be hungry," the dwarf said as though it were the most reasonable thing in the world.

Zarni shot Tobin a tentative glance before asking, "Is Milirore love here now?"

The mad sorcerer ripped a laugh so loud and hardy it startled the fork right out of Tobin's hand, the bite halfway to his mouth. His fork clattered to the table, and he moaned as though he'd just lost a long-time friend.

"Milirore love visits orcs," Jorbinan said again. He wiped jovial tears from his eyes. The dwarf tickled Gibs on the table and jutted a thumb toward Zarni, shaking his head.

The goblin wasn't sure what to think, but he knew they couldn't linger there forever.

"Is Milirore love your wife?" Tobin asked, retrieving his fork. He examined the bite of flapjack speared on its end, deemed it was still edible, and popped it into his mouth.

"Milirore love does this!" Jorbinan said, widening his eyes at the halfling before shoveling a bite into his own mouth.

"Oh ..." Zarni hummed. He was starting to get the picture. "And Milirore went to visit the orcs?"

Jorbinan pointed at the goblin with his fork and nodded enthusiastically. "Milirore love does this!"

Realization dawned on him, and Zarnikorek wondered what really happened to the dwarf's wife. The thought must have hit Tobin too, for the halfling met his gaze with an equally concerned look.

"Jorbinan," Tobin started softly. "How long has Milirore been gone?"

"Forever!" the dwarf said with a great huff. "Milirore love visits orcs forever! Jorbinan misses Milirore love. Jorbinan thinks Milirore love come back hungry."

Zarnikorek's stomach sank. Had the dwarf's wife gone north? He hated to think his own people might have killed the sorcerer's wife. But their peoples had been enemies for so long ...

The goblin wondered just how long Jorbinan had been alone out here. He could never replace the loss of the dwarf's wife, but maybe by establishing the wagon route through the area, they could bring some company for him on occasion. At least Zarni and Tobin could stop by and visit from time to time. Guilt sat in his stomach like a stone block.

"Hey Jorbinan," Zarni spoke with gentleness. "We're establishing a wagon route between Tobin's people and my own people."

"Wagons and orcs? Wagons and halflings?"

"That's right," Zarni said. "We're going to drive wagons between two cities for trade. Maybe we can come visit you sometime. And maybe others can visit you along their journey?"

"Others can do this!" Jorbinan said cheerily. As bad as Zarni felt for the dwarf, the sorcerer seemed to maintain an upbeat attitude. That fact warmed Zarni's heart.

"Good! Good!" Tobin said. "You know, you could open up a flapjack house here and feed wagoners along the trail. You'd have quite the business, I'd wager. Good eating like this on a long road. You'd be rolling in coin."

"Jorbinan cannot do this. Jorbinan clears snapplers. Keeps wagoners safe."

"Yeah ..." Zarni said, trying to sound encouraging but sharing a sad look with Tobin. "Well ... hey, listen. We need to get back on the road. Our boulder goat, Gregory, has been alone for far too long. But I'll put your cabin on the map. Maybe we can bring the route closer to your house."

As Zarni pulled the map from his pocket and splayed it out on the table before him, Jorbinan jumped to his feet.

"Jorbinan helps!"

Admittedly, Zarni had not reacted with abundant enthusiasm when the mad sorcerer offered to help. He wondered what kind of curse the dwarf would heap upon them in his excitement. Or maybe Jorbinan would turn them into mountain mules to help Gregory pull the wagon. Or maybe, more disastrously, the dwarf would want to come along.

Instead, Jorbinan piled random things onto the table, some of them tumbling down and smashing the pancakes on the serving plate, much to Tobin's chagrin.

"Ah, this! Ah, this!" Jorbinan kept repeating as if he were rediscovering old treasures as he gathered more contraptions and oddities.

"What is all this?" Tobin whispered to Zarni.

"I'm not sure. I think he wants us to take these things with us?"

"Ah, this!" Jorbinan said. Suddenly he stood straight and threw a perplexing device that Zarni could only guess was of gnomish design. The part crashed against a wall and shattered, pieces skittering everywhere. The dwarf knelt reverently and lifted a scaly egg in both hands.

"Is that ...?" Zarni whispered.

"A wyvern's egg?" Tobin continued the thought. "I've only seen them in books. Have you ever seen one yourself?"

"I have," Zarni said. "They had a hatchery in Ruk for the wyvern riders there. There's also a hatchery in Ghun-Ra, but I've never been in that one. But this ... This is the smallest wyvern egg I've ever seen. They're usually ... maybe eight times that size."

Jorbinan handed the egg to Zarni gingerly. "Zarni takes this."

"I couldn't," Zarni said, though he took the egg, worried the dwarf would drop it. He gulped his emotions back. His green nose twitched as he tried to bite back the growing tingle behind his eyes.

"It's beautiful. Zarni—wait. Are you alright?" Tobin asked.

"Yes," Zarni choked out. "It's just ... This reminds me of something I read in one of the historical texts my pa has in his library. In the ancient days, when the nation of Drelek was yet to be united under one orc king, the tribes were led by gars. We still have gars in every major orc city, but back then, there was no king. Each tribe was isolated. Each tribe, its own. But when the orcs came together, the gar from each tribe brought a wyvern egg to Ruk. They handed the eggs over as a sign of friendship, honor, and loyalty. The act symbolized the giving of oneself to the cause of the leader. It's from those original eggs that the first wyvern squadron of Ruk was formed. It's how all the orcs were united, and of course, the goblins and trolls of Drelek as well."

"I never knew that story," Tobin said quietly.

Jorbinan merely stared with a soft smile.

"This is a beautiful gift. Thank you, Jorbinan," Zarni said as a tear rolled down his cheek.

"Jorbinan does this. Zarni takes this. And ah, this!" the mad sorcerer dashed to a side table to grab a bottle filled with some sort of amber liquid. When he opened it, the potent scent of alcohol assaulted their noses. Jorbinan sniffed the bottle and waggled his red eyebrows. A strange glint shone in his yellow eye before he tipped the bottle back and took a long swig.

Zarni and Tobin shared a glance and chuckled along as the dwarf came up for air with a belch that dissolved into manic laughter. Zarni couldn't be sure how old the liquid in that bottle was, but judging by the smell, it had lost all good flavor long ago. Jorbinan shook the bottle in front of them, making sure they understood what was in it, before he splashed some all over the Traitor's Map.

Zarnikorek and Tobin leapt to their feet. "No!"

CHAPTER 20
ON THE ROAD AGAIN

As Tobin leapt to wipe the alcohol from the map, Zarni turned on the mad sorcerer. "Jorbinan, you can't do that. We need that map. You can't destroy other people's maps."

"Jorbinan does not do this," the dwarf said before releasing another roaring laugh.

"Of course you did this! Who else ...?"

"Zarni looks. Zarni looks."

"What?" the goblin said, not understanding. "You can't just do stuff like that to get reactions out of people.

"Not this!" Jorbinan laughed hard. "Not this! Zarni looks!"

"What?"

"Zarni ..." Tobin said, confusion lacing his tone. "What is this?"

As Zarni turned to face the halfling, he realized something about the wet parchment held Tobin captive—new markings had appeared. "What in Finlestia?" he wondered aloud, clutching the egg in the crook of one arm as he drew nearer. "Those markings weren't there before."

"Aye," Tobin said softly. "You think the alcohol did this? How does alcohol ink a map?"

"Milirore love does this," Jorbinan chimed.

"Wait," Zarni said. "Your wife, Milirore has something to do with this?"

"Milirore love does this!" the dwarf repeated with gusto. "Koris does this!"

"Koris!" Tobin gasped. "Are you saying your wife and Koris knew each other?"

The halfling glanced at the goblin. Each of their faces crinkled.

"How is that possible?" Zarni mused.

"Milirore love does this! Koris does this!" Jorbinan repeated, seemingly very excited that his guests finally understood. In truth, neither of them understood anything.

Zarni inspected the map, which now had a square of text written in an old elvish that he recognized, but couldn't read. He'd seen the script before in one of his pa's history books. Not particularly helpful now. "Do you read elvish?"

"No ..." Tobin said, examining the map himself. "Not a lick. Lenor knows some ancient dwarvish. Her father made her and Lotmeag study it while they were growing up. She taught me some of that. She's teaching Button. Though this doesn't look anything like that. I suppose that doesn't do us much good," the halfling chuckled to himself, but then forced a serious crease to his brow as if he realized he had been over-speaking again. "Sorry."

"It's alright," Zarni said. "Wait. Jorbinan, do you read old elvish?"

"Jorbinan does not do this," the dwarf said, shaking his head. "Milirore does this."

"Are you saying Milirore is an elf?"

Tobin turned to Zarni, as if it suddenly clicked for the halfling as well.

"Ah, this!"

"Tobin, that's it!" Zarni exclaimed.

"Yes!" the halfling cheered. He scrunched his nose and pursed his lips. "What's it?"

"Elves are the longest lived of all the known peoples of Tarrine. Some have been known to live a couple thousand years. It's entirely possible that Milirore was alive during the Second Great Black War."

"You mean when this map was made!" Tobin said, catching on.

"Yes! Exactly. And when Jorbinan said, Milirore and Koris did this," he said, turning toward the dwarf, who watched and nodded along excitedly as the goblin pieced it all together, "you really meant that Milirore and Koris knew each other."

"Ah, this!" the mad sorcerer bellowed.

"Milirore may have been one of Koris's contacts for the people of the south."

"Milirore love does this!"

"And she may have helped Koris to craft a secret message on this map."

"Milirore love does this!"

"And she would have been instrumental in aiding Koris in his mission and guiding him through this wilderness without him getting caught."

"Milirore love does this!"

They all laughed at Jorbinan's excitement. Even the dwarf himself.

"That's amazing," Tobin mused as he chewed on his unlit pipe. "Too bad neither of us knows how to read elvish. I have a friend back in Galium who's somewhat of a scholar. He'd have this read up in no time. Although, I'm sure Master Argus would be excited to read it himself. Though that's a long ride back. I suppose it doesn't make sense to drive all the way back to Galium at this point."

"No," Zarni said before Tobin could continue. They couldn't go back. "No, that wouldn't make sense."

As much as Zarni wanted to know what the block of text said, it likely wouldn't help them much. The more interesting thing about the new markings was that the path dots seemed to branch in the direction Zarni had mentally marked off in his mind as he'd followed the sorcerer to his home.

"Jorbinan, thank you for showing us this," Zarni said, patting the dwarf on the shoulder. "This is amazing. I'm looking forward to finding someone to read this for us when our quest is finished."

"Milirore love does this."

"Yes," Zarni said kindly. "Yes, she did. Thank you again. Tobin, we need to get back on the road."

"Aye," Tobin said. "Keep thinking about that Flapjack House, Jorbi. I'm telling you; those jacks are something fierce. Would give Lenor a run for her coin, I'd wager." He leaned in conspiratorially. "Though don't go telling her I said so. I don't like to bite the hand that feeds, you know?"

"Jorbinan does not do this," the mad sorcerer said with all seriousness.

Tobin chuckled as he made his way out of the house. Zarni looked down at the small wyvern egg he still held close, then back to the dwarf.

"Are you sure?"

The dwarf tickled Gibs affectionately one last time and placed the horned marten on Zarni's shoulder. "Zarni takes this." The goblin smiled as Gibs wrapped himself up on his shoulders. Jorbinan then nodded to the egg and placed an oddly comforting hand on the goblin's other shoulder and said, "Zarni takes this."

Zarni nodded. "Thank you."

Jorbinan waved to Zarni and Tobin for a long time as they made their way through the woods back toward their wagon. He hollered "Zarni beware snapplers" and "Tobin beware snapplers" and "Gibs does this," until long after they walked out of earshot.

When they reached the wagon, Tobin ran to greet Gregory with a hug. The boulder goat pranced about in his harness and nuzzled the halfling with his massive beard. *So, he does have a heart,* Zarni mused. With the reunion completed, Tobin set to work, checking over the wagon to ensure everything was in order. Zarni stopped a few paces away from the boulder goat. Gregory eyed him, but his normally aloof look was absent. Instead, Zarni could have sworn the boulder goat nodded to him. Whether in appreciation that the goblin had saved his friends—or at least the halfling that showered him with affection—or out of respect for the force with which Zarni had spoken to him the night before, the goblin wasn't sure. Either way, he nodded to the boulder goat and climbed into the driver's box.

"Ah, you ready to take a turn at the reins?" Tobin asked as he climbed up and sat on the red cushioned bench next to the goblin.

"Oh, no," Zarnikorek said quickly. "I can't do that."

Tobin eyed him as the halfling lit his pipe and puffed a few times to get it going. "You *can't*?" he asked, emphasizing the negative word.

Zarni chuckled and heaved a heavy sigh. "No. Maybe later. I just ..." A yawn interrupted his words. "I thought I might like to sit with you here in the driver's box for a little while. But now that I think about it, I've been up most of the night chasing after a mad sorcerer I thought was going to turn my friend into a mountain mule."

"Could you imagine the look on Lenor's face?" Tobin said, biting hard on his pipe so it didn't fly from his grin as he laughed and snapped the reins. Gregory seemed no worse for wear and pulled the wagon into motion. "Not sure she'd want to kiss my face if I had mule whiskers. She likes me clean shaven. Don't think she'd be too fond of a furry snout. Though Button would probably get a kick out of it, I'd wager. She'd be climbing all over my back and leaping to the chairs in the sitting room. Though Lenor might not want me to bring my muddy hooves in the house. I'd have to sleep out in the stables with Wendra and Kelli. Wouldn't that be a sight? I'd wager ..."

Tobin's words slowly faded away as the rocking of the wagon lulled Zarni to sleep. He fought it for a while, forcing his heavy eyes to open. But the pure relief of knowing his friends were safe and the exhaustion of the previous night added their input to the matter, sending him into a sleep he could not deny.

Gibs butted his head against Zarni's face, over and over again, waking the goblin. Zarni rubbed his eyes and sat up. The sun had moved over the western slopes of the majestic Drelek Mountains and hidden behind formulating thunder clouds—a common occurrence in the elevated lands. *How long have I been out? And how did I get into the back of the wagon?* he wondered as he pulled the blankets away from himself. He let out a long yawn and stretched his hands high.

"Well, good morning, there!" Tobin said cheerily as he ripped a bite of jerky with his teeth. He laughed to himself and said, "Well, I suppose it's afternoon now. You were out for quite a while. Jorbinan must have been asleep, too. Imagine he'd have been outside waving to us again as we passed the house earlier. But I suppose he was up all night too, 'clearing snapplers.' Probably sleeps most during the day, I'd wager. And what do you think snapplers are? I had some friends who traversed the Tandal Sea. Told me a story about faeries. Nasty, horrible story. I wouldn't want to run into their ilk. Likely as not ..."

Zarni had stopped listening. He was still waking up, wondering how he'd gotten into the back of the wagon.

Gibs butted his head against Zarni's feet. "Yes. Yes. I'm up. I'm up." He turned to the forward railing and spoke to the halfling. "Tobin, how did I get back here?"

"Ah, well," Tobin said through a bite of jerky. "You were falling asleep here on the bench, but I suggested you move to the back of the wagon to get more comfortable. Figured it's better to be comfortable when you sleep. You'll get better rest, waking up refreshed and renewed, you know. Then, you just stood up, didn't even open your eyes, climbed over the railing and buried yourself in blankets. Might as well have been sleep walking like I did last night. For a minute I thought Jorbinan was using his firepops again, but then I remembered it only affects halflings—"

"Ouch!" Zarni cried.

Gibs had butted the goblin's foot, leading with his little horn.

"You alright?" Tobin asked, looking over his shoulder.

"Yeah, I'm fine," Zarni said, bending down to rub his foot. "Just not sure what's with Gibs."

"Is he hungry? Hey Gibs, I've got some jerky here. You want some?"

Gibs rubbed up against Zarni again.

"What? What is it?" the goblin asked, now giving the horned marten his full attention.

Gibs scurried to the wyvern egg nestled on a small pile of unlit coals they used for their evening fires. The horned marten bobbed his head, emitting an adorable rhythmic purring noise.

"Yes, it was a very nice gift. Are you missing Jorbinan already?" Zarni asked. He paused and wondered. "Hey Tobin, do horned martens eat eggs? And no, you can't eat that," he said to Gibs.

"I'm not sure. He seems to be happy eating just about anything," Tobin said with a chuckle. "If I didn't know better, I'd think he was a halfling at heart. Is he trying to eat the wyvern egg?"

"No," Zarni said curiously. "He's just standing by it and making weird noises."

"That's strange."

"Yeah ..." Zarni drew closer to the egg. "What is it?"

His long green ears twitched as he heard another sound. Something like a croak. His face blanched when he realized it hadn't been Gibs.

The egg teetered, and a crack etched itself across the scaly surface.

Chapter 21
Wyvern Cries

As the egg crumbled, a red, scaly head poked out. Round golden eyes blinked behind tired lids. Tiny horns framed the little wyvern's face, following the ridges of its skull. A horned sail ran over its head like a purple mohawk, the skin in between the horns purple, like its leathery wings.

The creature looked at Gibs and blinked.

Gibs chirped uncomfortably. Zarnikorek might have cursed himself, if he could put together a rational thought.

Using its two legs and the articulating claw at the fore bend of its wing, the miniature wyvern gingerly crawled out of its egg. Gibs stood on his hind legs, petrified. Zarni's eyes met the horned marten's. The goblin didn't know what to do either.

Then the wyvern did something neither of them expected. Slowly, it bobbed its head toward Gibs, as if feeling him out. Zarni thought it looked almost like a featherless and scaly plains chicken. Gibs didn't move as the wyvern clicked and cooed and nuzzled against the horned marten's furry belly.

"What's going on? What's happening back there?" Tobin asked, turning and leaning back over the railing to see what he'd missed. "Well, I'll be ..."

"The egg ..." Zarni coughed, trying to clear away the shock. "The egg hatched."

"I can see that," Tobin said. "Have you ever seen such a lizard?"

"Yes … I …" Zarni shook his head, a million thoughts flooding his mind. How could this even happen? He huffed a heavy breath, trying to center his thoughts. The wyvern turned to face him.

"Easy there," Tobin said as they both recoiled.

The wyvern merely looked at them, angling its head so his golden eyes could take them in. It turned back to Gibs and chirped as though it were asking for the horned marten's appraisal of the duo. Gibs stood petrified for a moment, until the wyvern started rubbing up against him again.

"I think … I think it might believe Gibs is his pa." Zarni strung the words together, even though he hardly believed what he was saying.

"Does that make us a wyvern's uncle?" Tobin asked with a laugh.

The wyvern looked back to the front of the wagon, and the two recoiled again.

"I'm not sure it knows what to make of us yet," Zarni replied.

"Well, hopefully, Gibs tells him how nice we are. He seems a little small, don't you think? I've not seen a baby wyvern before, but I expected it would be bigger. I know they don't breathe fire."

"No," Zarni said. "Not like their dragon cousins. And they don't grow nearly as big as dragons. But this one is small for a wyvern. Smallest I've ever seen. Might be a runt."

"He'll fit right in with us," Tobin chuckled. "Only big member of our crew is King Gregory!"

Zarni wasn't sure, but he thought the wagon got a short burst of speed—likely the boulder goat surging with pride at the comment.

"What are we going to do with a wyvern?" Zarni asked, genuinely lost for ideas. He had initially thought he'd be able to bring the egg to King Genjak as a symbol of this new venture between their peoples. But now ...

"I don't know. Doesn't seem like he's going to grow big enough to ride. But I'm no wyvern expert."

"Who knows ..."

Tobin stroked his chin before popping another piece of jerky into his mouth. "Do we know how to take care of a baby wyvern?"

Zarni didn't respond as he watched the odd interaction between Gibs and the baby wyvern as the little creature nuzzled into the horned marten's furry belly.

As it turned out, they had no idea what to do with a baby wyvern. At first, the wyvern climbed around the wagon, following Gibs. The horned marten seemed to be trying to get away from the creature without making any fast movements. Zarni wasn't sure if Gibs was worried about startling the wyvern or not, but he seemed mortified by the situation. After a few hours of this, Gibs seemed to resign himself to the fact that the wyvern wasn't going to eat him, and even seemed curious about this creature that followed him around.

The two climbed on barrels and sacks of wares. Gibs even clambered to the railing, seemingly testing the wyvern's balance. It had been fascinating to watch the dynamic grow between the two creatures.

Eventually, the two had worn themselves out and Gibs curled up into the blankets. The baby wyvern followed suit, coiling up next to the horned marten and stretching one purple wing over his face and the other over Gibs. The horned marten's head popped for a second, his black eyes blinking curiously, before he laid back down for sleep.

They'd driven long into the evening, Zarni marking the map and asking Tobin to fill in the gaps from when he was asleep himself. That is, until the baby wyvern starting crying. The little creature reared his head back and bobbed his neck, letting out the most pathetic and heartbreaking cries—somewhere between a coo and a crackle.

Zarni had climbed into the back of the wagon, trying to help Gibs settle the baby wyvern. The wyvern even let the goblin pick him up. Zarni stroked the wyvern's scaly back, and the creature rolled into his touch like a house cat, enjoying the pets.

Still, the wyvern cried.

After several hours of this, Zarni called to Tobin. "We may need to stop for the evening. If we can't get it to stop crying, the whole mountain range will know where we are. Including any predators."

"That would not be helpful," Tobin agreed. "There's a stream up ahead. We can camp near there for the night. Have you tried feeding him? What should we name him?"

"Name him?"

"Yeah," Tobin shrugged. "I was thinking we should probably name him. No sense in calling him little lizard forever. Maybe something strong since he's so tiny. You know, make him feel big and tough. Something like Boulder. Or Mountain. Or Cliff."

"Cliff?" Zarni asked, wondering how they even managed to get into this situation. The wyvern stopped crying. "Cliff?" he said again. The wyvern eyed him, his scaly head popping to the side curiously. "Cliff?" Zarni said again. "He stopped. I think he likes it."

"Good. Cliff it is."

"But we have to spell it the orcish way with a 'k.' Kliff," Zarni said. The wyvern seemed intrigued by Zarni's voice.

"Sounds good to me," Tobin said. "Not many bigger and tougher than orc warriors. I'd wager there's a warrior or two in orcish history named Kliff."

"I'd bet you're right," Zarni chuckled, more out of relief that the wyvern had stopped crying than out of amusement.

It was then that he realized why the baby wyvern had stopped crying. His neck pulled away from the goblin's embrace as he angled his head to see what Gibs was dragging over to them. When Zarni saw the cloth, he said, "Hey. How'd you get those out of the barrel?"

Gibs didn't respond, but Zarni could have sworn the horned marten snickered. The furry creature pulled at the knot on the cloth, quickly dismantling it. Zarni pressed a bemused smile between his lips. *Looks like you were going to eat those gibs no matter how well I hid them or how tight I tied that knot.*

Gibs pulled one of the fish bone snacks from the cloth and the baby wyvern nearly flew out of Zarni's arms. The wyvern croaked and cooed as Gibs relinquished the snack. Kliff bobbed his head and neck with fervor as he gobbled it down.

"Great," Zarni said, grabbing one of the snacks for himself. He tried to savor it, thinking it may be the last one he got on the trip.

"What?" Tobin asked as he parked the wagon and turned to lean over the railing.

"Looks like we might need more gibs."

"You know how to make them on the road?" Tobin asked. "I suppose we'd probably be able to make something similar using the skillet, but it wouldn't be the same. I'm sure we could make it taste good, but I don't know how to fish. So, we may be out of luck. I'd wager we could—"

"That's it!" Zarni cut him off excitedly. "Fish! Wyverns love fish."

"Well, I imagine that makes sense," Tobin started to say, but Zarni cut him off again.

"Tobin, how would you like to learn how to fish?"

CHAPTER 22
JOY

*P*lunk!

"Well, I think we're done fishing for the evening," Zarni said through a laugh that ached his ribs.

Kliff screeched and flapped his wings wildly as he pulled himself back onto the bank of the creek. The wyvern had already taken bites of three of the trout they'd pulled from the river. Tobin had just pulled in another, and Kliff jumped and chomped at it like a cat attacking a dangling ribbon. Once the wyvern realized where the fish were coming from, he'd hobbled across the stones and dove in after one. Zarni was sure the creature hadn't expected the mountain waters to be so brisk. Kliff, with his tail tucked between his legs, crawled to Gibs who sat nearby watching.

"Oh, that pesky lizard," Tobin scolded, though couldn't help but laugh himself. The halfling had been having a blast. He took to the leisurely patience of fishing easily and had pulled in a couple himself. It did, however, take Zarni a couple of explanations before Tobin understood why he needed to stay quiet while they fished. But eventually, the halfling settled in, chewed his pipe, and enjoyed the game. "I suppose we should probably build a fire. Going to have to cook these fish up somehow. Though it doesn't seem like Kliff minds eating them raw."

"No," Zarni agreed. "I suppose most wyverns eat them raw."

The pair gathered up their basket of fish, and Zarni took both of the poles. He'd taught Tobin as much as he could think to teach him. The halfling had proven to be an adept student, eager to learn. Zarni showed him how to pick a branch to fashion the rod. Funny enough, Zarni had brought a fishing kit with him. When he unrolled the leather pouch that held his string, his hooks, and his flies, Tobin had looked on in wonder, as if the goblin were unveiling some sort of long-lost treasure.

"That was a lot of fun," Tobin said as they rejoined Gregory and the wagon. The boulder goat contentedly munched on the abundant mountain grass. "I could have done that all night!"

"Well, the fishing isn't as good when the sun sets. Better to hit the creekside in the morning." Zarni said. "But you did really well for a first timer."

"Thank you kindly. I appreciate you teaching me all that stuff. I'll have to keep practicing my flick," the halfling said, whipping his arm and wrist in a mock cast. "I can't wait to teach Button and Bandix how to fish. My father never taught me. He was a wagonwright. Whole reason I fell in love with wagons. When I was just a mite, I thought he had the neatest job in all Finlestia. But it didn't afford him much time outside the wagon yard. And I wanted to go out and see where the wagons were taking good folk!"

"And look at you now," Zarni said.

"Yes! On a wagon route that doesn't even exist yet. Driving through the Drelek Mountains with the strongest boulder goat in all of Finlestia. With good weather, fresh air, and as good a friend as anyone could ask for."

Zarni smirked. "Well, I appreciate that."

"Nothing but the truth," Tobin said as he set the basket of fish on the back of the wagon.

"Funny thing is," Zarni said slowly, "I've spent so much time looking at maps and reading books and wondering what places would look like. Just like you, I always wanted to go out and experience the world. But when the opportunity came, I almost said no."

"What?" Tobin gasped. The halfling eyed him with genuine disbelief.

"No, really," Zarni chuckled. He didn't think it would be so hard to believe.

"Why?"

The simplicity of the question struck the goblin. Tobin was getting better at asking questions and leaving the space for Zarni to answer. The goblin grumbled at how jarring it was.

"Well ..." he hemmed. "I'd just been stuck for so long. You know, settled into the idea I would never get to do something like this. I resolved myself to the notion that I couldn't."

"Ah," Tobin nodded with understanding as he lit his pipe. "There's that 'can't' again."

Zarni chuckled. "You picked up on that quick."

"Something of a gift," the halfling said.

"Yeah. Well, you were absolutely right. I just came up with excuse after excuse. I started believing some of the things others were saying about me. Well ..."

The goblin's words trailed off as he lost himself in what he was saying.

"Well, what?"

"Well, I'm just realizing that there was only one person who ever said those words to me. I've had others who only ever encouraged me. But the only words I believed about myself were the ones said to me by someone I knew was bad. How could I get so wrapped up in the words of someone who only used me? So wrapped up I couldn't hear the words of those who loved me?"

Tobin didn't respond right away, but Zarni could tell the halfling was pondering his words as he built the campfire. An uncomfortable shiver shook him. His stomach soured as he tried to replay his words. How foolish they seemed. Had he just lost the respect of the first person who'd called him friend in who knows how long?

"Tobin, I—"

"I'm not—"

They spoke at the same time, but halted quickly, each offering for the other to go first. With an incredible display of self-control, Tobin held firm. Zarni knew the halfling was working hard to hold his tongue, so he wanted to encourage his friend.

"I'm sorry," the goblin said, taking the lead. "I shouldn't be sharing all the messy thoughts that bounce around in my head."

Tobin laughed. "I think you have a much better handle on that than I do. But," he added pointedly, "you do know that's what friends are for, right? Friends are the ones who encourage you and see the best in you, even when you have a hard time seeing it in yourself."

"I suppose," Zarni agreed. Had he not just done that exact thing, trying to encourage Tobin in his own personal growth challenge?

"And as for what you said, it's always better to hear the things from the people that love us. Honestly, I don't know why we always take criticism so hard. Maybe because it pierces right to the heart of us. Words are powerful. Good or bad. That's why I've made it somewhat of a life mission of mine to bring as much joy as I can to every situation."

Zarni nodded thoughtfully as he handed Tobin another log for the fire. He'd seen that in the halfling a dozen times already.

"The way I see it," Tobin continued, "there are enough people who will bring negativity and hurt everywhere they go. But if I bring joy everywhere I go, at least I know there will be some joy in the situation. It doesn't always work, mind you. I'd wager there are loads of folk that find it rather uncomfortable because they don't know how to have joy with themselves. And certainly, I've heard the mean things people have said about me. It's hard not to wrestle with that. But regardless, I am determined to bring joy with me, even if others don't."

"But how can you be so confident in that? How can you not care what other people think and just show up, anyway?"

Tobin humphed, clearly burying a laugh. "I care. I just try not to live or die by the words of those who don't have my best interest at heart. Those that love me do. And therefore, their words hold more weight."

Zarni blinked at the halfling as Tobin gathered the skillet and a trout. Yet again, he'd surprised the goblin.

"But what about the things I've done ..." Zarni could hardly speak the words.

Tobin stopped. He turned to meet Zarni's eyes. A kind smile wrinkled the crow's feet at the corners of the halfling's eyes. "Everyone has a past filled with mistakes. But when you live moment to moment, you find ways to bring something better into the world. Remember what Master Argus Azulekor said? 'Even small things can have great impact on the world.' Small deeds, my friend.

"Look at me. When Lotmeag asked why I had to come, I told him it was because I didn't feel like I did enough during the Battle of Galium. And here we are. Small deeds."

Zarni nodded again, trying to hide the fact he was blinking back welling tears. *There's a lot of wisdom in such a small halfling.* He laughed at the notion.

"What?" Tobin chuckled along.

"Oh, nothing," Zarni said, waving the attention away. "I was just thinking, since you joined this quest with me, maybe I'd like to join your mission, too. Maybe I can bring some more joy to Finlestia everywhere I go, too."

"I have no doubt," the halfling said as he plopped a trout into the skillet.

"And maybe I can drive tomorrow."

Tobin burst out laughing, slapping his knee. When he could finally breathe, he turned a wide grin on the goblin. "You're already on mission, it seems."

CHAPTER 23
DRIVING

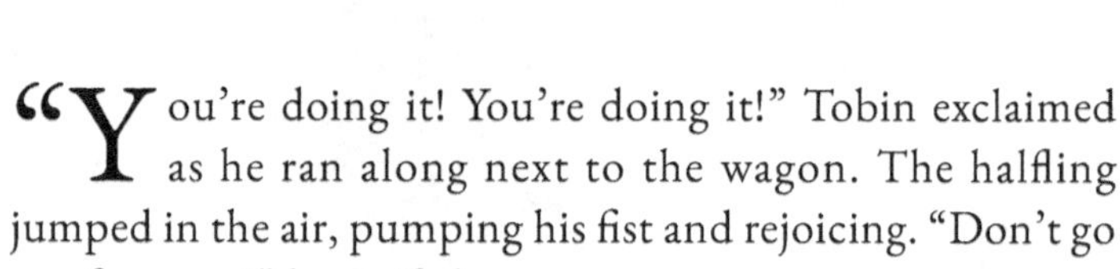

"You're doing it! You're doing it!" Tobin exclaimed as he ran along next to the wagon. The halfling jumped in the air, pumping his fist and rejoicing. "Don't go too fast now!" he puffed.

Warmth welled up inside Zarni as he held the reins and drove the wagon. Gregory pulled along, seemingly quite content to have the goblin take the reins. And if Zarni didn't know any better, he thought the boulder goat gave him a slight grin. But that'd couldn't be right.

Kliff clung to Gregory's horns, having climbed along the riggings and finding the perch quite appealing. The boulder goat didn't seem to mind, and the wyvern wasn't crying, so Zarni saw no need to remove him. Everyone seemed in good spirits, except Gibs who dug his claws into the railing behind Zarni and watched the wyvern like a worried father.

"Alright, now you have to get him to stop!" Tobin hollered, now trailing the wagon. "Remember, snap the reins with the wrist and say, 'slow.' Once he starts slowing, you can say 'stop.'"

Zarni gripped the straps in his hand, feeling the smoothness where Tobin's grip had already started to polish the leather. He flicked his wrists, just like the halfling had shown him, and called to Gregory, "Slow."

The boulder goat slowed his steady trot to a meandering walk.

"Alright, now stop."

Suddenly, Gregory bolted.

The wagon surged forward with such an alarming jolt that Gibs flew out of sight into the back of the wagon. Kliff's clawed feet gripped the boulder goat's horns, but his wings fluttered with the new speed.

"Stop! Stop! Stop!" Zarni hollered.

He thought he heard Tobin yelling the same thing far behind.

The boulder goat ran and ran, gaining speed until he planted his hooves into the dirt and the wagon skidded along behind him, nearly launching Zarni right out of the driver's box. Zarni clutched at his chest, his heart beating against his ribs. "What was that?" he growled. "I mean it! What was that?"

The goblin shot a glance into the back of the wagon and spotted Gibs. The horned marten shook his head dizzily, but otherwise seemed alright. Zarni climbed out of the driver's box and positioned himself just in front of the boulder goat, who stood tall above him.

"What? Are you trying to kill us?"

He fixed the beast with a glare that could turn a troll to stone. His hands pressed to his hips and his foot tapped impatiently.

Gregory stared back. And the creature's flat look made Zarni think the boulder goat *had* been trying to kill them. But in a sudden and rather confusing show, Gregory bobbed his chin high over and over again, eliciting several strangely pitched grunts.

"Are you ..." Zarni blinked, trying to regain his composure. But the boulder goat's display was so awkward, it was humorous. "Are you laughing?"

Gregory's quirky grunts grew louder and his front hooves started to dance.

"You're laughing," Zarni couldn't help himself. "That's how you laugh?"

The boulder goat nearly dropped to its knees, so overcome by its mirth. Gregory stepped from side to side to keep his balance. Kliff, along for the ride on the boulder goat's horns, squawked what Zarni assumed was the equivalent of a laugh for the wyvern.

Tobin huffed and puffed as he caught up. "Is every—" He paused, doubling over and removing the pipe from his mouth. "Is everyone alright?"

"Oh, yes," Zarni said, wiping the jovial tears from his eyes. The boulder goat nudged the goblin's head, nearly knocking his goggles off. Zarni grabbed them and petted the goat's big beard. "It seems Gregory likes to play pranks on people."

"What?" Tobin asked, still out of breath and clearly confused.

"I thought he didn't understand me so I just kept yelling, 'Stop! Stop! Sto—" A sudden fit of laughter cut off his own words. Zarni could hardly breathe. He felt like he had run just as far as Tobin.

"Well," Tobin gasped. "Maybe the mischievous king can wait until I'm in the wagon before he plays another prank?"

The companions laughed even harder. The entire group joined in the moment of mirth; save for Gibs, who now sat on the driver's bench, less than enthused by the boulder goat's prank.

Zarni got to drive much of that day, enjoying the pointers that Tobin gladly shared. The halfling seemed more than eager to repay all the goblin had taught him about fishing. And, in a boisterous show of confidence in his friend, Tobin had climbed over the railing into the back of the wagon to 'take a nap.' The halfling was up and talking with the goblin less than fifteen minutes later, putting the legitimacy of his 'nap' in question. But Zarni appreciated the show of encouragement.

The mountain passes and valleys they traversed throughout the day became more and more wild to Zarni's eyes. These were areas people did not travel. At one point, they stopped on a ledge that overlooked a wide-open valley filled with northern great white elk.

"Look at them all," Tobin said in awe as he packed his pipe. "I once saw one of them on a winter run to Crossdin. Came down from the mountain valleys to the warmer area. Funny, it was a cold day, anyway. Lots of snow in the area. But he was majestic."

Gregory snorted.

"Not as majestic as you, Gregory," Tobin cooed.

Zarni shook his head. He'd seen the great white elks before, but he'd never seen so many in one place. "They must gather in this valley because it's so remote," he mused.

The companions watched the enormous creatures for a long while before moving on. They even got to see some of the bull elks grappling with their enormous, pointed antlers.

Tobin had taken a long driving shift after that, giving Zarni the chance to consider the Traitor's Map and make any appropriate markings for their own purposes. He wondered what it had been like for the allied armies to walk this path all those centuries ago. He thought it rather strange that they'd seen nearly no sign of the army at all. Sure, the land had probably reclaimed much of the trail with its vegetation, but he thought they'd find ... something. A shield. A sword. A spearhead. Something steel. Something shiny. But perhaps anything that the army had dropped or left had rusted away generations ago.

He knew his fleeting hope to find a sign of them was unnecessary and nostalgic. Or scholarly at the very best. But a small doubt nagged at him. If he could only see a sign, he'd feel a lot more confident in their direction.

Geological formations determined much of their route. Driving straight up a mountain was illogical and would make for an unreasonable wagon road for trade. Much of the time, they followed curves and hillocks and wound around boulders and through waterless canyons. Tobin had explained to him the system that wagoners used in the south to take breaks midway between their destinations. This route had required a few, and Zarni marked spots where he thought wagoners would naturally gather. The halfling confirmed his own thoughts on the matter, mentioning again how well Jorbinan could do if he turned his home into a flapjack house.

That evening, they came to the edge of a river and Tobin suggested he would prefer to cross in the morning, bright and early. It was only after they'd unloaded for camp and decided to find the best fishing spot that they discovered the first sign of the ancient allied army.

"Look at that!" the halfling shouted, pointing to a wide stone bridge nearby. Several of the stones had crumbled, and mountain grass and moss clung to the cracks, but overall, the bridge seemed structurally sound. Zarni was no engineer like his pa, but he guessed it would hold their wagon just fine.

"I can't believe it!" Zarni said, excited to finally find the proof he'd hoped for. A wave of relief washed over him. He'd wondered if he was leading them in the right direction, but this bridge proved it.

"You better believe it," Tobin said through a laugh, clapping the goblin on the shoulder. "I'd been wondering when we would see some sign of that old army. Looks like you were leading us right to it."

The companions settled in for bed that evening, well-stocked on mountain trout and high-spirited. They were finally getting somewhere. But as their eyes closed for what they expected to be a good night's rest, other eyes watched in the darkness.

CHAPTER 24
SNAPPLERS

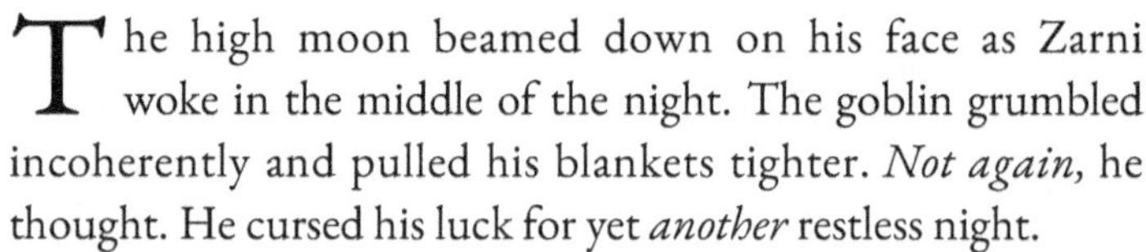

The high moon beamed down on his face as Zarni woke in the middle of the night. The goblin grumbled incoherently and pulled his blankets tighter. *Not again,* he thought. He cursed his luck for yet *another* restless night.

Zarnikorek popped up suddenly, and patted Tobin's bedding. The halfling rolled away from the patting hand and his snores rumbled out louder. *Thank the Maker,* the goblin thought. When his fingers landed on a furry ball, half-covered by a leathery wing, relief began to slow his heart. A quick glance under the wagon railing told him Gregory was fine as well. Everyone was here. Sleeping soundly. Why couldn't he?

The goblin grimaced and pulled his blankets up on his head. He curled his body inward, trying to ball himself up in a cocoon. The blankets twisted around him as he rolled over several times, his ears taking in every snore the halfling breathed. Eventually, he pulled his head out of the blankets and eyed Tobin's round form, rising and falling with the blissful peace of sleep.

Zarni reached over to poke his shoulder, and Tobin rolled again. In this position, his snores lessened to a quiet breathing. But as soon as Zarni settled back into his own covers, a rumbling growl vibrated in his ears.

"Ugh!" he groaned as he sat up again.

"Grrrrr ..."

Zarni's ears twitched, and his brow crinkled. That noise hadn't come from Tobin. The goblin clambered to his knees and moved to the back of the wagon. Holding onto the railing, he peered out over the landscape that surrounded them. The creek flowed nearby. Though deep, it ran quietly through the night.

"Grrrr…"

Zarnikorek winced. This time, the growl seemed to come from a different direction. He shuffled to the other side of the wagon.

"Grrrrr…"

He froze. The growls were coming from all around them. *Gregory!* Zarnikorek panicked. "Gregory!" he exclaimed under his breath as he threw himself to the side of the wagon to check on the boulder goat. The massive beast slept away, his big furry body looking an awful lot like a hairy boulder.

Zarnikorek narrowed his eyes and scanned the area, but he couldn't identify any predators that might be stalking them in the night. The moon was high enough to light the area well. And even if it wasn't, goblins had the ability to see in much darker conditions, like those in the depths of the mountains or even so far beneath the surface as the Underrock. But his eyes gave him nothing.

Was he imagining it?

"Gregory!" he croaked again.

"Gregory!"

"Gregory!"

"Gregory!"

Quiet, vibrating voices echoed his call from all directions. The boulder goat raised his head at the many mentions of his name.

"Who's there?" Zarnikorek said.

"Gregory!"
"Gregory!"
"Gregory!"
The voices called back, laced with a vibrating laughter.
"Tobin ..." Zarnikorek said slowly.
"Tobin!"
"Tobin!"
"Tobin!"
"Tobin, wake up!" Zarnikorek said, leaping next to the halfling and shaking him.
"Oof, wha—"
"Tobin, something's happening. Someone's here."
"Tobin!"
"Tobin!"
"Tobin!"
The voices buzzed.
"What in Finlestia?" Tobin mumbled, shaking his head and forcing himself up.
By now, Gibs had arisen to his hind legs and was looking about warily. The snoozing Kliff clicked, talking in his sleep as he adjusted to the horned marten's movement.
"Grrrr ..."
"Grrrr ..."
"Grrrr ..."
The growls came from all around them, followed by laughter.
"We need to go," Zarnikorek said.
"What is this?" Tobin whispered.
"I have no idea. But I don't like it one bit."
"Could it be ...?" the halfling's words trailed off but his eyes locked onto the goblin's.
"Snapplers?"

Neither of them had actually believed such creatures existed, for Zarnikorek had seen nothing but the mad sorcerer's firepops the other night. But now, the only thing he could remember with certainty was the mad sorcerer's concerned look and the way he said, *"Zarni beware snapplers! Tobin beware snapplers!"*

"We need to get out of here. I'll get Gregory strapped up," Zarnikorek said firmly. They didn't have time for Tobin to dote on the boulder goat to get him ready. "You gather the unloaded supplies, and we'll get out of here. They haven't attacked yet. Let's not make any sudden movements to excite them."

"Right you are," Tobin agreed. "I'm starting to think we should have asked Jorbinan for more information about the snapplers. Would have been wise, I'd wager. Don't suppose we have any way to defend ourselves. If they're like faeries, my crossbow won't be much use. You don't know how to wield magic, right? I certainly don't. Never had the aptitude for such things as—"

"Tobin!" Zarnikorek cut off the halfling's nervous rambling.
"Tobin!"
"Tobin!"
"Tobin!"

The voices cooed. Cackling laughter bounced around the night.

"No sudden movements," Zarnikorek urged him, as they climbed out of the back of the wagon.
"Grrrr…"
"Grrrr…"
"Grrrr…"

Zarnikorek slowed his pace, moving as if he were stuck in a bog. "Gregory!" he called as quietly as he could.
"Gregory!"
"Gregory!"

"Gregory!"

The voices repeated.

A creeping sensation slithered up Zarnikorek's spine. The boulder goat seemed to be on alert now and watched the goblin approach. "We have to get out of here. Now. I need you hooked up. Don't give me any guff."

Gregory rose to his feet without hesitation.

"Grrrr…"

"Grrrr…"

"Grrrr…"

"Easy now…" Zarnikorek said to the boulder goat. He looped some of the goat's leathers around Gregory, and the pair ambled slowly toward the wagon.

"Zarni," Tobin called quietly.

"Zarni!"

"Zarni!"

"Zarni!"

"What is it?" Zarnikorek choked out. The way the snapplers said his name nearly stole the heart right out of him.

When Tobin didn't reply right away, Zarni looked away from his work. The halfling stood, paralyzed. His eyes, like saucers, stared at something above Zarnikorek's head. The goblin couldn't move his own muscles as fear crept from every limb up to his throat. He knew without looking that the halfling was staring at the exact same thing he was looking at above his friend.

Glowing orbs of warm light floated about. It was hard to discern any details, but inside each amber orb of light appeared to be tiny, people-like creatures. *Snapplers!*

Krakoom!

The night exploded into chaos.

Firepops erupted in the air all around them. Bursts of colorful fire appeared out of thin air and ruptured the quiet of the night. Snapplers scattered and buzzed about, the color of their glowing orbs changing to match the most recent firepop. The erratic lights were almost hypnotizing.

Boom! Crack!

The loud explosions were less so.

"Hurry!" Zarni hollered to Tobin.

The goblin finished cinching the boulder goat to the front of the wagon. Zarni had never seen fear in the goat's face, but Gregory stamped at the ground, clearly uncomfortable and ready to get them out of there. Zarni whirled to the side of the wagon and hurtled toward the back.

Bang!

The explosion threw Zarni to the dirt. He pushed himself up quickly and churned his feet. As he rounded the back of the wagon, Tobin struggled to heave the last barrel back into the wagon. Zarni threw his shoulder into it and the two of them pushed it inside without bothering to upright it.

Zzip! Kroom!

"Get in! Get in!" Zarni yelled.

They climbed into the wagon through the back. Zarni and Tobin ran past Gibs, who was burying a squealing Kliff with blankets and standing over him protectively. Zarni reached the front first, leaping over the railing into the driver's box. He grabbed the leather reins and snapped. "We're ready Gregory! Go! Go! Go!"

The boulder goat didn't hesitate. His legs had already been tensely coiled, and with one heaving leap, he charged through the night. The wagon lurched into motion with such force, Tobin nearly didn't make it into the driver's box with Zarni.

Bam! Clack!

Explosions continued to fill the sky above them.

"Where are we going to go?" Tobin hollered over the cacophony.

"We have to get to that bridge. After that, I don't know."

Boom!

Zarni saw the bridge, only a short distance away. The stone structure's silhouette broke the moonlit, reflective waters of the creek. Motion caught his eye, and he turned to see a figure on the far side of the water. With a grace unlike Jorbinan's, the figure maneuvered almost in a dance. Zarni's keen ears picked up the figure's voice, clearly identifying them as the one who was conjuring the firepops. Whoever they were, they were saving the companions' bacon.

"Across the bridge, Gregory!" Zarni hollered. The boulder goat muscled the wagon into a turn, and they bounced across the uneven structure.

"Careful!" Tobin yelled. As they rolled onto the other side of the river, he quickly glanced down each side of the wagon. "Phew," he exhaled, wiping his brow. A relieved smile crossed his round face, and he laughed. "Didn't want to break a wheel."

The time between explosions extended as the group rolled into a wooded area and hid behind a large boulder. Once Gregory had them parked, Zarni and Tobin climbed out and used the boulder to get a better view. They crawled to the peak and, laying on their bellies, watched the rest of the light show. They couldn't see the figure from their vantage, but they could see the firepops and the ever-dissipating snappler lights.

Eventually, the firepops ceased altogether, and neither of them could see a single snappler. The night fell quiet once again. Zarni leaned closer to Tobin. "Can you see the mage?" he whispered.

"I can't see anything," the halfling replied, adjusting the butt of his crossbow in his shoulder. "Who do you think that was?"

"No idea," Zarni said. "I didn't think we'd actually run into *anyone* on this journey. Then we ran into Jorbinan."

"That wasn't him, right?" the halfling wondered aloud. "He couldn't possibly have kept up with us on foot."

"No. No ..." Zarni said, shaking his head. "Jorbinan was really easy to see at night with his glowing green staff. And that golden eye. This figure was cloaked. I couldn't make out any of their features."

"They're probably still out there," Tobin said.

The thought did not melt the brick of concern in Zarnikorek's stomach.

"Might be nice to thank them for the help."

Zarnikorek looked the halfling dead in the eye. Tobin stared back. A completely unexpected grin crept across the halfling's face. Zarni couldn't help but match it. "What?" the goblin asked.

"Tobin beware snapplers!" the halfling said, doing his best impression of Jorbinan.

The two of them dissolved into laughter. Zarni couldn't understand why. They must have been so full of nervous energy after their encounter that they were bursting at the seams.

"Zarni beware snapplers!" the goblin said, trying to do his own impression through the uncontrollable chortles.

"Ha!" Tobin cried, his laughs becoming a ridiculous roar.

Soon, neither of them could breathe. They clutched their aching ribs as they gasped for air. The crisp mountain breeze blew over them, and they sucked it in between bouts of reverberating laughter. Tears streamed down their faces and into their ears as they stared up at the stars high above them.

"You were amazing!" Tobin said, when he finally composed himself enough to speak. "You were like, 'I'll get Gregory hooked up. You get the supplies!' You were so decisive."

Zarni chuckled at the compliment. "I don't know. I just wanted to get us out of there."

"I was scared out of my wits," Tobin said with another chuckle.

"Me too."

"Well, you hid it very well. I'd wager even an orc gar wouldn't have been so composed."

"Ha!" Zarni spit a laugh.

He rolled back onto his belly and peered in the direction of the river. The whole thing had been a blur. His heart was still slowing, either from the excitement or the exorbitant laughter. Either way, he imagined there wouldn't be any more sleep this night. He smirked as he remembered how grumpy he'd been about the notion when he'd first awoken.

He watched through the dark, hoping to catch a glimpse of their savior. But with no sign of the mysterious figure, he resolved to at least take a look in the morning before they vacated the area.

Tobin had also turned over to watch again. After a long while, laying there in silence, the halfling nudged the goblin with his elbow. "Hey."

"What?"

"Zarni beware snapplers!" he said again.

But their laughter was cut off when a voice from the dark said, "Where did you hear those words?"

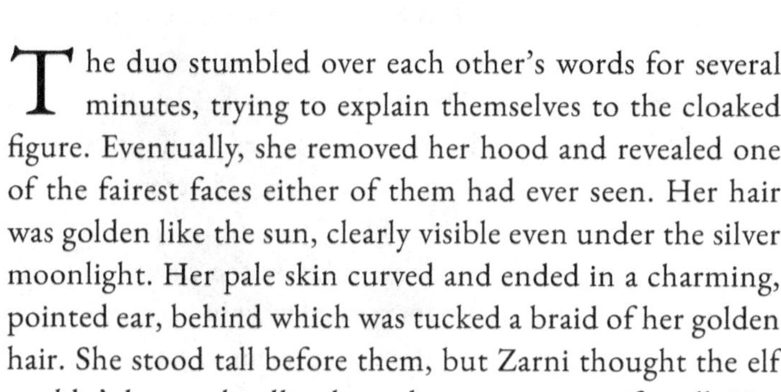

CHAPTER 25
MAVRO'S BOW

The duo stumbled over each other's words for several minutes, trying to explain themselves to the cloaked figure. Eventually, she removed her hood and revealed one of the fairest faces either of them had ever seen. Her hair was golden like the sun, clearly visible even under the silver moonlight. Her pale skin curved and ended in a charming, pointed ear, behind which was tucked a braid of her golden hair. She stood tall before them, but Zarni thought the elf couldn't be much taller than a human woman, if at all. Her amused smile put them at ease.

"How *is* my husband?" she asked.

Zarni and Tobin shared a glance, their jaws unhinged.

"Are you ..." Zarni started.

"Milirore?" Tobin finished.

"I am," the elf woman said with a short giggle. "And who do I have the pleasure of speaking with?"

"Zarni ..."

"Tobin ..."

Each stood dumbfounded, barely able to answer.

She smirked. "My husband clearly warned you about the snapplers. You did not take his warning seriously?"

"Well ..." Zarni hemmed. His green cheeks rosed. He didn't have the heart to tell her he hadn't believed her husband, thinking him somewhat of a loon.

Her smile didn't fade, but somehow, her look turned compassionate. "He is ... eccentric, to be sure."

Tobin laughed. "Maybe one of the most eccentric people I've ever met, my lady."

She nodded to the side. "He was not always that way. Long years have not been kind to him. But inside, he remains the dwarf I married long ago."

Zarni shook his head. He could hardly believe it. When they had talked to Jorbinan, the goblin had gotten the impression his wife was long since passed. But here she stood before them.

"I'm sorry to say ... my lady," Zarni added the last part quickly. He wasn't sure how to address the elf woman, but nothing but the highest honor seemed to fit in his mind.

"Milirore is fine," she said, putting them at ease. "I've been called worse."

Zarni couldn't believe anyone would say anything negative to her. "I just mean to say, I ... I mean, we got the impression that you were ... well ... passed."

Milirore let another giggle escape her lips. "What did my husband say?"

"Well," Tobin jumped in. "He said that you've been gone forever!" He emphasized the word just as the mad sorcerer had.

She snorted. "My dear husband says that even if I'm gone for a day. I've only been gone three days this time. I was just on my way back."

"In the middle of the night?" Zarni asked.

"I try to travel by night. I like to clear the snapplers. In Jorbinan's addled state, he is rather obsessed with the little monsters. I try to do my part to alleviate the stress for him."

"What were those things anyway?" Tobin asked.

"Distant cousins to faeries," she said, the words sour off her tongue. "More depraved though. You two are lucky I came along. They would likely have flayed the flesh from your bones after they got bored of terrifying you."

Zarnikorek and Tobin shared an uncomfortable look. Neither seemed to think the situation very funny anymore.

When they didn't respond, Milirore changed the subject. "So, you said you're establishing a new wagon route?"

"Right!" Zarni said, snapping back to the conversation. Suddenly, he remembered the map. He pulled it from his pocket and held it up to her. "I believe you may recognize our path."

Milirore took the map from the goblin as if he'd handed her a delicate work of art. "Koris ..." is all that she managed to whisper. A silvery tear streaked from her eye, down her cheek, and dripped off her chin. Regret slammed into Zarni. He wished he could have caught the tear before it fell to the ground.

"So, it's true then?" Tobin asked. "You really were there. You really knew Koris?"

"I did," she said, her nostrils twitched as she composed herself. "He was a dear friend. I have not seen this map in hundreds of years," she said, tracing the text with her fingers. "Where did you acquire this?"

"A master mage in Galium gave it to us. Said it would help us on our journey." Zarni paused for a moment and watched her. "Do you know what that text says?"

"I should hope so," she said with a weak smile. "I was the one who inked it."

Tobin gasped as though some unexpected truth had just rocked the world. Zarni smirked.

"It is an ancient elvish script that says, 'Should you lose your way, be sure to set your sights. No path leads straight through the mountains. Follow the curve of Mavro's bow.'"

"Mavro's bow," Zarni repeated. He rolled the words around in his head. They sounded familiar. Where did he know that? He looked up to find the elf mage watching him expectantly. He held her eyes momentarily before glancing away. A billion stars shone through the night. "Mavro!" he said.

Milirore nodded to him.

"What?" Tobin asked.

"The constellation," Zarni said as he hurriedly climbed into the back of the wagon. He retrieved the stello glass and rejoined them. "Mavro is one of the ancient constellations. One of the ones I didn't recognize. When I couldn't sleep, I was familiarizing myself with some of the ancient constellations. See? This one right here!"

He held the stello glass up above himself and Tobin drew closer to gaze at the stars through the magic item. The glowing blue lines marked out the constellation for them to see. And before their eyes, Mavro and his bow were clearly visible.

"That's why the map wasn't clear," Zarni said. "It was a Traitor's Map." Milirore winced and her cheek twitched at the name. "I only mean," Zarni continued quickly, "that it was a map used during the Second Great Black War and needed to be secret. It needed to be coded, so that if it fell into the wrong hands, no one would be able to figure out the allied forces' plans."

"Correct," Milirore offered, seemingly impressed with the goblin. Zarni blushed under her praise.

"But the Trait—" Zarni paused to correct himself. "But the Map of Koris would never have gotten us to the route they used because we didn't know what the text said."

"We could only follow it so far before we needed to follow the stars," Tobin added excitedly.

"Well, not quite," Milirore said. She reached her hand out toward the duo. "May I?"

"Of course," Zarni said, handing the stello glass over.

She held it before them. "Can you still see Mavro?"

"Yes, my lady," Zarni said. He flinched. "I mean, Milirore."

She pressed her lips into another smile as she lifted the Map of Koris to the back side of the stello glass. Now, the constellation of Mavro glowed on the parchment. His bow curled along a path that matched much of the markings Zarni had added. Realization dawned on them.

"We had to use the stello glass and the map together!" Zarni uttered.

"That's right."

"This is incredible," Tobin murmured. "Have you ever seen such magic? I'd wager even Master Argus had no idea about this. You'd think he would have told us if he did. This wouldn't be something he would keep from us. Considering how important this quest is. I suppose—"

"I don't think he realized," Zarni stopped the halfling.

"Well," Milirore said. "I think your quest is more important than even you realize."

KRIK

CHAPTER 26
KRIK

When they rolled into the canyon of Krik, Zarni couldn't believe his eyes. Orc and goblin children ran and played with each other. They jabbed wooden swords and axes at each other, clearly fending off some pretend evil. Adults moved from one merchant stall to another, each stall pouring out of one of the myriad alcoves in the canyon walls. Certain spaces were empty, and as they passed, Zarni noted them as tunnels that led deeper into the stone. Red stone mixed with grey to create what looked like waves that painted the canyon an awe-inspiring color. High above, several wyverns and their riders sat perched on the cliff edges.

"What is this place?" Zarni asked. He'd never seen this place on any map. To his knowledge, there weren't supposed to be any people out here, let alone a whole orc community.

"This is Krik," Milirore said, a hint of amusement lacing her words.

"How ...?" The goblin could hardly string his thoughts together. His mouth gaped as an elderly goblin woman peered around the tapestry she'd been weaving and fixed him with a suspicious glare. He waved to her, and her whole body shivered as if to shake the scandal from her skin. "How long has this place been here?"

"Since Koris founded it," the elf said with a hint of pride.

"Koris founded this place?" Tobin asked. The halfling was getting as excited at every mention of Koris as Zarni was now. "He was quite the orc."

"He was," Milirore said fondly. The elf's eyes shimmered, and Zarni wondered where her mind went with that far off stare.

"How has no one known of this place? How have they been here so long without trade or ... or ..." he just couldn't seem to wrap his head around a whole orc community so isolated from the rest of Drelek that they didn't even know it existed. Sure, there were small towns scattered throughout the mountains. But one to the south of a major city like Ghun-Ra? Especially one that rested between them and their old enemies?

"Krik has been forging their own path for generations," the elf explained patiently. "Just to the west of here is where the farms are located. The same farms Koris planted all those years ago. They're the farms that feed this place."

"But what ... I mean, why?" Zarni wasn't even sure how to ask what he wanted to.

"Koris was an honorable orc. He only wanted to do what was right. But he was playing a dangerous game. If he kept his family in Ruk, he would have been endangering all of them. So, they moved out here from Ghun-Ra. And he wasn't the only one. Several folks from the valley moved with them."

"Valley folk?" Zarni mused. His own people? Or, he supposed, the predecessors to his people. If they'd left hundreds of years earlier, it made sense that others would fill the valley, taking up residence in the free opportunity. In a strange way, he felt connected to these people. Even oddly beholden to them.

They parked the wagon next to a wide gap where the canyon wall recessed. A sign above a door in the stone said 'tavern,' and Zarni shook his head. *They have a tavern and everything.*

A goblin came scurrying out as if he'd been watching them through some unseen peep hole, awaiting his chance to greet them. But Zarnikorek learned quickly it had nothing to do with him or Tobin.

"Greetings, Missus Milirore!" the goblin said with a low bow. "I am delighted to see you. I did not expect you'd return so soon. I have already cleaned your room, and it is ready for you to stay again, if you'd like. I'd be so honored to have you stay at *Krik's Hollow*. As always, my lady."

Zarni smirked. *Seems she has that effect on everyone.*

The goblin clerk spoke with nervous energy and the way his green cheeks rosed made Zarni wonder if his own cheeks had been so obvious when he'd met the lovely elf. The thought made him blush again.

"Hello, Lenk. I am grateful for your warm welcome, as usual. I hope to ask you to extend it to my new friends as well."

"Of course, Missus. Of course. Happy to oblige! Can I help you with your—" Lenk's words halted as he caught sight of Gregory. The boulder goat stood with his chin held high, eyeing the goblin that wasn't Zarni.

Tobin laughed. "I think I'll get Gregory unhooked, but maybe you can help me get him to a good spot? Is this area over here alright? He's a fine beast. Mighty fine. Maybe even the strongest boulder goat in all Finlestia. But he's a might touchy when it comes to new folks. But look at that beard. Have you ever seen the like? He's easily—"

"I'm sorry," Zarni cut the halfling off. "Over there is fine?"

"Oh ... Uh, yes," Lenk responded, now curiously staring at the halfling with the same bewildered look he'd just been giving the boulder goat.

"Are Master Gahljik and Katonka here for breakfast?" Milirore asked.

The sound of her voice seemed to snap Lenk back to the situation at hand. "Aye, Missus. They only just arrived."

"Fantastic," she said, walking over and giving Gregory a loving pet. She stroked the boulder goat's beard as Tobin unhooked the beast. Gregory leaned into her affection, clearly unable to resist the elf's charm either.

Krik's Hollow bustled with the morning crowd. Again, Zarni found himself with open-mouthed wonder. *How big is Krik?* he wondered. Sconces burned with firelight along the rough-hewn stone walls, allowing Tobin to see inside the place without needing a dark sight spell to aid his vision. The halfling ate with fervor, surprising their hosts. Zarni found their bulging eyes rather humorous.

Gahljik and Katonka, as Zarni had come to find out, were not married as he'd initially assumed. Gahljik had been the leader of Krik for years, but Katonka and her people had only arrived several months earlier. The orc woman's eyes looked tired. Her face had a softness to it, as though she had painted a fierceness upon it for years before a long jaunt of worry washed over it.

"When Ruk was lost," Katonka explained, causing a brick to form in Zarnikorek's stomach, "myself and several of my fellow wyvern riders fled to the south. Though we didn't make it very far. My own wyvern, Kahren, had been mortally wounded in the battle. We lost two others while we were on the run. But we knew we needed to get as far away from Ruk as possible."

Katonka paused for a long time, her gaze falling to the wooden table in front of them.

Gahljik placed a comforting hand on her arm. "Krik is a safe haven," he said. "Not many people know of this place."

"We didn't even know about it," Katonka continued. We traveled around the mountains, not staying in any single place for too long, for fear of being discovered."

"Why were you hiding?" Tobin asked, between bites.

"Because we were on the wrong side of a war that we never wanted to fight," Katonka said coldly.

Gahljik patted her arm. "You're safe here. Among friends. Tell them the rest."

Katonka growled, but heaved a heavy sigh. "We had no food. No home. We snuck into towns and raided what we could in the night. We tried not to take more than we needed, but we were desperate."

Zarnikorek shook his head, and his brow crinkled with compassion. He couldn't imagine.

"One night, one of my orcs decided to visit a local tavern. He was distraught. Hadn't seen his family in months. The isolation was getting to him. He snuck into town without my permission, but when he returned to us the next morning, he brought news of a town of rebels. A myth, really. Hearsay at best. But we had no other hope. What choice did we have but to believe it possible?"

"Hope is a powerful thing," Milirore said from behind her steaming mug of tea. "A beautiful thing."

"Aye," Katonka grumbled. "So, we searched. And searched. And searched."

Gahljik chuckled. It was a warm and hearty chuckle. "The canyon is well hidden. Unless you know where to look," he said with a wink toward Zarni.

Katonka snorted and gave him the closest thing to a smile the goblin had seen on the orc woman's face. "Then eventually, we did find Krik. And we weren't the only ones. Apparently, some of the warriors who'd marched south for the Battle of Galium had found their way here as well. All warriors without a home. None of us able to go back to our towns. None of us able to see our families. None of us ..." Her words faded as she tried to check her growing emotions. "But you ..." she said, turning to face the goblin directly.

Zarnikorek's stomach flooded with bile.

Katonka's tired eyes seemed to glass as she stared at the goblin intently.

Zarnikorek hesitated, and silence fell on the table so thick it could have been a traditional troll mushroom cake. Her eyes locked onto his, and every muscle in his body tensed. He wanted to jump up and run out of the tavern. But her stare. Those eyes. Piercing ... Knowing ... "You ... you know who I am, don't you?"

"Yes," she said.

The goblin nearly vomited. Of course she did. If she was a wyvern rider of Ruk, she would certainly have seen the old king. And wherever King Sahr went, Zarnikorek had always been scuttling along behind him. All those months he'd worried what people in Ghun-Ra would think of him, and here in this isolated place, a place he hadn't even known existed, someone had recognized him. Part of the reason he'd been so excited about this quest was the utter impossibility that he'd run into anyone who recognized him. And yet ...

"How is it that *you* got this quest from the new king?" she asked quietly.

Her question struck the goblin as odd. "King Genjak's mage adviser sought me out in Ghun-Ra."

"You mean, you were in Ghun-Ra? Living among the people there?"

"Yes," Zarnikorek said awkwardly.

Katonka leaned back and ran her hands through her thick black hair. "How?"

"How, what?" Zarnikorek asked tentatively.

"You were the king's aide!" Katonka nearly spat the words as she heaved herself forward. Her chair went clattering to the stone floor behind her.

A squeak escaped Zarnikorek, but as his heart nearly hammered out of his chest, he found two hands holding him. Tobin stood on his chair, leaning forward to meet the orc's outburst and shielding the goblin. He held a single hand back to touch the goblin's chest as though to make sure he was still back there and safe. The other hand belonged to Milirore. This one comforting.

Gahljik's hand clamped around Katonka's arm. Tension hung in the air between them.

Zarnikorek let a tear escape his eye. After everything, his past was catching up with him. How could he be so foolish to think this quest would help him overcome his past? How could he be so foolish to think he could build a bridge for the future and leave Drelek better in some way when he'd been a part of something so ...

But those hands. Hands of friends who cared deeply for him. Hands of friends who would protect him in the face of an orc warrior six times the halfling's size. The hand of a friend who would comfort him when he was scared. Bridges were already being built.

Tears streamed down Katonka's face, her tusks quivering.

Zarni slowly stood on his own chair. Rising to meet the orc's gaze. He slowly patted the hands that held him, indicating he was alright. Even on the chair, he looked up to Katonka. "I am so sorry," he said quietly.

Katonka burst into sobs.

"I'm sorry for everything you've endured," Zarni continued. "The truth is, I have lived in Ghun-Ra for a year. Not truly living. Every day I looked over my shoulder. Every day I prayed no one would recognize me as King Sahr's aide. Would they shun me? Would they hate me? Would they exile me?" Zarni's words slowed, as realization continued to unravel the tangled knot of thoughts he'd wrestled with for so long. "But I was fooling myself. Of course, they knew who I was. How could they not? My pa is too social for them to not have known. It wasn't any of them holding me back. It wasn't even my past. I was holding myself back."

Katonka sat back into her chair, Gahljik having retrieved it and guiding her. "But how can we go back? How can we face ..."

Zarni swallowed the lump in his own throat. He understood how hard this was. A kind smile lifted one corner of his lips. "When I got back to Ghun-Ra, my pa raced down the dirt path from his house to greet me. I remember it. I was so tired. I had been gone for so long. When his arms wrapped around me, I melted. We fell to our knees in the dirt. I wept and wept. My pa held me the whole time, even shedding tears of his own. He let me cry until I had no tears left. He just held me. Because he loved me. Because he had missed me. He didn't care what side of the war I had ended up on—of my own volition or under compulsion. The only thing he cared about was having his son back."

Zarni gulped the emotion that gripped his throat. He glanced from side to side, gathering the courage to continue from the nod Milirore gave him. "Surely, there are folk that miss you and your riders. And the warriors who'd marched to Galium."

"Many," Katonka choked out. "Some haven't seen their orclings in a year. But how can they ever forgive us for what we've done?"

Zarni smiled at her as he patted Tobin on the shoulder. "When I started this quest, I couldn't fathom what I was going to learn. Back in Ghun-Ra, I didn't give people the chance to know me. I was too afraid it would end up in disaster. But as I've traveled in the south, among the people that have been enemies of Drelek for as long as history remembers, I've come to learn that people can surprise you. Sure, not everyone will, but more than you think. If only we'd open up just a little and give them a chance. We may find more joy than we ever expected."

Tobin's smile grew into a wide grin. "And who doesn't need a little more joy in their lives?" the halfling asked. And to his credit, he left it at that.

Zarni chuckled. "I'm driving a wagon through the Drelek Mountains with a halfling from Galium, stopped at a tavern in a town that I never knew existed, in the presence of an elf who has been in contact with the people here for centuries. It's hard not to believe that the seemingly impossible could very well turn out to be possible."

Katonka nodded, unable to regain her words. Zarni could see the thoughts running through her mind as she weighed the options.

"Perhaps," Zarni offered. "Perhaps we can all help each other."

Katonka's eyes shot up to his. Gahljik patted the orc woman's arm comfortingly, before turning his attention to Zarni. "What do you have in mind?"

CHAPTER 27
A PLAN

Gahljik called a council meeting that night. Zarni found it interesting to note the different folks who came. He learned that the warriors from the Battle of Galium had been led to Krik by a goblin who stood three full heads taller than he. Also among the leaders of Krik were a merchant master, Katonka, and a farmer's guild representative. Zarni thought it only right that Milirore sat among them in some esteem. She spoke only rarely during the discussions, but when she did, everyone listened intently, and her words held great weight.

Not everyone was enthusiastic about Zarni's proposal to make Krik an official stop along the wagon route between Ghun-Ra and Hill Stop. The farmer's guild representative shifted uneasily, and his apprehension was not idly assuaged. But the benefits of integrating Krik in such a pivotal role for the alliance's first trade route far outweighed the hesitations.

The merchant master eloquently expressed his excitement over the growing trade opportunities. He also mentioned the opportunity for expansion for the town's only tavern, stating clearly a plan that would not only benefit the growth of *Krik's Hollow* but also the opportunity for a new tavern to crop up. Plus, the added work for construction and engineering in the canyon.

Zarni listened to the proceedings with great interest. But it was the goblin leader of the warriors who'd fought at the Battle of Galium who spoke about some of the most fascinating things. Apparently, there were several of his unit who would rather stay in Krik. Even more interesting, Katonka agreed that some of her unit would likely stay as well. Not all of the displaced warriors had homes to go back to. Some of them were quite content to stay in Krik, having built something of a life for themselves there in the canyon city.

In the end, the vote among the council members was unanimous for Krik to become an official way stop for the new wagon route on the singular condition that the warriors who'd found sanctuary there wouldn't be chained up and hauled away. After the council meeting, Milirore caught up with Zarni and Tobin, an odd look on her face. Her normally pale cheeks and nose were rosy, and her eyes looked as glass.

"Are you alright?" Zarni asked the elf.

"I am," she said, her nose twitching slightly, as though she was working hard not to cry. "I was just thinking Koris would be so proud to see what this place has become. He would be so proud to know that it will become a bridge of peace after all these centuries. After everything he sacrificed."

Zarni sniffed, trying to quell his own burbling emotions. Had he not wrestled with the idea of his own legacy? Maybe he was more like Koris than he'd initially thought.

"I'm sorry for my outburst yesterday," Katonka said as Zarni followed her up a winding staircase that carved up the side of the canyon wall. "I didn't mean to scare you or cast blame … I just …"

"It's alright," Zarni said.

She glanced down at him. He gave her a smile and a nod of assurance.

"Well, I'm sorry nonetheless," she said, trudging along.

"Have you ever seen the like?" Tobin asked, puffing extra hard on his pipe as they climbed the stairs into a long hallway that led to several openings. Inside each alcove was a nest, a single scaly egg resting in each. The eggs were easily three times the size of the one from which Kliff had hatched.

"No … I haven't …" Zarni whispered. He remembered visiting the hatching ground for the wyvern riders of Ruk. It had been a rocky area on the top of a sloping mountain, the nests scattered without any sort of uniformity. These nests had clearly been set up in alcoves specifically chiseled out of the side of the canyon wall by the wyvern riders.

"Before we arrived, Krik didn't have any wyvern riders," Katonka explained. "In fact, they actively avoided wyverns. There's a wyvern cauldron that inhabits a nearby canyon called Wyvern Alley. Until we arrived, they were known to steal sheep from the farmers on occasion. Since, the farmer's guild has been rather fond of our wyverns. I think it's a territorial thing. Now that ours is here, the other cauldron doesn't come around."

Katonka led them down the stone hallway to the very last alcove. She turned in and knelt next to a large wyvern egg with reverence. Zarni watched her curiously as she placed a hand on it, gently caressing the egg.

"This one was supposed to be my new wyvern," she said solemnly. A long silence lingered. Zarni could sense her worry from where he stood. She turned to look him up and down. "You really think this will work?"

"I do," Zarni said.

"How can you be so confident?" she asked, shifting her small tusks from side to side uncomfortably. She clearly didn't like showing this amount of emotion. But something about her vulnerability warmed his heart.

Zarni huffed a small chuckle. *Confidence.* That was something he hadn't experienced a lot. "I have to believe it will work. This is bigger than all of us. This whole thing is about bridging the gaps between our people and the rest of Tarrine. If we can't extend grace to our own, how will we make good allies with the people we've been enemies with for generations? There has to be grace on all sides."

Katonka nodded. "But did you raise an axe to your own people?"

A pang of regret rippled in Zarnikorek's stomach. "Maybe if I had, I could have prevented some things."

"King Sahr?" Katonka guessed correctly.

"Yeah."

"You weren't the only one who could have done something. There had been several hushed discussions about the mad king amidst the wyvern riders of Ruk. We might have been more capable of doing something, but we were all too afraid of rocking the boat." She shook her head in disgust at the memory.

"How easily you extend grace to me, but withhold it from yourself," Zarni said with a wry smirk.

Katonka almost gave him a smile.

"Still, I was afraid," Zarni continued. "I spent far too much of my life being afraid. I'm choosing to walk each day with a different mindset. A different attitude. Someone I know inspired me to bring joy into every situation."

The halfling, leaning on one of the nearby walls, enjoying his pipe and listening quietly to the conversation, bobbed in amusement.

"Perhaps," the she-orc said slowly, "I could consider that when my people can go home to their families without fear."

Zarni nodded thoughtfully. "You served Drelek with honor for years. Just because the situation changed and our enemies changed, doesn't negate the character with which you served. King Genjak has to see that. I don't know much about the new king. I haven't met him yet. But the impression I've gotten from one of his closest advisers suggests that he is wise beyond his years and approaches situations with deliberate consideration. I don't think we could say anything less of the first king in Drelek history to forge an alliance with the folk of the south."

Katonka shrugged to the side as she lifted the egg and stood. "I suppose you're right. You know, you're awfully wise for such a little goblin."

And that time Zarni was sure she smirked at him.

"I think Tobin is rubbing off on me."

CHAPTER 28
PREY

Leaving Krik left a bittersweet taste in Zarni's mouth. The people of the canyon town had been more than hospitable, and he particularly disliked leaving Milirore, not knowing when he'd see the she-elf again. Not only had he quickly grown fond of her presence, a quality he guessed fell upon most who met her, but he also worried about running into more snapplers. Though, the elf mage had assured him, most of the snapplers dwelt in the mountains and valleys south of Krik. Plus, they weren't as common as he had experienced. Usually.

As the wagon rolled along through the beautiful summer morning, Zarni couldn't help but reflect on all the people he'd met on the journey so far. Deklahn and Argus, two mages from different peoples, but both so encouraging, pushing him to find strength within himself. He'd met the king of Galium and the foredwarf of the famed garvawk warriors. Dwarves! And speaking of dwarves, he'd befriended some who taught him how to beat members of the fabled Griffin Guard in a game of Castle Brick. And Jorbinan ... Come to think of it, he'd met a lot of dwarves. It was funny to think that dwarves had been the most hated of their enemies for so long, and on a single trip Zarni had befriended so many. Sure, most of them could probably only be considered acquaintances at this point, but he looked forward to visiting all of them again and further growing in fellowship.

Zarni absently stroked Gibs' back, the furry horned marten happily sitting next to him on the driver's bench. Kliff gripped the railing of the wagon with his feet, letting the breeze billow his wings. The little wyvern chirped cheerfully. Tobin talked Katonka's ears off in the back of the wagon. He hadn't even hesitated when Zarni asked to drive.

"Ahhh," Katonka said, letting out a long, contented sigh as she stood in the back of the wagon and stretched her back. "That is the smallest wyvern I've ever seen," she said for the third time that day. Apparently, Kliff was quite the anomaly.

"He may be small, but he is mighty. Just like most of us," Tobin replied with a laugh. "You and Gregory are the biggest of us, but we've all got our strengths."

Katonka laughed. "I just mean, normally, wyverns don't have runts. The runt eggs are usually destroyed in the nest and never hatched. His egg must have been truly tiny."

"Very," Zarni agreed. "In truth, when Jorbinan gave it to us, I wasn't sure it was even a viable egg. But I think that mad sorcerer is keener than folks give him credit for."

"No doubt," Tobin agreed, shifting his pipe to one side of his mouth. "I'd wager he's smarter than most. You just have to sift through the sand to find the gems."

"Definitely," the goblin replied. "I wonder what he was like before. It's quite beautiful that he has someone like Milirore."

"I have this feeling she'd say it's quite beautiful that she has someone like him," Tobin said. "Though I don't doubt there are those of us who are luckier than others to have our spouses. Maker knows I married up. I don't deserve Lenor."

"Having met her, I'd agree," Zarni said before he could pull the humorous jab back.

"Whoa!" Tobin said through a roaring laugh. "Flying arrows!"

Zarni smirked over his shoulder. He was teasing, of course, but he couldn't remember the last time—if ever—he had a friend he could rib like that. "No, I'd bet Lenor would say she's the luckier. Maybe that's how it's supposed to be. Each thinking they're the luckier of the two. Thinking of the other first."

"I'd say that's about right," Tobin said, stroking his chin.

"And having met your family, I can say from the outside that you *all* bring love and joy to the table."

"Too true. Too true," the halfling agreed. "I remember some friends asking how we felt about having another baby when Lenor was pregnant with baby Bandix. 'Tobin's on the road so much. It must be hard with him gone all the time. It can't be easy to have one little gem, let alone two.' And Lenor, full of grace as she is, only told them that another one only brought more love into our world."

"She sounds lovely," Katonka said.

"Oh, she is! Maybe the loveliest dwarven woman in all Tarrine. Maybe all Finlestia, I'd wager. Not that you're not lovely, mind you. But you're not a dwarf." Tobin chuckled. "I mean, you're a mighty fine orc warrior. I imagine you're one of the finest. But of course, I married Lenor because she was just the loveliest. Well, she *is* the loveliest. She does her hair in this net braid with beads. Prettiest thing you ever did see. I bet she'd show you. I'd even—"

"And what about you, Zarni?" Katonka asked the goblin. Zarni snorted a laugh. Only a few hours into the drive and she'd already figured out that she needed to cut the halfling off every once in a while.

"Ah, well ... Someday. If I have a family half as nice as Tobin's, I'll be a happy goblin."

"Don't be coy, now!" Tobin said as he rummaged inside one of the barrels, looking for a pouch of jerky. "Zarni's got a girl he's keen on back in Ghun-Ra."

"Oh, is that so?" Katonka said. Her tone told Zarni she could tell the topic made him uncomfortable. So, of course, she pressed. "What's her name?"

Zarni shook his head, unable to mask his smile. His cheeks rosed, and he bit at his lip. "Her name is Jileva. She's a bard at *The Wyvern's Wish*."

"Ooooh, a bard," Katonka cooed.

"Yes," Zarni said.

"She even dedicated a song to him," Tobin said through a bite of jerky.

"Well, I mean ... she ... well ..." Zarni struggled to put two words together.

"Wow. How romantic," the big orc heaped on.

"Well, I don't think it was romantic ..." Zarni hemmed. "I've barely spoken to her."

"Look how frazzled he is," Katonka said to the halfling.

"Ha!" Tobin barked a laugh, rather enjoying the orc's company. Zarni regretted teasing the halfling. *Well, I suppose if you dish it out, you have to be able to take it.* Tobin continued, "I've been telling him he should ask her to go on a date with him. I think it should be breakfast."

"Why breakfast?" Katonka asked incredulously.

"It's perfect!" the halfling proclaimed as if it was the most obvious thing in the world. "First of all, hash browns and eggs and sausage. Oh, and bacon. Oh, or even flapjacks!"

"What? How does that make it perfect for a date with Jileva?" Katonka asked, genuinely confused. But she still managed to say Jileva's name with a swoony drawl.

"Well, besides breakfast food being the best, showing that Zarni is a goblin of true class and taste? Because again, breakfast foods are the best. It also works perfectly because Jileva is a bard."

When the halfling shoved a big bite of jerky in his mouth and stopped at that, Zarni turned on the driver's bench. He shared a confused glance with Katonka, who shrugged. And maybe for the first time in the halfling's life, someone asked him to elaborate. "What are you talking about?" Zarni asked.

"It's obvious!" Tobin said, gulping down his bite. "She's a bard. Bards play at the tavern at night. I don't know if she plays every night, but most of her nights are probably booked. So, breakfast is the perfect time for a date. Plus, breakfast foods are the best. I can't stress that point enough. I'd wager it's the most important meal of the day," he said with a slap on his belly.

"That ... actually makes a lot of sense," Katonka said slowly.

"Ha!" Zarni laughed. "I told you he was wiser than he looks."

Tobin's teeth glimmered in a wide smile, then his brow creased. "Wait."

They all laughed.

"But the problem is," Zarni continued, "she probably doesn't even like me like that. I mean, we only just met. And of course, she might already be courting with someone else."

"Mate, she dedicated a song to you and called you her hero," Tobin said matter-of-factly.

"She called you her hero?" Katonka said with whimsy.

"I delivered a package for her. It was new strings for her lute."

"What a hero," Katonka crooned.

"Alright, alright," Zarni said, waving the relentless pair off. Though admittedly, he rather enjoyed the banter.

"It does sound like she would say, 'yes,' if you asked her," the orc said. "You should go for it. If she's anything like me, she'd appreciate the effort."

"Yeah? What about you?" Zarni said quickly, seeing his out.

"Ah ... well ..." Katonka hemmed. Zarni had to look over his shoulder again, trying to get a read on her. The orc warrior's face was a mix of emotions.

"Katonka?" Tobin asked softly.

"Gronk," she said quietly.

"Who's Gronk?" the halfling pressed, though Zarni was impressed with Tobin's gentleness.

"Orc blacksmith back in Ruk. We were supposed to be married. But then ... everything happened."

A long silence fell between them. Gregory's rhythmic hoof beats, Kliff's cheerful chirping, and the creaking of the wagon wood as the wheels lumbered over bumps were the only noises.

"Is he still there?" Tobin asked.

"I'm sure he is."

"You don't know?" Zarni asked.

"His smithy was in one of the deeper caverns. Much of the battle took place on the king's landing. He would likely have been safe. There were a few cave-ins, but most of those were near the surface."

A sadness gripped Zarni's heart. He hoped Gronk was alright. It sounded as though he probably was, but Katonka had lived all this time not knowing. He couldn't imagine that. The thought motivated him to accomplish their mission even more. That's what this quest was about, bringing people together. And if he could be a part of helping Katonka come back together with Gronk ...

"It doesn't matter, though. He probably thinks I died in the battle. He was a rather eligible orc bachelor. I'm sure someone else has ..." her words choked off.

"Katonka ..." Tobin said, patting her arm.

The big orc melted and enveloped the little halfling in a hug. Her body heaved over him, sobbing. It was short-lived though, for her orc warrior side came back with a vengeance and she composed herself with a sharp sniff.

"I don't know what happened with Gronk," Zarni said. "But I promise you this; I'll do everything I can to help you find out."

They drove on until evening drew near. Zarni could feel their proximity to home. From his estimations with the map and the stello glass, he guessed they'd arrive at Ghun-Ra the next day. He couldn't say when, but he could just feel it.

The thought of being reunited with his pa welled a deep joy in him that nearly brought him to tears. He hadn't realized how much he missed home. He wondered where Yan and Grahk might be. He thought about the duo on the *Helgar*, navigating the waterways of the Fork. Zarni looked forward to seeing the pair again. He felt like he owed them a round. Not that they would require it, but he wanted to explain himself. And what a story he had to share now.

Tobin drove along, humming a quiet tune to himself. Zarni opened his eyes and noticed Katonka and Gibs near the back of the wagon. The orc and the horned marten both stared out over the land in silence.

"You two alright?" Zarni asked, thinking the orc might be getting sick and Gibs, being as good as he was, might be trying to comfort her. The notion vanished quickly though as Zarni remembered Katonka had trained on the back of wyverns and had flown through the sky. A wagon ride was tame by comparison. He maneuvered his way to the back of the wagon to join them. "What are you two—"

"Shhhh," Katonka shushed him.

Zarni inspected them. They both sat rigid, scanning their surroundings. The goblin turned his gaze outward, his eyes seeing nothing but jagged, rocky mountains, and smaller hills covered in trees. In one direction, there was a rather lovely mountain covered in colorful summer wildflowers. The blue sky was dashed with the regular white clouds that formed over the region every afternoon. The colors hadn't started changing yet, but the sun would pass over the western slopes soon enough.

After a long silence, he whispered, "What is it?"

"I saw this one watching our back, and I wondered what he was looking at." She pointed at Gibs, but her eyes remained vigilant.

"Did you see something?"

"Not yet ..." she said. And the way she let her words linger ominously left a lump in Zarnikorek's throat.

"Should we stop for the day? Maybe find shelter for the night?"

"I'm not sure ..." she said slowly. "But I can't help feeling like prey."

Just then, a roar ripped through the sky like thunder.

CHAPTER 29
AN ANGRY WYVERN

"Drive! Drive! Drive!" Katonka hollered.

Tobin stood in the driver's box, gripping the reins and biting hard on his pipe. Gregory's hooves pounded as he rushed onward. The wagon jarred to the side as they hit a bump, sending Zarni tumbling into the side of a barrel.

"Sorry!" Tobin yelled back over his shoulder. "Sorry!"

"Just drive!" Katonka emphasized.

Zarnikorek pulled himself upright, catching another glimpse of the fully grown bull wyvern that soared above them. He'd seen big wyverns, but those were tamed and trained by riders. This one was wild. Zarnikorek knew it wasn't as big as a dragon, but that knowledge did little to assuage his terror.

"Hold on!" Tobin hollered.

Zarnikorek barely had time to turn toward the front when the wagon banked hard to the left.

"Rrraagghhh!" Tobin roared as he pulled on the reins to avoid a boulder. As sturdy as Gregory was, he scampered in a mad dash to flee.

Crack!

Whump!

One of the wheels splintered into a million pieces. Shattered wood flitted away as if it had been thrown in an explosion. The front corner of the wagon dropped into the hard dirt, sending dust into the air, and halting the wagon almost instantly. The force launched Zarnikorek forward, slamming him into the arms of Katonka, who'd wedged herself at the front railing. They laid in place for a long moment, coughing the dust from their lungs.

"Argghh," the orc woman groaned. "Is everyone alright?"

Zarnikorek pried himself upward. Everything hurt. And he'd had something soft to land on. Or at least, the she orc had been softer than the wagon wood. He clambered to the front railing. "Tobin are you—Maker, no ..."

The halfling's limp form lay several yards ahead of them on a flowery berm. Gregory stamped in his distress. The immediate stop had likely jarred him as well.

"Tobin!" Zarnikorek cried.

The goblin climbed over the railing and leapt from the driver's box. He landed hard on the ground, sending shooting pains through his bones. He forced himself upright and sprinted toward the halfling.

"Zarni ..." Katonka called to him.

Roooaaarrr!

The bull wyvern let out a cry and swooped so low overhead that the force of its wings lifted Zarnikorek from his feet and sent him toppling. The goblin spit the dirt from his mouth, pushed himself up, and dashed the rest of the way. He slid to his knees at the halfling's side and turned him over. "Tobin!"

White fur, grass, and flowers covered the halfling. Grass stained his tunic, and dirt covered his face.

"No ... No. No, no, no," Zarnikorek moaned, inspecting the halfling through his forming tears. "Tobin, say something. Come on, say something!"

"Mumph," the halfling spit out a mouthful of white hair and flowers. He coughed and sucked in heaving breaths.

"Tobin, it's alright. I'm right here."

"Ugh," he blubbered with agony. But shortly, a painful smirk crossed his face. "Not everyday folks ask me to say something."

"What?" Zarni asked, not understanding.

"Tobin, say something," he croaked his best Zarni impression.

The goblin let the tears fall from his face as he laughed.

"Usually the opposite," the halfling mused.

"Maker. I thought you were dead."

"Hit Gregory as I launched from the wagon. Might have broken some things. But it probably saved my life. That beautiful beast."

Zarni shook his head, still reeling over the whole thing. All he could think was how glad he was the halfling would live.

"Oh, no ..." Tobin said with a cough. He gripped at something on his backside, and dread crawled up Zarnikorek's throat. *Maker, no ...* Had he missed something, some injury he didn't see when he turned the halfling over? *Maker please, don't let him die. He's my best friend.*

"Just leave me," Tobin said as he strained. "I'm not going to make it."

"What? No," Zarnikorek said through more tears. "Don't say that. You're going to be just fine. By my estimations, we could make Ghun-Ra tomorrow."

The wyvern bellowed another sky shattering roar.

"Zarni! It's coming back!" Katonka called from near the wagon.

"I'll never make it," Tobin bemoaned. "I won't survive a whole day without ..." the halfling paused as he heaved with great effort and pulled his arm from behind his back. In his hand dangled his pipe, broken in half, barely held together by splinters. The halfling's eyes welled with despair.

"You idiot," Zarni said, punching the halfling in the arm.

"Ow, ow," Tobin said with a pained chuckle. "That actually does hurt."

"I thought you were going to die! You can't do that!"

"It's a terrible loss," the halfling whined.

Rrroooaaarrr!

The bull wyvern tore through the sky, just low enough to let them feel his wingwash again.

"Come on!" Zarni yelled and heaved the halfling to his feet. Tobin favored the arm Zarni had punched and limped along on one of his legs. As much as the goblin thought the halfling deserved the pain in his arm, he helped Tobin hobble over to the wagon. "What did we do to make this wyvern so mad?" he asked as they rejoined Katonka.

"Ahhhh," Tobin groaned as he inspected the shattered wheel. "We're not going anywhere fast."

"Did we encroach on his territory?" Zarni wondered aloud.

"No," Katonka said with a grimace. "He's been trailing us since we left Krik. We just didn't know it."

"Since Krik?"

Katonka didn't respond as she watched the bull wyvern. The beast angled its wings and turned into another dive.

"Well, you're the wyvern expert here," Zarni continued. "What does it want?"

"It wants the egg," she growled.

"The egg?" Zarni and Tobin asked at the same time.

Katonka growled again and gripped the egg in a defiant hug. "Yes. The egg. Our wyverns only laid three of the eggs in Krik. We collected the rest from nests near Wyvern Alley."

"You mean that's his egg?" Zarni spluttered.

"His mate's. But yes."

"Are you serious?"

"It's an old method to grow a dwindled cauldron that doesn't have enough wyverns to produce enough viable eggs. We didn't take too many. Only one per nest. This wyvern might have been the bull for several of the nests."

The ground rumbled as the wyvern crashed to the ground nearby. Bits of earth splattered away from the impact. It roared a hideous cry and bared its fangs.

"Give it back to him!" Zarni said quickly.

"We can't! We need this egg to give to King Genjak. He'll never pardon us without it!"

"What are you talking about?" Zarni yelled back. "That won't matter if this wyvern kills us here and now!" Katonka had to see the reason in that, but the she orc hugged the egg tight. Zarni stepped closer to her. "Katonka, please."

He placed a hand on the egg. She glared at him, but her defiance soon turned to defeat. Slowly, she let the large egg slide out of her hands and into Zarni's. The goblin gulped. What was he doing? He wanted to throw the egg back at the orc warrior. She was way bigger than he was. She was brave and strong. She was the expert. She should face the wyvern. But the tears that fell from her chin told him exactly why she couldn't.

Zarni cleared his throat, to no avail, and spun on his heel. He walked out toward the wyvern, shaking in his boots.

"Zarni ..." Tobin called to him.

The goblin glanced back. His friends all watched, terror in their eyes.

He couldn't do this ... He shook the thought away. He had to do this. If he didn't ...

Zarni turned and marched forward. The monster growled as it watched him approach. It turned its magnificent head, which

Zarni noted was big enough to chomp him in one bite. But the wyvern merely hissed and eyed the goblin as he drew near. His steps slowed, and he knelt to the ground to lay the egg out as an offering.

To his surprise, Gibs stood on all fours next to him, bearing his tiny fangs. "Gibs," Zarni whispered. "Back away slowly."

Gibs seemed to get the message and backed away, matching Zarni's pace, and keeping himself between the wyvern and the goblin. If he wasn't completely overcome by terror, Zarni's heart would have swelled at the horned marten's display.

It was then that a red and purple blur flew past his shoulder and landed on the egg. "Kliff, no!" Zarni breathed out.

The bull wyvern reared up as Kliff clicked and lifted his wings high. The tiny wyvern cooed and screeched. The bull's long neck bobbed, and guttural clicks emanated from his throat. Zarni watched in horror. And though he couldn't read the faces of wyverns, he thought the bull looked just as confused as he did.

Kliff gripped the egg under his feet and draped his wings over it as though he were covering and protecting it. The bull wyvern blinked its reptilian eyes and swayed its head back and forth. It stamped its feet and dug at the dirt with its wing claws.

Like a viper, it darted its head forward with a growl that made Zarni wonder if he'd wet his breeches. In a flash, Gibs stood next to the egg, baring his teeth at the enormous creature. Zarni wondered how he'd gotten there. But Kliff and Gibs stood their ground, unflinching.

A long moment passed where no one moved a muscle.

The bull huffed out a grunt and reared itself up, flapping its wings with such force, Zarni dropped to one knee. The wyvern bellowed one final roar as it took to the sky and flew away.

No one moved for another minute.

When Zarni finally got up the courage to speak again, he petted the little wyvern and said the only thing he could think, "You're as mad as Jorbinan."

Kliff cooed and clicked happily, relishing in the pets.

CHAPTER 30
HOME

It took some time and clever ingenuity for the crew to get the spare wheel onto the wagon. With Tobin's injured arm and leg, he ended up doing a lot more instructing than physically helping. He cleverly guided them through the process of rigging up a pulley system around the boulder and attaching it to Gregory. The boulder goat heaved the wagon into a position where they could get the spare wheel on. By the time they'd finished with repairs, Zarni knew without a doubt why Tobin was considered one of the best wagoners in Galium.

Funny enough, Zarni was starting to feel like he was getting the hang of it himself. Tobin deferred driving duties to the goblin again, the halfling's bum arm making it difficult for him to manage the reins. Gregory listened to Zarni without reservation—something for which the goblin was immensely grateful. And aside from the repairs taking a significant amount of the morning, they made great time on their drive, and Zarni soon recognized a hill in the distance. He and his pa had summited the hill many times. One of their favorite fishing spots was in the creek that bent around the other side.

"That's it," he whispered as the mountain breeze streaked a tear sideways on his face.

"What is it?" Katonka asked, leaning over the front railing.

"That hill right there," Zarni pointed with one hand as he held the reins with his other. "That hill is called Pickers Peak. It grows all the best mountain berries around. I bet you the griffinberry bushes are loaded right now. And the huckleberries will be delicious too. Maybe even raspberries, if we're lucky."

"Almost home, then," Katonka said quietly.

"Yeah," Zarni replied, reaching up to the railing and patting the she-orc's hand. "Almost there. Don't worry."

Her small tusks shifted from side to side nervously, but she nodded anyway.

A bump jostled the wagon, waking Tobin with a startled snort. "What? What'd I miss?"

The halfling jumped up far too quickly, forgetting in that moment that his leg was injured. Gibs and Kliff, who had been cozily cuddled up next to the halfling chittered grumpily as Tobin fell over. Katonka lifted the halfling with one hand, hoisting him upright and holding him near the front railing so he could grab it.

"Thanks," Tobin said sheepishly. "Forgot I'm not quite at my best. Also," he continued with a groan, "somehow, a lot more things hurt today than they did yesterday. I've got this great wrench in my back. A big old bruise in the shape of my pipe."

Katonka laughed and shook her head. "You're lucky your whole body isn't just one big bruise."

"He's lucky he's not dead!" Zarni added. "The way he got thrown from the wagon. And then, nearly giving me a heart attack. I almost killed him myself."

Zarni shot the halfling a bemused smirk.

Tobin sniffed an overly dramatic sniff, and his face wrinkled in utter pain. "It was a good pipe. Best one I ever had. You know Lenor got that one for me when we had Button? Nicest gift she's ever given me. I suppose pipes aren't meant to last forever. Though I'd wager that one was one of the best."

Zarni shook his head, trying not to laugh, but the huffing he heard from Tobin behind him told him the halfling was teasing.

Zarni steered Gregory around Pickers Peak on the west side, where the sun was still bathing the hill in its warmth. The goblin parked the wagon and hopped out. "Gibs," he said. "Come on over here. I think you'll like this."

Katonka climbed out of the back of the wagon to join them, happy to stretch her legs.

Tobin worked his way over to one of the railings so he could watch. Kliff climbed onto the railing and nudged the halfling. Before long, Tobin was chatting away with the wyvern, who happily listened, accepting the halfling's pets like a house cat.

Zarni was happy to find that one of the raspberry bushes hadn't been picked clean, yet. He plucked a couple of ripe berries from the bush and plopped them into his mouth. The warm berries burst, filling his mouth with a sweet tang.

"Mmmm!" Katonka moaned in delight next to him.

"Right?" was the only word Zarni could get out of his mouth as he shoveled more berries in.

They spent a long while picking the delectable treats and loading a couple of baskets Tobin had emptied along the journey. They wandered leisurely from bush to bush, enjoying the afternoon sun and the quiet of the day. Not being chased by a wild wyvern helped. But being so close to home, a weight had lifted.

After a long time, they loaded back into the wagon and continued on their way.

"Pa will be happy to make us some berry juice with all these raspberries. We don't always get to Pickers Peak in time to get raspberries," Zarni said.

"Raspberries in juice?" Katonka asked incredulously.

"You've never had raspberries in juice?" Tobin asked, aghast. "My lady, you are missing out on one of the finer things in life."

Zarni chuckled. "I don't know if I'd consider it one of the finer things, but I like it."

"Anything that adds flavor and zest to your life is a fine thing, indeed!" Tobin pressed. "I have a friend in the Garome District back in Galium who owns an herbs and tea shop. She's used raspberry in some of her blends. You should see the tea blends she comes up with. I'd wager there's no larger selection in all of Tarrine. She *does* live in the garden there. Suppose she's got the space to grow whatever she wants. And she has this house made of glass behind her home. It's almost all windows. Strangest thing. But it helps her keep her plants growing in the winter. She calls it a greenhouse. Which didn't make much sense to me at first, since it's made of glass and you can see through it. But she says it's because it keeps her plants green in the winter. Ha! When she told me that ...

Tobin's words faded from Zarni's hearing. A toothy grin spread from ear to ear as he guided Gregory along the path toward home.

"Zarni!"

The goblin heard his pa before he saw him.

"Zarnikorek? My boy?" Grinble called out again.

Katonka and Tobin both appeared over the railing behind the goblin.

"Pa!" was all Zarni could say as tears welled in his eyes.

"Zarni!"

Grinble had been walking down the path, his arms loaded with his fishing rod and a basket dangling on the top of his cane. At the sight of his son's wagon, the goblin engineer lost all decorum and chucked the gear to the ground. He churned his feet and hobbled as fast as they could carry him, his cane thudding in the dirt, barely helping.

Zarni pulled Gregory to a stop and tumbled out of the driver's box in his own excitement. He popped up from the ground quickly and ran.

The two goblins collided into the kind of embrace that only a father and son share. "Pa! I made it," Zarni cried, sobbing into his pa's shoulder.

"I had no doubt, my son. I had no doubt," Grinble whispered to his boy. For no matter how old he got, Zarni would always be his boy.

They hugged each other for a long time, Zarni thinking how strangely similar this embrace was to the one his father had given him when he'd first gotten back to Ghun-Ra after King Sahr had been killed. And yet, in that previous hug, he'd been broken. He'd been beaten down. In this hug, he was certainly tired. He was certainly overjoyed to see his pa. But this time, he was returning triumphant.

After a long while, Zarni pulled away and said, "Come on. Let me introduce you to everyone. And maybe I can give you a ride back to the house."

Grinble eyed his son, and his head bobbed in proud approval.

"Lotmeag has been raving about omelets ever since he got back from his joint mission across the sea," Tobin said through a mouthful of omelet. "Spent a lot of time with orcs on that one, he did. Came home raving about the cook on the ship that took them across the Gant Sea to Kelvur. Blueberry scones and omelets. I didn't think he ever ate anything green, but apparently spinach in omelets changed his world! I never quite understood the attraction to it until now. You've got quite the skill with the skillet, Mister Grinble. Ha! Skill with the skillet."

"Why, thank you," Grinble said as he finished his own omelet.

The travelers had stayed up late into the night regaling the old goblin engineer with tales of their adventure. Grinble had gotten up at his usual time, but decided to let the weary crew sleep in a while. As they'd begun to stir, he cooked them up quite the breakfast. Zarni was so happy to see his pa. A sense of gratitude swelled in his heart. But even more, he saw a new look in his pa's eyes.

Zarni tried to tell the story of their travels, but it came out as facts, lacking the flare that Tobin happily added into it. And Zarni had caught his pa glancing at him wide-eyed many times as Tobin described one event or another. Zarni thought Tobin's beaming words of his courage and deliberateness in the face of danger were a little bit overzealous, but the halfling praised him with the utmost sincerity. When Grinble looked to his son for confirmation that what he was hearing was true, all Zarni could do was shrug and smile. Nothing the halfling said was inaccurate to the actual events.

Katonka had been particularly quiet, only piping up to explain their encounter with the bull wyvern. The only reason she could come up with for the wild wyvern leaving as it did was that somehow Kliff had convinced the other wyvern that the egg was under his protection now. Other than that, the orc warrior remained stoic. Zarni was sure she was waging an internal battle. He knew how nervous she was. He knew how much this all meant to her.

"Oh, I meant to tell you last night, but I was so enthralled with your tales, I forgot," Grinble said suddenly. "King Genjak is here in Ghun-Ra!"

"The king is here?" Katonka gasped.

"Aye. Been here a couple of days. I'm not sure how long he was planning on staying, but he's been here talking to the leaders of the city. Guess he's been on a tour of all Drelek. Visiting every town and city to firm up the new direction he's leading us in. Deklahn is here too. He stopped by and mentioned they planned the stop specifically, hoping you would arrive while the king was here. That way, he didn't have to make a separate trip. That's why I've been going fishing every afternoon near Pickers Peak. I hoped I'd be out there waiting for you as you rolled into town."

Zarni patted his father on the shoulder. "Beat you to it yesterday," he said with a wink.

"Ah, well, you have wheels, and I have ... well." He lifted his cane with a chuckle. "Not as fast as I used to be."

"That's fair. I suppose I should probably report to Deklahn then, now that our quest is complete. Do you know where he's staying?"

"He said they were staying in the mountain. You'll have to meet him there. But," his pa said with a pop of his brow and a smirk. He gathered up a couple of plates, which Tobin quickly took from the old goblin. "Well, thank you."

"My pleasure, sir. My pleasure. I can't wait to tell Lotmeag that I finally get why he likes these orcish omelets so much," the halfling said with a wink. "Yours were way better than the ones he's tried to recreate."

"Ah, well, thank you," Grinble said with a chuckle. "But what I was about to say is, I want to show you what we've been working on while you were gone."

"Oh?" Zarni said.

A twinkle glinted in the old goblin's eye. "I think you're going to like it."

Massive wooden beams, made from the biggest mountain pines, crossed overhead as Grinble gave the crew the tour of Ghun-Ra's new wagon depot. The previous one had been a quarter of the size, as wagoners in Ghun-Ra were far less frequent than boaters. The roads between orc cities were difficult and often treacherous in the rugged Drelek Mountains.

Goblin engineers worked away, measuring and cutting and hammering and chiseling. Some walked atop the beams high above their heads. Some worked together to carry large planks of wood, while a couple of trolls handled heavy beams by themselves.

"They started building it even before we completed our quest?" Zarni asked. He clamped his jaw shut, realizing he'd been staring in awe again.

"Aye," Grinble affirmed. "A raven arrived for me. A message from Deklahn sent from Galium. In it, the blueprints for a wagon depot. Same exact plans they used to build the one in Galium."

"I thought this looked familiar!" Tobin exclaimed. "It may be the finest wagon depot in all Tarrine. Although, now that you're building the same one here, I suppose this one will be the finest. Being newer and cleaner and all."

"I guess so," Grinble chuckled. "As soon as I received the letter, I went into the mountain for an audience with the gar to get approval and start work on it right away."

"And he approved it? Even though we hadn't made the journey yet?" Zarni could hardly believe it.

"Aye," Grinble said. "The gar knew how important this is for our people. Plus, when he asked if I held equal confidence to that which Deklahn stated in his letter about you completing the task, I said I had no doubt."

Zarni blinked, his eyes getting oddly watery. His nose prickled, and he twitched it to fight back whatever mixture of emotions was trying to work its way to the surface. He noted how everyone always seemed to have more confidence in him than he did. *No more*, he thought, as his chin quivered, pressing a smile onto his face.

"Thanks, Pa."

Grinble didn't reply. He merely gave his son a proud nod.

"So, this is where the stables are going to be," Tobin said excitedly. "And that over there is where the dais will be for the wagon master to call out all the transports. And that back there is where the storage area is going to be. And ..."

CHAPTER 32
AUDIENCE WITH THE KING

Zarni, Tobin, and Katonka stood in the gar's hall, deep within the mountain of Ghun-Ra. All was quiet, save for Katonka's nervous shifting from one leg to the other. The stone hall where the gar of Ghun-Ra held hearings was eerily quiet when it was empty. Zarni had only ever been in the hall when it was filled with people. Standing in the middle of the empty stone hall, stalactites hanging down from the ceiling, and the echoes of the she-orc's shifting feet forced his heart to speed up. He knew he wasn't the only one feeling it. Even Tobin said nothing.

Zarni sucked in a deep breath, breaking the silence. He let it seep out of him as his companions turned to the noise. He smiled at them both, narrowed his eyes, and gave them a confident nod. Tobin smiled back, but Katonka stared, petrified.

"We've got this," Zarni said, reaching over and grabbing the orc's big hand in his own.

On her other side, Tobin grabbed her other hand. The act seemed to crack whatever hardened wall Katonka had been building within. Her chin quivered, and a tear streaked down her cheek. It changed direction as the corner of her lip turned upward and her eyes lit up.

Off to the side of the empty gar's seat, a door clanged open and Deklahn entered the room. The tall orc mage swished past the chair and posted himself next to it. Ghun-Ra's gar came into the room next, proudly taking a spot on the other side of his seat, and leaving it empty for the last figure who entered the chamber.

King Genjak strode to the chair and sat. Zarni had spent years watching King Sahr sit in a throne, his oversized body lumpy and sluggish as he melded into the seat. But King Genjak was different. His posture was upright and his body rigid. Zarni could see the orc's wyvern rider training merely in the way he sat.

Zarni gulped and glanced to Deklahn. The orc mage winked, and it was like all the nerves in the goblin's little body dissipated. They'd told Deklahn the whole tale of their quest earlier that day. The king hadn't been available until now, and Deklahn assured them that he'd relay all of it to King Genjak before their audience with him.

"Zarnikorek," King Genjak said.

Hearing his name come out of the king's mouth in the otherwise silent room was strange. For some reason, he thought he'd wince. He'd always hated when King Sahr called upon him. But for whatever reason, Zarni's chest filled, and he replied, "My King."

The king's eyes narrowed, and he leaned toward Deklahn. "Seems you were right."

"I told you he was the right goblin for the job," the orc mage said with a chuckle.

A broad smile spread across the king's face, his tusks gleaming as he addressed Zarni again. "And from what I hear, you performed the duty admirably."

"Thank you, My King," Zarni said with a nod. "But I couldn't have done it without the help of my friends here."

"Ah, yes. Of course. May I relay my deepest thanks to you as well," he said. He looked directly at Tobin and said, "The bridge we build here between our peoples will be remembered for generations to come. I should tell you, Deklahn has been good at recommending historical texts for me to read. I have been reading up on our people's history, and I have come across few halflings of note. It should bring great honor to your family to know that you will be remembered forever in the annals of our people."

"I am honored. Truly," Tobin said. "I hope that I have represented my kind well."

"You have," Zarni said. "You've been a greater friend to me than any I've ever had."

The goblin winced when he realized he'd spoken out of turn in the presence of the king. But he found King Genjak watching with a kind smile.

When he said nothing for a long moment, Tobin filled the silence.

"Well, it was easy with such a kind friend as yourself. I only hope I am the first of many halflings to make a good mark in your historical texts to come."

Zarni smirked at his friend's incredibly controlled response. Tobin was doing great. It was then that the goblin realized he couldn't feel his fingers. He hadn't even noticed how tightly Katonka was squeezing his hand.

"As for you, Katonka, daughter of Ganjor," King Genjak continued. Katonka squeezed harder. "I hear we have much to discuss."

She looked to Zarni. The goblin gave her a confident nod. The she-orc relinquished his hand, and his fingers tingled as blood began to recirculate inside them. Katonka took several tentative steps forward and swiveled her pack around to the front. She knelt on one knee and lifted the wyvern egg in both hands before her. She bowed.

"King Genjak, in the tradition of our peoples in the establishment of our nation as one tribe from many, I present to you this wyvern egg as a symbol of my loyalty to your cause and the future causes of Drelek on behalf of myself and my people."

Silence fell in the chamber. A lump formed in Zarni's throat. He wanted to say something. He wanted to praise Katonka. He wanted to tell King Genjak to see the honor this orc warrior still had. But he couldn't. He knew in his heart he couldn't do that. This moment was between the king and this wyvern rider. All he could do was hold his breath and hope the display was enough to move the king toward compassion.

King Genjak stood from his seat and Katonka bowed lower.

"Listen," the king said. "There are only a few of us in here. Would it be alright if we dismissed the formalities?"

Zarni blinked in confusion, and Tobin shrugged as they shared a glance. King Genjak knelt and grabbed Katonka's elbow, guiding her to stand with him. "Let's talk. One wyvern rider to another. You *do* realize that only a year ago, I was part of the wyvern riders from Borok."

Katonka audibly gulped and straightened herself. "Whatever you wish, My King."

King Genjak suppressed a laugh and shook his head. "I have spent the last year traveling to all our cities and towns in Drelek. I've been visiting all our peoples, trying to share with them the future hope we are aiming for. Not only for Drelek but also for Tarrine as a whole. It's not as easy as you think to explain that we're now allies with those that feature most in the scary bedtime stories we tell our children. Many of them still warn their young ones not to wander off alone in the mountains lest the Griffin Guard carry them away."

Tobin chuckled, but quickly clamped a hand over his mouth. "I'm sorry, My King. I've just met members of the Griffin Guard and they're quite an honorable lot."

"I agree," King Genjak said. "It's amazing what we can learn if we're willing to give each other a chance. And that's my point," he said, turning back to Katonka. "The Griffin Guard has been our nation's greatest enemy since the beginning of our history. If we're willing to give them a second chance, how much more should we show that grace to each other? Everyone deserves a second chance, no matter how much they condemn themselves."

Tears streamed down Katonka's face. "After everything ..." her words choked off.

"I served as a member of the wyvern riders of Borok under King Sahr's reign. I merely became privy to different information than you and ended up on the opposite side of the battle. I can't, and I won't, hold that against you. Or," he added, "any of the others with you."

"Thank you ..." Katonka said, barely able to get the words out. She held up the wyvern egg.

"No," King Genjak said, placing a hand on top of the egg. "From what I've been told, you lost your wyvern during the Battle of Ruk. Seems to me you'll need that one if you're going to come back and rejoin the wyvern riders of Ruk."

Zarni stepped forward to support his friend, who seemed as though she were about to melt into a puddle. But the she-orc pulled herself together and said, "It would be my honor."

King Genjak nodded his approval. "Also, I'd like to induct the town of Krik as an official town of the nation of Drelek. I'm very much looking forward to visiting soon, though I have to return to Ruk for a short while before I can make it over there.”

“It’s a wonderful place,” Tobin piped. “The people are lovely. And the canyon walls ... I haven’t seen the like. It’ll make quite the waypoint for the wagon route.”

The king chuckled. “And I imagine you’ll be retracing the route home? I wonder if I might ask you to carry a letter to Krik for me. I’d consider it a personal favor.”

“Of course. Of course!” Tobin said. “Happy to be of service. This whole quest has been a pleasure. I mean, aside from the snapplers and the wild wyvern and the crash and the bumps and bruises along the way. And my pipe.” The halfling grumbled the last one.

King Genjak laughed out loud. “As Deklahn explained it to me, you’ve all had quite the harrowing adventure. And that reminds me,” he said, turning to Zarni. “You, Zarnikorek, have done your country proud.”

“Thank you, My King.”

“I know you served King Sahr before the rebellion took Ruk.”

Zarni’s stomach churned.

“And,” King Genjak continued, “the whole reason Deklahn suggested we seek you out was the good work you had done. The work that is all the more impressive due to the conditions you faced. It’s not easy to do good work with a bad boss. It got me wondering how good your work could be under someone who would treat you with respect.”

Zarni’s brow crinkled. “My King?”

“I thought, perhaps I could honor you with a position among my advisers in Ruk. That is, if you would be interested in coming back to the capital.”

Zarni blinked. Was the king serious? The goblin's mind reeled. Could he really go back to Ruk? Would it be any different? *Of course it would*, Zarni thought. King Genjak was proving his quality in this meeting, unlike the goblin had ever seen before. But did he want to go back?

"My King," Zarni started slowly. "I am honored you'd even consider such a thing."

The king's eyes narrowed, and a smirk crossed his face. "But ..."

"But ..." Zarni continued, gathering his thoughts. "I spent so long isolating myself. I worried so much about my past. I used to worry what people would remember about me. Would they only remember I was the aide to the mad King Sahr? But I've learned so much on this quest. Which, admittedly, I originally thought was a way for you to dispose of me."

"Oh, really?" the king asked, his brows popping up in surprise. He shared a glance with Deklahn and the mage shrugged and nodded. "To be clear, that was never my intention. Deklahn and I just thought you would be perfect for the task."

"I understand that now," Zarni chuckled sheepishly. "I got to meet so many people, and I instantly saw the future hope you speak about. But not only that, I saw a new hope for myself. Hope for a life filled with joy and not just worry that people would judge me for my past affiliation. Going on this journey, I met people that reminded me of the things I really want in this life. And it's not the accolades and the honors of a position so near the king. It's much simpler than that."

"As I've been wading through this whole being king thing, I've come to find, sometimes the simplest answers are the best," King Genjak said with a wink. "What is it that you want?"

"I just want to bring joy with me wherever I go. After spending so much time isolating myself, I see there are so many relationships out there to be had. I want to build friendships. I want to have a family that's half as nice as Tobin's." The halfling shared a smile with the goblin. "I want to raise children and encourage them half as well as my pa. And I want to make the world better in simple ways."

King Genjak nodded approvingly. "So, perhaps you can take lead as the wagon master here in Ghun-Ra? It seems you've done a marvelous job representing our people."

"Well ..." Zarni hemmed. "I feel like I've finally started something. As if my life can finally begin again. If it's all the same to you, I'd like to go my own way. And maybe do a little more wagoning."

"Yes!" Tobin whispered with a fist pump.

"Then it shall be done," the king said, placing a hand on the goblin's shoulder. "I have no doubt, you will continue to be a wonderful ambassador to our allies in the south, just by being who you are. Thank you for your service to our nation, Zarnikorek."

"I am honored to have been a part of this," the goblin said, unable to hide his grin. "Oh, and sir, you can call me Zarni."

With those words, a weight slipped off of his chest. For the first time in ages, it was like he could breathe again. He no longer felt like he had to hide. He no longer felt like he had to prove something to the new king or anyone else.

He was finally free.

CHAPTER 33
A SWEET TUNE

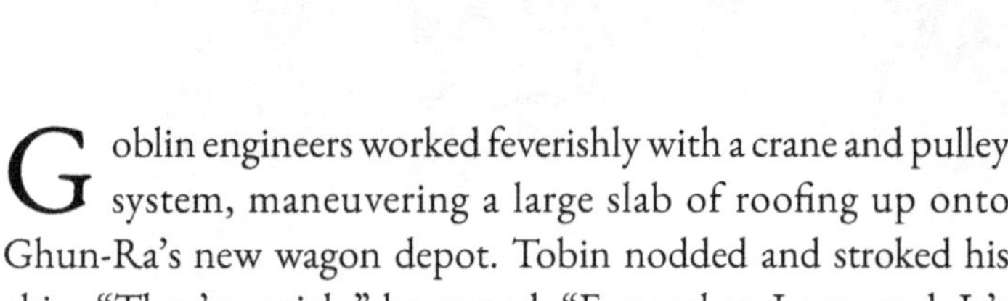

Goblin engineers worked feverishly with a crane and pulley system, maneuvering a large slab of roofing up onto Ghun-Ra's new wagon depot. Tobin nodded and stroked his chin. "They're quick," he mused. "Faster than I expected. It's rather impressive."

"They're good at what they do," Zarni agreed as he thumbed a leather pouch.

The duo had stayed in Ghun-Ra for several days, helping where they could to prepare the new wagon depot. The few wagoners of the city stopped in and out to check on the depot's progress, and an excited buzz hung in the air. A couple of the wagoners expressed some nerves about the new route, but the younger wagoners were zealous to see the new map Zarni offered.

Ghun-Ra's gar was still looking for the right person to take the lead as the city's new wagon master. From what they'd been told, it sounded like he had a troll who'd been apprenticing with the city's merchant master, who might be interested. Zarni had assured the gar, he'd be glad to help whoever the gar ended up choosing. Though they'd had only a few wagoners for years, Zarni guessed with the new depot and the new route and all the excitement, opportunities for wagonwrights and wagoners would draw an influx of new folk to the area.

The goblin rolled the leather pouch in his hand. "Hey, Tobin."

"Aye?" the halfling replied, turning away from the impressive display of the engineers. "Sorry, got distracted there. Not sure I'd want to be up on top of that roof myself. I'm sure they'll have it secure in no time, but looks precarious to me. Though I suppose I don't really care for heights. I would be scared out of my mind to fly on wyvern back. Even watching Katonka take off with Deklahn a few days back churned my stomach. Didn't think I'd eat for a whole day."

"You were eating gibs when she took off," Zarni pointed out.

"Nervous eater," Tobin said nonchalantly. "But that's beside the point. You really rode on Deklahn's wyvern with him?"

Zarni chuckled and nodded as they started the walk back to his pa's house. "I did." He held the leather pouch up, trying to get to his intention before the halfling could take them on another rabbit trail. "I picked this up yesterday while I was out securing some of the supplies we need for the trip back to Galium."

"What is it?" Tobin asked, eyeing the pouch suspiciously. "I was glad to have that time with the gar. He's a decent orc. Very hospitable. He wanted to show me all the great things about Ghun-Ra. He was very adamant about me going home and telling all my fellow wagoners about how great it is." The halfling paused to chuckle. "I wouldn't have minded procuring some supplies, though."

"I think I got us squared away with everything we need," Zarni assured him. "Including this. Because I need you to survive the trip home."

Tobin took the pouch and gave the goblin a side eye. "What is ..." The halfling gasped as a brand-new pipe rolled out of the pouch into his hand. The long stem was stained slightly lighter than the bowl at the end, accentuating the lovely grain patterns of the cherry wood. Intricate gilded script ran the length of the stem. Tobin twirled it in his fingers and inspected the bowl. An etched engraving of a wyvern adorned the side of the bowl with expert artistry. "This is ... Wow ..."

Zarni laughed. He hadn't seen the halfling speechless often, and knowing that he was the cause of his friend's awe brought him a deep joy. "So, I take it you like it? I got it from a pipe maker in one of the market caverns. He said it was 'made with the finest cherry wood in all Finlestia.' And that sounded like just the right pipe for the finest wagoner and friend I've ever known."

Tobin marveled at the pipe for a long time before he popped it in his mouth and breathed through it several times, testing it. "This is a fine pipe," he exclaimed, clamping the long stem in his teeth. "Thank you."

"Of course," Zarni said. "I couldn't have done this without you. And well, I figured, you couldn't do the return journey without a new pipe."

Tobin laughed. "Ha! I did have this one," he said as he pulled the corncob pipe he'd cobbled together to hold him over until he got home. Just the sight of it in light of the new cherry wood pipe made him shudder. He shoved it back into his pocket. He twirled the other one in his hand again, looking at the gilded script intently. "But this one is much better. What does this say, anyway?"

Zarni smirked. "It doesn't look familiar?"

"It does ..." the halfling said, pursing his lips and scrunching his face. He brought the pipe stem right up in front of his nose to inspect it better. "Wait ... this is ancient elvish ..."

"'Should you lose your way, be sure to set your sights. No path leads straight through the mountains. Follow the curve of Mavro's bow.'"

Tobin looked to the goblin, his eyes like wet glass. His lips pressed awkwardly to the side as his face fought between a smile and tears.

"I know we're going to be really establishing the road by traveling it multiple times over the next few months. We'll be leading other wagoners until the ruts are deep. But I figured, just for the first while, if you ever get lost, I want you to be able to find your way back."

Tobin shook his head, nearly tackling the goblin in a hug. "Come here, you. This may be the best gift I've ever received," he said, squeezing the air out of Zarni's lungs. Zarni patted his friend's back desperately, and Tobin released him. "But don't go telling that to Lenor. I don't need to be getting in trouble with her now. The pipe she gave me was lovely. And well-loved," he added with a chuckle. "But it wasn't going to last forever, anyway. But this one ... I can't wait to show it to Milirore on the way back. And Jorbinan. And Katonka. Although, I suppose she'll still be in Ruk for a few more days, so we'll probably miss her."

"Oh! That reminds me, I ran into Pa earlier when I went by the docks. He mentioned she sent us a letter."

Dear Zarni, Tobin, and Grinble,

I know Zarni and Tobin are preparing to head back to Galium to establish the wagon route, so I hope this reaches you before you leave. I'll ask the owl master to send his best.

Anyway, I'm back in Ruk, and while I was nervous to see it at first, I cried the moment I set foot on the king's landing. Deklahn's wyvern, Gloh, is a beautiful beast. But that's not the point of my letter.

When I set foot in Ruk, I felt like I was finally home. This is what it must have felt like for you, Zarni, when you saw Pickers Peak.

Anyway, I was right. Most people thought I had died in the battle. A nice young family of goblins bought my old dwelling. The mother just started working at a tavern that serves this really interesting glorb wine. It's all the rage here in Ruk.

But I'm rambling, and I'm going to run out of parchment before I get to the point.

I went to see Gronk.

It was weird at first. When he saw me, he froze. Like he'd seen a ghost. He moved so slowly, pawing at my face as if to see if I was real. But finally, he grabbed me and pulled me in for a kiss. That's probably too much information, but it was ... Well, it was amazing.

Turns out Gronk had mourned for months. That, of course, is heartbreaking. But apparently, after months of mourning and others telling him to move on, he had a dream one night. And in the dream, he saw our reunion. And he knew I was alive.

Can you believe it?

Anyway, everything is wonderful here. I've got a lot of work to do here to help organize the return for some of the others in Krik, because I'm not the only one who they thought was dead. It'll take some time to get everyone squared away, but the new commander of the wyvern riders here in Ruk has been extremely helpful.

Anyway, Grinble, thank you for all your hospitality. The gibs you slipped into my bag before I left were delicious.

Zarni and Tobin, happy trails, and I'll see you back in Krik in the coming months. When we do, the glorb is on me. I can never thank you enough for what you've done for me and my people.

Sending much love,
Katonka

Yan slammed a fist onto the table and shouted, "No way! You really survived an encounter with a bull wyvern?"

"It's true!" Tobin countered between swigs from his mug. "And Zarni walked right up to it with the egg. I thought he was dead for sure."

"No way," Grahk said behind his own mug.

"Me? I thought you were dead, for real," Zarni said. "Tobin flew out of the driver's box. And notice," he emphasized, grabbing at the back of the halfling's tunic, "he doesn't have wings!"

Everyone around the table laughed, adding to the general buzz of merriment that permeated *The Wyvern's Wish.* Zarni had been nervous to catch up with the boating duo, but, right off, they'd embraced him with excitement, and he wondered why he'd ever worried.

"Another round on me," Grinble said.

"Yeah!" Yan, Grahk, and Tobin cheered.

"Pa, you've bought the last two."

"With you headed out wagoning again, how often am I going to get the chance to buy drinks for my hero of a son and his friends?"

"'e's right, you know?" Yan said.

"Between that and us navigating the rivers, the chances are going to be difficult to predict," Grahk added.

Zarni looked to Tobin for help, but the halfling merely smiled and said, "Too true. Too true."

"Madam, another round for the table!" Grinble said to the barmaid, who just happened to walk by at the perfect time.

"Yeah!" the others cheered.

Zarni just laughed and shook his head.

"Oh! Zarni, there she is," Tobin said, nudging the goblin with his elbow.

"Oooh, is Zarni interested in Jil?" Yan asked, wriggling his dark eyebrows.

"Interested?" Tobin asked. "She's the only girl he talked about the whole trip. I see why too. Prettiest goblin I've ever met. She's awfully sweet, too. She looked at me a little funny when Zarni introduced me the other day. But so did you two."

Yan and Grahk barked laughs.

"But now look at us," Tobin said. "It's like we've been friends forever. I think that's the way it's going to be for a while, as everyone gets used to all the different people coming around."

"True enough," Grahk said in his deep baritone. "But the real question is, are you going to ask her out?"

"Yeah!" Yan piled on. "We've known Jil for years. Even back in Lakjo. She was the prettiest goblin there, too."

"I'm telling Lonka you said that," Grahk teased.

"Scorch me! Please don't," Yan said, cringing at the thought. "She'll have my hide."

Zarni hardly heard his friends' words as he watched Jileva on the other side of the tavern. She inspected her lute, turning the pegs at the top and plucking at the strings to make sure it was properly tuned. As if she knew he was staring, her eyes fluttered and looked his way. Their gazes met for a moment, and her face spread into a coy smile before she looked away. Was she blushing?

Could she possibly ... No. I can't ... Wait.

Zarni shook his head and took a long swig of his mug and handed it over to Tobin. *I can.* "Hold my glorb."

"What?" the halfling stammered as he caught the mug.

"Alright!" Yan shouted.

"Go for it!" Grahk called.

But his friend's shouts of encouragement drowned out behind him as he strode toward the small stage.

Jileva looked up to see Zarni approaching and inclined her head. She knelt on the stage so she could be face to face with him.

"My hero," she said by way of greeting.

Zarni's cheeks burned so much his ear itched. "Hi, Jil," he said awkwardly.

"Hi," she said with a giggle.

"I just ... well," Zarni's brain seemed like it was shutting down. *Think. Think,* he scolded himself. "Do you like breakfast?"

"What?" She let out a laugh that sounded like the cheerful ringing of bells.

"What I mean is, breakfast is the best meal. I mean, for a bard. Well, I guess you would know. Since you're a bard. I'm just a wagoner. Well, I suppose, I'm just really getting started with that. We leave tomorrow, actually. And I might be gone a couple of weeks. But then I'll be back."

Jileva inclined her head to the other side and reached out to grab Zarni's chin, forcing him to meet her gaze. "Are you trying to say you'd like to have breakfast with me tomorrow morning before you leave?"

Zarni's eyes bulged, and his heart pounded. The lump in his throat forced him to respond with a nod for fear that any words would come out as merely a croak.

She giggled again, and even her beautiful blue eyes seemed to be smiling. She pushed back several wavy ringlets of her red hair and said, "You know, breakfast is the best time for bards to go on a date. I mean, if a date is what you meant by wanting to have breakfast?"

Zarni nodded again.

"Then it's a date," she said with a wink.

Relief washed over Zarni in waves, and he couldn't control the goofy grin on his face.

"Is it alright if I dedicate this next song to you, or will you run out of here again?"

Zarni scratched at the side of his head sheepishly. "Yeah, sorry about that. I was having a bit of a rough day."

"Oh good. I thought it might have been my singing."

"No!" Zarni said faster than he meant to. "You sing like the stars in the sky."

"Oooh," she cooed. "You're a romantic."

Zarni chuckled at her light teasing. "So, tomorrow morning?"

"I'll see you then."

Zarni nodded and turned around to hurry back to his table. His friends all leaned in, watching, eyes wide as if they wanted to know what happened. Zarni gave them an excited fist pump, and they went into raucous cheers. Behind him, he heard Jileva giggle. And all Zarni could do was smile.

EPILOGUE

Three months later ...

Zarni looped and hooked the leather straps to the latch system on the front of his wagon. He strode around to the front of the boulder goat and dug his fingers into the deep fur of Gregory's beard, scratching wildly and cooing, "You ready for a good ride today, King Gregory?"

After all the time they'd driven together, the goblin had developed a soft spot for the stubborn boulder goat. For his part, Gregory nuzzled and gently butted heads with the goblin, nearly knocking his goggles off.

"Alright, alright," he said with a laugh. "You ready to see Tobin? We should be running into him and Kliff in Hill Stop, if we timed it right."

The boulder goat stamped happily, ready to get moving. He still loved the affection that the halfling inevitably lavished on him every time they got together. At the mention of the wyvern runt, Gibs's furry horned head popped up over the railing of the wagon.

"You ready to see Kliff?" Zarni smirked. "In Tobin's last letter, he said Kliff is as big as a dog now. But Master Argus expects he won't get much bigger."

The horned marten clambered into the driver's box and perched himself on the bench. Zarni climbed in next to him and took the reins. Gregory needed no prompting and pulled the wagon into motion.

Zarni breathed in the crisp mountain air. It was cooler now, with autumn around the corner. The smell of warm flapjacks filled his nostrils as he waved to Milirore who sat on the front porch of the newly built restaurant in which, Zarni knew, Jorbinan was happily humming his tunes and serving up flapjacks to weary wagoners. The she-elf adjusted her woolen blanket around her shoulders and blew the steam off her morning tea.

Soon, she was out of sight through the trees as the goblin's wagon rolled out onto the main wagon route. The ride had gotten smoother as experienced wagoners had traveled it more and more, removing dangerous rocks that posed a risk to wagon wheels. And Zarni's wagon drove smoothly as well. Tobin had gotten him connected with the wagonwright who built the halfling's own wagon. And after the goblin's was built, Tobin said he might have to have him build a new one for himself, because Zarni's "must be the finest wagon in all Finlestia."

The goblin smirked at the memory as he pulled a gib from his oiled leather bag. He munched half of it and eyed the horned marten, whose nose twitched with interest. Zarni popped his brow and handed the other half over to the creature. Gibs, of course, gobbled it down.

Zarni laughed into the mountain air, happy to be on the road again, knowing he rolled onward to good places and even better friends.

Acknowledgements

Thank you for reading my book! I hope you had as much fun on the trail as I did writing this adventure. If so, please leave a wonderful review. Reviews are the lifeblood of indie authors like me. The more positive reviews we have, the more likely it is that others will pick up the book as well.

Just like Zarni, I had several people helping me on this journey in various capacities. A quick thank you to Aleksa and Megan for helping me make this book so pretty with art and edits. And thank you to Peter for not only your friendship, but also for breathing life into the world of Finlestia with your extraordinary voice talents.

A special thanks to my local coffee shop folks who kept me fueled and provided me with a great place to write this book.

And to my wife Brittany and our kids, you've encouraged and inspired me to chase after this crazy dream. You have sacrificed time on countless days to allow me to blaze trails through this fantasy world. I love you guys.

ABOUT THE AUTHOR

Z.S. Diamanti is the award-winning author of the *Stone & Sky* trilogy, an epic fantasy adventure and *Guard in the Garden,* the first book in the *Fables of Finlestia* cozy fantasy series. He went to college forever and has too many pieces of paper on his wall. He is a USAF veteran of Operation Enduring Freedom and worked in ministry for over 10 years. He and his wife live in Colorado with their four children, where they enjoy hikes and tabletop games.

You can get the *Stone & Sky Preludes Series* of stories for FREE at zsdiamanti.com

Connect with him on social media: @zsdiamanti

CONNECT

A COZY FANTASY!

READ THE NEXT BOOK IN

Fables of Finlestia

ORDER NOW!

WANT MORE FROM THE WORLD OF FINLESTIA?

JOIN THE
GRIFFIN GUARD
TODAY!

JOIN Z.S. DIAMANTI'S
OFFICIAL READERS LIST
AND GET EXCLUSIVE ACCESS TO NEWS,
SHORT STORIES, EVENTS, AND MORE!

Good reviews are vital for Indie Authors. The importance of reviews in helping others find and take a chance on an indie author's book is impossible to overstate.

If you enjoyed this book, would you help me get it in front of more people by taking a minute to give it a good review?
I can't tell you how thankful I'd be.

Check out this link for the best places to review this book and help me get it to more readers who love good books just like you and me!